THE WHEELWRIGHT GIRL

A captivating wartime saga of love, loss and self-discovery

TANIA CROSSE

Revised edition 2020
Joffe Books, London
www.joffebooks.com

ISBN 978-1-78931-322-2

CHAPTER ONE

'Call that a full can?' Martin Vencombe chided as he took the watering can from the young woman and handed her the empty one.

Grace Dannings bunched her mouth in mutinous indignation. She had been chatting with her neighbours as they waited in Vencombe's Yard. But as soon as Martin's father had called out to them to look sharp as the first wheel was coming, all conversation had at once ceased. As always, Grace felt the simmering excitement froth up inside her. She had spent her entire young life in the tiny Dartmoor village of Walkhampton which was famed for the wagons and particularly the wheels produced at the wheelwrights' mill. But no matter how often Grace took part in bonding day, she never ceased to be caught up in the fascination of watching the iron tyres being fixed about the wooden wheels.

Her heart fluttered with anticipation as the men from the wheelwrights' used special tyre irons to lift the white-hot iron rim from the bed of glowing coals and timber off-cuts. She watched as they then carried the metal tyre the few yards to the wheel fixed onto the bonding plate. The tyre was carefully dropped over it and then knocked and levered into place with tyre dogs, tampers and sledgehammers. It was a task

1

that required both skill and strength, and the men's faces were serious with concentration. But when Grace had caught Martin's eye, he had winked mischievously at her across the noisy clamour of hammering and grunts of exertion.

'There we go, then!' Martin's father proclaimed with satisfaction when the sweating men had stood back for their boss to inspect their work. Now they would douse the rim of the wheel with cans of cold water while the village folk kept them refilled from the barrels in the yard. As the metal cooled and contracted, it pulled together the already rock-solid wooden joints under huge and permanent pressure. Hence a Vencombe wheel would see many decades of heavy service.

'All hands to the wheel!' Grace's neighbour, Martha Redlake, had chuckled at her own habitual pun, and they had both gone to plunge an empty can into one of the barrels.

Now, as Grace glared at Martin Vencombe, she saw the light dancing rakishly in his eyes. She realized he was teasing her and she was ready for the game.

'You get on with your own work!' she retorted playfully, nodding to where his elder brother and some other men were already lowering the next tyre onto the fire on the ground in the yard.

Martin threw up his head in laughter, his fashionable pencil moustache echoing the curve of his mouth before he indeed turned back to his work. As the men carefully emptied their watering cans along the outer curve of the wheel, a great whoosh of spitting, furious steam hissed into the warm morning air like a dragon breathing fire and smoke. The whole exciting event resembled a celebration, bringing the small community together, and happy jubilation radiated from every face. It might be hot, strenuous toil, especially on such a glorious, late spring day, but as everyone rushed to replenish the watering cans, jolly pleasantries were exchanged and spirits were high.

'Reckons as he'm sweet on you, I does,' Martha whispered in Grace's ear.

2

'Who, Martin?' Grace's cornflower blue eyes widened in surprise at the older woman's suggestion. 'No! He and Larry are more like brothers to me. Besides, they'm far too old, and Martin wouldn't be interested in the likes of me. Not in that sort of way.'

Grace had to hide a secret smile. Something of a matchmaker was Martha. She had successfully married off two of her three older sons and now she and her husband Barry only had their fourth and youngest lad living with them in the cottage adjacent to Grace's chaotic family home. Before Grace had taken up her live-in position with the Snells when she had left school, Martha's home had been an orderly haven for her. She would often take refuge there, basking in Martha's friendship despite the difference in their ages.

But as they jostled among the other villagers to refill their watering cans yet again, Grace looked across at Martin. She supposed he was rather attractive, but having known him all her life, she had never really thought about it. Besides, the Vencombe sons had been well educated before going into the family business and would surely seek their spouses among less humble folk than her kind.

Grace tossed the thought from her mind and turned her attention back to the wheel that was being bonded in the yard. Steam no longer spewed up from the bevelled iron rim, and very soon Mr Vencombe would pronounce it fully cooled. The heavy wheel would then be rolled away and stacked in the village square — which was actually more of a triangle in shape — on the far side of the little bridge over the stream that ran along the far side of the wheelwrights' workshop. The Black Brook cut right through the centre of the village, but much of its rushing water was directed into a wooden channel or launder and thus it drove the waterwheel that provided power for the machinery in the wheelwrights' mill.

'Mind your back, Grace!'

Grace glanced over her shoulder at Martin's elder brother, Larry. The jab of his head warned her that the blacksmith was approaching with a wheelbarrow full of white-hot coals to stoke up the circle of fire where the next tyre was being heated. Grace pulled Martha aside, and once the danger had trundled past, they made their way back to the barrels. The area around the bonding plate was awash with water, and Mr Vencombe indicated that the first wheel was fully bonded. Activity among the helpers would be less frenetic now, and Grace allowed her eyes to drift back to Martin's lithe, athletic form as he lounged against the wall, lighting a cigarette and chatting to Agatha Nonnacott. Grace had never liked the older girl particularly, but she was nearer the Vencombes's class and so would be far more suitable to be courted by Martin than she was.

'Always good of Mrs Snell to give you the morning off.'

Martha's comment distracted Grace from her ponderings as they set to work again. While everyone was waiting for the next tyre to reach the required temperature, the villagers took buckets to the stream so that they could top up the depleted barrels in the yard. It would take another twenty minutes or so for the tyre to be ready, and so they could work at a more leisurely pace now.

'Well, she knows how I love bonding day, and Farmer Snell says the wheelwrights' is good for the economy of the village,' Grace said wisely, remembering her employer's erudite words.

'It were certainly a good thing when old Mr Vencombe chose to set up his business here back along,' Martha concurred. 'Us is mainly farm labourers in the village, and a few workers on the Princetown railway, of course. But the wheelwrights' certainly helps to make us the thriving place us is now with two village stores and one of them a Sub-Post Office and all. And look at your Stephen, apprenticed to Mr Vencombe. Without that, he might've had to leave the village to find work, like my elder two did once they was married and had responsibilities. Or join the Navy down in Devonport like our Horace did.'

Grace nodded in agreement. Old Mr Vencombe, who had established the wheelwrights' about seventy years previously in the 1840s, had died when she was a small child and so she had no memory of him. But his son had helped him develop the business into a successful concern with a reputation that had spread far and wide, and *his* sons, Larry and Martin, had followed in his footsteps. Now the Vencombes employed several men: a couple of wheelwrights, a carpenter, two general labourers and the painter who decorated the farm wagon wheels in their traditional bright colours and patterns. And then, of course, Grace's brother, Stephen.

Here he was now, propelling the next wheel towards the bonding plate. At eighteen, and a year or so older than Grace, he had virtually completed his apprenticeship. Mr Vencombe had promised him full employment, but Grace had a suspicion that Stephen wanted to spread his wings. He had pretended to joke that there were no girls in Walkhampton who took his fancy, but Grace believed that in reality he was being serious and meant to go off in search of a young lady who did!

'Just a few more minutes,' Mr Vencombe announced, and Grace took the opportunity to look round at her companions.

Most of the village had turned out for bonding day, at least everyone who didn't have other employment they couldn't afford to neglect. Martha's Barry, for instance, was a tenant small-holder, and with only their 13-year-old son, Peter, to help him, he had no spare time on his hands. Then there was Grace's father who was a farm labourer and lucky to be in a permanent job. Ernest Dannings worked for Farmer Snell just outside the village on the road to Horrabridge. It was he who had procured Grace's position as general maid in the farmhouse. She assisted Mrs Snell in every way, sometimes helping to make butter in the dairy, but mainly carrying out duties of a domestic nature which kept her busy from early in the morning until she fell into bed at night.

'How do, Martha? And young Gracie?'

'Morning, Mr Brown.' Grace turned to the man who had come up behind them. 'Come to watch, have you?'

'Yes, but not for long. Got to make sure everything's shipshape in the tap room for this lot when they've finished. Thirsty work, this.'

'Good for business, in it?' Martha nodded her head vigorously. 'Us was just saying that the wheelwrights' be proper good for the village.'

'Certainly is. Take my inn, for instance. No good having a coaching inn with no coaches no more if you hasn't got local trade to rely on. Must've been grand back along seeing they fine coaches and their horses arriving all the time. Afore the new main road and then the railways changed everything. Still, there are worse things. God knows what the future holds for us all just now.'

'You means all this talk of war?' Martha scoffed. 'Aw, it'll never happen.'

'Wouldn't be so sure,' Mr Brown replied.

Grace saw his eyebrows arch, and a strange coldness shivered down her spine. War. Her young mind had little concept of what it meant, besides some vague image from learning about the Zulu War at school, of vast grasslands, blistering heat and frightening natives wielding spears. But British soldiers sweltering in their red uniform jackets seemed to have little to do with the festive atmosphere in Walkhampton on this fine May morning in 1914. Now Mr Vencombe declared the next tyre to be hot enough for fitting, and all was forgotten again in the wonderful excitement of bonding the next wheel.

It was in the interlude after its completion that Grace spied the young woman sidling into the yard. She was struggling to support a tiny babe on one arm, while her other hand gripped firmly onto a small child tottering about her knees. The poor woman looked ghastly, more as if she should be in bed than jostling among the crowd, and Grace flew across to her.

'Nan, let me take the baby! Surely you shouldn't be out and about yet? He's, what, barely two weeks old?'

Nan Sampson's pale face melted with relief as she gratefully relinquished the bundle into Grace's willing arms. 'Aw, that's master kind of you, Grace. I be mortal tired, like, but you knows how John insists I always comes to bonding day. Show my respects to the Vencombes, he says.'

'But not when you've only just had a baby!' Grace was appalled, but almost instantly, an enchanted smile crept onto her lips as she glanced down at the snuffling little creature in her arms. 'He'm adorable. So tiny,' she breathed, and watched the weary wonderment on Nan's face.

'Yes, but you wouldn't think such a tiny thing could keep you up all night. And then just as I gets him off to sleep, this one wakes up, full of the joys of spring for the new day. And I has to keep him quiet till John wakes up, and so it starts all over again.'

'What?' Horror flashed in Grace's eyes as she glanced across at John Sampson, one of the Vencombes' general labourers. 'You mean, John will sleep all night, and then won't get up a bit early so that you can get some sleep yourself? That's disgraceful! Well, we'll soon see—'

'No, Grace, please.' Nan caught her arm as she went to stride purposefully across the yard to where John was helping Larry and Stephen lower the next wheel onto the bonding plate. 'He gets, well, proper angered, like, if I doesn't do what he says.'

Grace stared at Nan's pleading expression, trying to control her own outrage. Poor Nan, browbeaten by her own husband — and when he had given her two children in such quick succession. Grace sighed in exasperation. Whenever the day came when she got married, it would be to someone who knew how to contain his ardour. Or at least would use those rubber things she had heard about. It was Martin she had learnt about them from, as he joked in some whispering attitude that had made her feel confused and uncomfortable — and Larry had told him in no uncertain terms to shut his mouth in front of her. At the time, Grace had felt grateful to Larry, but on the other hand, she was pleased to be armed with such knowledge. Not that it was of any help now, though.

'Well, come and stand at the front for a few minutes so as John can see you'm here,' she instructed, ushering Nan forward. 'And then go home and put your feet up. Sally still

7

has an afternoon nap, doesn't she? So try and get the baby asleep at the same time.'

'But then John's supper won't be—'

'Let him wait for his supper. He'll eat well enough this dinnertime.'

'Yes, I supposes so,' Nan relented, although Grace was not at all sure she had convinced the poor girl. But there was little more Grace could do except chase Nan and her children out of the yard once John had acknowledged their presence. She watched them go back inside their cottage in one of the rows opposite the inn. At least they only had a few yards to go, but Grace shook her head. It baffled her why such a meek little mouse as Nan had agreed to marry such a man as John Sampson. But maybe she had been afraid to say no!

Life could be strange sometimes, Grace mused as she turned back into the yard. But as the morning continued, her enjoyment of the friendly village camaraderie was tempered by the vision of poor Nan huddling against the wall. Her thoughtful mood, though, was eventually diverted when the bell rang out from the roof of the school house, heralding the coming of midday. Children from the outlying farms stayed there to eat their meal, but the village children spilled out of the gate to go home for dinner.

Lady Modyford's School was but a stone's throw from Vencombe's Yard, and everyone knew it was bonding day. The draw was simply too irresistible even to stomachs rumbling with hunger and the yard was soon bristling with little people. Most found members of their family and stood watching, their eyes bright with expectation. Yet others were so infected by the sense of celebration that they darted and dodged about, playing tag or other games.

'Hey, you!'

Grace looked round as Larry Vencombe caught two young boys each by the collar, his face stern as he glared at the other accomplices.

'Stop running around before someone gets hurt! How many times have I told you this is dangerous work! If you can't behave, I'll have to arrange for you to stay in school on bonding day.'

He released his captives with a little jerk to lend emphasis to his words, meeting Grace's eyes with an exasperated twist of his mouth. One of the boys he had been holding shrugged his tattered jacket back into place while the other sniffed and wiped his nose on his sleeve.

'Spoil sport,' he retorted rudely.

Larry lifted his arm as if he would cuff the child, but Grace knew it was only a warning. As soon as Larry had turned his back, however, the little scamps were making derogatory faces at him. Grace knew, though, that they would obey him now, even though they were trying to make fun of him. Poor Larry. He had learnt to be thick-skinned. He had needed to.

They had finished bonding the iron tyres to all the waiting wheels, but now it was the turn of the naves. The heavy hubs — or naves as they were more often called — were fashioned from huge logs of three to five year seasoned elm, and the central hole for the axle and the mortices for the spokes were then drilled and chiselled out. Iron hoops would then be fitted around the two sides to give the nave extra support in much the same way as tyres were fitted to the completed wheels. Several nave hoops could be heated at the same time and so bonding day always finished in a frenzy of activity to complete the process in record time but without compromising the quality of the work.

'Well done, everybody!' Mr Vencombe called when it was all over. 'Many thanks for your help. Pasties and pints on me for all of you at the inn as always.'

The usual cheer went up from a score of parched mouths. Grace found herself standing by Larry and gave him a broad smile, but her fine brow knitted when she saw the grim expression on his face.

'Enjoy it while you can,' he muttered. 'It could be gun-carriages we'll be making before too long.'

Grace flashed him an irritated glare. Why spoil the day with such comments? Typical of Larry, who must be the most sombre person she knew. And she was sure he must be wrong about this war business anyway!

Everyone trooped across the narrow road to the old inn. Faces were grimy with dirt and sweat, and throats were gasping for a thirst-quenching drink. Grace and Martha jostled in through the lounge bar at the front of the inn to the taproom at the back. It wasn't the usual place for women to go. Indeed it was frowned upon for any lady to enter even the lounge bar except when dressed up for a special occasion and accompanied by a male member of the family. But on bonding day, all the rules were broken.

Grace and Martha weren't the only females to go through to the back. Anyone over fourteen, as the law allowed, of whatever sex was welcome to partake of Mr Vencombe's generosity. A trestle table had been set up on the flagstone floor, groaning under the plates of pasties and sandwiches piled onto it. While Mr Brown pulled pints from the massive barrels for his eager customers, chalking them up on a board for Mr Vencombe's tab, people helped themselves to food. Within minutes, the room was vibrating with lively voices vying to make themselves heard.

'Crazy if you asks me, they Suffragette women,' John Sampson commented to his neighbour as he chomped voraciously on his pasty. 'What does women know of voting? Woman's place be in the home. And what does you think about that lunatic throwing herself under the king's horse last year? Completely daft.'

Grace caught their conversation as she sipped her ginger beer, and felt the hairs bristle on the back of her neck. After talking to Nan just now, she was just in the mood to confront the poor girl's husband. Before she could control her tongue, the words blurted out of her mouth, 'If you'm referring to Emily Wilding Davidson, then you'm wrong. She were very brave to do that for summat she believed in so passionately. And she weren't trying to kill herself. She were just trying to throw a banner over the horse.'

10

John snorted so violently that he spluttered into his beer. 'Well even if that were so, she must've realized it were mortal dangerous to run out in front of a field of galloping horses!'

'Exactly! That were the whole point, to show that—'

'Personally I believe we'll soon have more than votes for women to worry about,' Larry put in from behind her. For a moment, Grace filled up with resentment at his interruption of the heated argument, for the Suffragette Movement was very close to her heart. But when Larry concluded with the comment, 'Important issue though that is,' she felt her annoyance drop away. Proper clever was Larry, and Grace respected him for it. Serious of character he might be, but she had always enjoyed his conversation since she was a child. That, and Martin's constant joking was what had made her from a very early age want to join in the threesome of the two Vencombe brothers and her own brother. They had accepted her into the fold, taking care of her like a little sister, and she had joined in their escapades ever since.

'Doesn't really think there'll be a war, does you, lad?' another voice chimed in.

'Unfortunately, yes, I do. This thing's been brewing for years. Decades even. Some say part of the problem dates back as far as the Franco-Prussian War, and I'm inclined to agree. What do you think, Dad?'

Grace turned as Geoffrey Vencombe shouldered his way through the crowded room. 'I'm certain it has something to do with it, yes. But basically it all boils down to the fight between imperialism and nationalism.'

Grace noted the bafflement on John Sampson's face, and arranged her own features into an expression of intelligent interest. But she said nothing, not wanting to admit to anyone that she didn't really understand Mr Vencombe's words either! She had loved school, priding herself on being a most diligent pupil, and had been devastated when she had reached her twelfth birthday and had to leave at the end of term. But she did read the newspapers, trying to keep up with all that was happening in the world, even though she didn't always understand everything she read.

'In my opinion, we'll be at war before the year's out,' Mr Vencombe continued, 'and Heaven knows what'll happen to us all, then.'

'It'll be unprecedented, that's for sure,' Larry agreed, swilling the beer in his tankard before taking a deep draught.

'It's being so cheerful that keeps you going, brother!'

Martin clapped his elder brother so rumbustiously on the shoulder that Larry momentarily lost his balance and spilled some of the bitter liquid down his shirt. Grace's heart lurched. Martin's boisterous show of sibling affection was all very well, but he should have thought about Larry's affliction first.

'Well, *if* it happens,' Martin went on with one eyebrow raised sceptically, 'it'll be over in a few months, mark my words. We'll give the Germans a bloody nose in no time. Could be a chance for anyone who goes to fight to see a bit of the world, mind, while it lasts. Now who's for another pint?'

Grace stood back pensively, sinking beneath the waves of raucous chatter, munching jaws and the occasional satisfied belch. While she chewed on a tasty pasty, nodding at Martha's jolly laughter, her mind shifted back to Mr Vencombe's words. War before the year was out? It seemed inconceivable on such a perfect day.

'I'd better be going,' she told Martha. 'I promised to be back by two o'clock and I want to call in to see Mummy and the tackers on the way.'

'All right, my lovely,' Martha answered through a mouth full of food. 'See you soon. I's just going to have another pasty. Mighty tasty, they be.'

Grace nodded, nailing a smile on her face. Her enjoyment of bonding day had dissipated into thin air. The atmosphere in the room was suddenly oppressive and she felt she must escape. She slid outside unnoticed, and gulped at the fresh country air, leaning back against the wall of the inn as she did so. Only part of Walkhampton fronted what was, for want of a better word, the main road through the village. Other buildings were tucked away in alleyways and lanes behind the inn or in the odd area where the grocers-cum-Post Office stood at a strange angle to its neighbours. Grace sometimes imagined that a wilful giant had rolled some dice there and turned them into houses wherever they came to rest. All so familiar to her, so peaceful and reassuring.

So why was talk of war on everyone's lips?

She sighed deeply and glanced towards the little bridge over the brook. On the far side of the village square, just where the road towards Woodman's Corner began its long ascent, was Vencombe's timber yard. Next to it tottered the tumbledown row of higgledy-piggledy stone cottages where Grace's family squeezed together in one downstairs room and the bedroom above. The ceilings were so low that Grace could easily touch them if she stretched upwards. But it was home. And although she sometimes found the chaos within exasperating, she loved it. And perhaps a cup of tea and a quick chat with her mother would allow her to cast all thoughts of war aside.

For now, at least.

CHAPTER TWO

'Grace.'

Before she brought herself to move, however, Larry appeared beside her as if out of nowhere. His voice portrayed only the faintest surprise. He hadn't noticed her leave the taproom and so hadn't expected to find her outside leaning back against the front wall of the inn.

'You left early,' he commented.

'So did you.'

'Yes, I suppose I did. I felt . . . I don't know . . .'

'Stifled?' she finished for him.

He looked at her askew and a wry smile tugged at his mouth. 'I was going to say unnerved, but stifled is just as good a word.' He took a lop-sided step to join her in leaning against the pub wall. For several moments, they remained in an easy silence, Grace returning to her contemplation of the peaceful village. Just up the road, afternoon school had begun and through an open window, they could just hear the chanting of times tables above the muffled babble from the taproom at the rear of the inn.

Larry heard Grace sigh, drawing him from his own reverie. 'It's all this talk of war, isn't it?' he murmured.

It was a few seconds before she replied, watching her toe as she ground it into the hard-baked earth. 'Yes, I reckon so. Life is so . . . so perfect here, I just can't imagine . . . I thought Mr Asquith were trying to sort things out.'

'He is. But it seems to me that all this prevarication is simply allowing more time for all sides to build up their armaments. And in the meantime, the balance of power in Europe is becoming increasingly unstable as well.'

'That's what everyone keeps saying, but I don't understand it all. Not properly, like. And I want to. Can you explain it to me, in simple terms? You know I'm not that clever. I don't mind admitting it to you.'

Larry tipped his head sideways. 'That's not true at all. You shouldn't have had to leave school at twelve. You should have had the chance to go on . . .' He broke off, his voice sounding strange, and Grace's eyebrows met in a frown. But the moment was forgotten as Larry went on in a more matter-of-fact tone, 'Well, can you imagine a map of Europe from when you were at school?'

'Yes. At least, I think so. I remember France and Spain because they'm easy, and the boot of Italy and then Greece next to it. But there are so many countries in the middle, it's all mixed up in my mind.'

'And that's precisely one of the reasons it's all so complicated. You have Austria-Hungary on one side vying against the Serbs on the other. A lot of it's historical, of course. And then Germany will always support Austria-Hungary, and the Russians support Serbia. Then there's the French who I'm sure would welcome any opportunity to win back the territories they lost in the Franco-Prussian War in the 1870s—'

'And now we'm allied to France and Russia.'

'Exactly. So you see, you do understand. As much as the majority of people do, anyway. Things are spiralling out of control and if you ask me, it will only require a spark for the whole tinderbox to explode.'

Larry pushed himself forward from the wall, and Grace fell into step beside him. They ambled along the road back towards the Vencombes' substantial residence that stood in front of the yard, making the peaceful harmony of the morning's work rush back into Grace's thoughts.

'Why can't people just be friends and get on with their lives like we do in the village?'

'But you were arguing with John just now about the Suffragettes.'

Grace had to bite her lip. It wasn't just about the Suffragettes, was it? But for Nan's sake, she would keep their conversation a secret. So she replied simply, 'But I was hardly going to have a fight with him over it.'

'Well that's because—'

'Because I'm a girl?' she rounded on him.

'I was going to say because you've got more sense than that.'

'Oh.' Grace twisted her lips. No, Larry wasn't like that, and she felt a trifle embarrassed. 'I'd better go,' she said quickly to cover up her feelings. 'I'm calling in to see Mummy afore I go back to work.'

'Give her my best wishes, then,' Larry nodded at her with a smile.

'I will.' Grace paused a second before she turned away. He looked nice, did Larry, when that rare smile lit his face. But as she had said to Martha, the Vencombe lads were more like brothers to her, and it was no more than a fleeting thought as she skipped over the little bridge.

Larry watched her go, and then limped towards his own home.

* * *

Grace hurried across the square and past Vencombes's timber yard on the left. Immediately after it was the row of humble cottages that was home, cobbled together with random extensions here and there that appeared to prop each other up in defiance of gravity. But it was thought that the major part of the building dated back three hundred years, and so it would doubtless still be standing in another three centuries.

Grace's family occupied the cottage tacked on at the lower end. It seemed that it had originally been a small stable or cowshed as the timber lintels of a blocked up hayloft door were still visible high up on the gable wall. The chimney stack inside was built of brick rather than stone, indicating that it had been added later. No one in the village seemed to know when it had become living accommodation, but with a proper little range and flagstone floor, it was mortal cosy even in winter. After all, the stone walls were nearly two foot thick and kept out the wind and rain. Certainly upstairs where they all slept in one crowded room, Grace had rarely felt cold. At the farmhouse, she had her own room which was sheer luxury in the summer, but it had no fireplace so that in winter it could be freezing. Mrs Snell insisted she took a stone hot-water bottle to bed, but it wasn't the same. Even after five years, Grace still sometimes missed cuddling down in the big warm bed with her younger brother and sisters.

Her heart lifted as she pushed open the front door. 'Hello!' she called, proudly using the new word with which Martin had told her people answered that newfangled machine, the telephone. At least, the word had been invented over twenty years previously when the contraption had been in its experimental stages. Her family were never likely to own one, of course. Such wonders would be far beyond their financial reach. But Grace felt very pleased with herself that she knew the word was beginning to spread as an every day greeting, too.

Her mother was busy at the range, stirring what smelt like mince and onions in a giant saucepan. 'I were hoping you might call in, cheel, it being bonding day,' she smiled over her shoulder. 'Is it all over now?'

'Yes, it is, so you can let the tackers outside now.'

'Oh, good. Go along now then, you two,' Temperance Dannings ordered her younger daughters who were playing

17

with their rag dolls on the rug. 'Outside with you. I want to talk to your sister.'

'Where was George today?' Grace asked as her mother shooed the little girls outside. 'He didn't come out of school at dinner time, at least I didn't see him.'

'Got a bit of a cold, so he'm upstairs in bed.'

'Oh, yes?' Grace inwardly groaned. Swinging the lead, more like. Unlike herself, George hated school, but at ten years old, he was savvy enough to know that at the slightest sign of illness, his mother would keep him home. Temperance was far too protective of her children although Grace understood why. There had been two other children between her and George, both lost to pneumonia that had developed from coughs and colds. Temperance was determined to preserve the rest of the family, even if it meant mollycoddling them to the extreme.

'You don't have to keep Faith and Maggie indoors on bonding day, you know,' Grace suggested gently.

'And have them wander down to the village and get theirselves burnt with everyone dashing about?'

'But Faith is very sensible. She'll be starting school herself in the autumn. And Maggie never lets go of her hand. And if they did end up at the wheelwrights', I'd take care of them.'

'I's sure you would, cheel. But what if you wasn't there? Pass me they carrots, would you? And that's what I wanted to talk to you about. Are you certain Mrs Snell don't mind you having time off for bonding day? Wouldn't want you to lose your job.'

'No, Mummy, you don't need to worry,' Grace answered as she tipped the bowl of chopped carrots into the saucepan. 'I work really hard so Mrs Snell's happy to give me time off occasionally. You know, you really shouldn't worry about things so much.' She wrapped her arms about her mother, hugging her so that they all but waltzed about the room.

'Aw, you'm a good girl, Gracie,' Temperance told her fondly. 'And I swears you get taller each time I sees you. Tall as a bean pole, you'll be soon.'

Grace tossed a laugh into the air. 'I hope not. Now let's put the kettle on and I'll go up and have a word with young scallywag while it's boiling.'

The rickety stairs protested even under her light weight as she scampered up to the room above. It gave George just enough warning so that when she pushed open the door, she caught him scooting back into bed and pretending to cough as he pulled the worn blankets up to his chin. The sun was just coming round to the front of the cottage and was streaming through the low window, showing the particles of dust dancing in the air. Grace shook her head as she approached the bed, her face stern and menacing.

'Busy gazing out the window, weren't you? Well, you don't look very sick to me.'

'Oh, I am, Gracie,' he tried to croak, but she knew him of old.

'You don't fool me. If I catch you doing this once more, I'll tell Constable Rodgers.'

George's face dropped. 'You wouldn't,' he whispered in horror.

'I would. So no more play-acting. It's not fair to worry Mummy like this.'

'All right. But you won't say ort about today?'

'Not if you promise on your heart not to do it again.'

'Yes, I promises,' George gulped, his eyes wide with fear.

Grace turned away, trying to keep the smile from her face. He was a good boy, was George. He just hated school. He would rather be out in the fields with their father, or up on the wild moorland, his heart flying free. Grace knew how he felt. She would love to spend her own life up on the moor, to be swept up in that sense of immensity and timelessness that filled every fibre of her being whenever she could escape for a few hours. But there were more important things in life that must come first. Work, for instance. And family.

Twenty minutes later, after a quick mug of weak tea with her mother, Grace was hurrying along the lane towards Horrabridge. The farm stood but a few hundred yards away, so that you could see it from the bedroom window of the Dannings's cottage. On the bank of the ancient hedgerow, bluebells were beginning to unfurl, proud and erect among the delicate stems of red and white campion that were coming into bud, while here and there, primroses nestled daintily in the protection of their taller brethren.

This was Grace's favourite time of year, all was so fresh and young and with the promise of the long summer days ahead. Her heart swelled with gladness and anticipation. Oh, all these people who believed that war was approaching, they couldn't possibly be right when the world was bursting into life. And even if they were, it would all be far away and nothing to do with the peace and harmony that reigned in Walkhampton and similar villages all over the country. And nobody from here was in the army. The men mainly laboured on the land. Two or three villagers worked on the railway that snaked its hazardous way up over the moor to Princetown, passing not far from Walkhampton itself, while others, of course, were employed at Vencombe's Yard. No. Life here was safe and secure.

Satisfying herself that nothing could ever change, Grace's heart took a happy bound and she skipped down the long front garden to the farmhouse. She found Mrs Snell in the spacious kitchen, stirring something on the large range in the inglenook fireplace — much as her mother had been, except that Grace knew the ingredients in Mrs Snell's pan would be far superior.

'I'll do that,' she offered, going to the sink to pump water into the enamel bowl. 'Or would you like me to start on the ironing?'

'The ironing, I think, maid,' Mrs Snell beamed at her. 'And how was bonding today?'

Grace dried her freshly washed hands and went to stand the flat irons on the range with a thin cloth between to prevent any smuts being transferred onto the ironing plates. 'Good as ever. But everyone's talking about a war coming. Larry's convinced there's going to be one.'

'Aw, that boy's too serious by half. And he won't be doing any fighting himself, will he, poor fellow? Not with that leg of his.'

'No, I suppose he won't.'

Grace frowned as she spread the thick ironing pad on one end of the vast table, for why should the mistress think that anyone from the village was likely to go off to fight? Not unless they *wanted* to. And why anyone would want to leave the peace of Walkhampton for the battlefield was beyond her. But this was all speculation and only time would tell what was really in store.

'When I've finished this,' Grace said, nodding at the overflowing laundry basket, 'I'll bring in the coal and then I'll wash the floor. And the dairy needs scrubbing ready for tomorrow. I assume we'm making butter as usual on a Tuesday?'

'Certainly are.'

'And I'll give the furniture in the sitting room and the dining room a good polish, too.'

'By the time you've finished that there mountain of ironing,' Mrs Snell chuckled, 'it'll be supper time. You're a good worker, young maid. But just because I give you a few hours off every now and then doesn't mean you have to work like a slave to make up for it. I give you that time off because you deserve it. And how was your mother, by the way? How are her nerves, poor soul?'

'She'm still worrying about the tackers. Reckon she always will.'

'Well, I suppose that's one thing about never having been blessed with chiller of our own. We don't have to worry about them. Now, we've a spring cabbage ready in the vegetable plot, so I'm just going to fetch it in.'

Grace was left alone with her thoughts for a few minutes, but soon Mrs Snell came back in with the said vegetable and they chatted away the afternoon while Grace ploughed through the ironing. She had indeed scarcely finished turning the crumpled heap of laundry into beautifully pressed items of clothing or smooth bed and table linen before Farmer Snell returned for the evening meal. Afterwards, he settled himself in his easy-chair by the empty fireplace in the sitting room to read the paper, and his wife sat opposite him knitting.

In the kitchen, Grace washed up, scouring the pans until they shone. Then she cleaned the dairy so that it was spick and span and ready for the morning, and went outside to lock the hens away for the night. It was almost dark before she came inside and met Farmer Snell coming out of the kitchen.

'There you are, cheel,' he smiled benevolently. 'I've put the newspaper on the table. All yours.'

'Thank you. I'll read it afore I go to bed.'

'Don't stay up too late. Need your beauty sleep,' he winked.

'I won't. Good night, then.'

Grace turned up the lamp. She loved her work, helping the bustling, jolly mistress all day and living as one of the family. But she had to admit this was the best time of day when she allowed herself ten minutes to look through the paper. Recently Farmer Snell had taken to having a daily national delivered in addition to the weekly local — to keep abreast of the times, he had said casually. But after all the talk that day in the village, Grace realized he was trying to conceal his concern over the current situation.

The first few pages were full of conjecture and Grace tried to understand it all in the light of Larry's earlier explanation. And then horror darted into her stomach as she recalled Martin's words. Give the Germans a bloody nose. Be a chance to see something of the world. Surely he wouldn't consider going to fight himself? He might even encourage her brother Stephen to join him. Grace knew that Stephen had a yen to travel beyond their Dartmoor home, and he had always been easily influenced, especially by the persuasive Martin. Oh, God. It would destroy their mother if her eldest son went off to war! Grace really must have a quiet word with Martin and beg him not to get Stephen involved even if he was determined to go himself.

Pleased with her plan, Grace turned back to the paper and another article caught her attention, one that she felt more comfortable with. More than that, she felt inspired and invigorated by it as if her life had suddenly expanded and begun to mean something radically important.

It was another piece about the Suffragettes.

Grace devoured every word. Men like John Sampson were entirely wrong. Women bore and brought up the children who would be the future of Britain and its empire. They worked as hard as men — at least all those Grace knew did — so surely they had just as much right to vote for the country's future. If only she knew more.

But there, at the end of the article, was an address to write to for more information. Surely it wouldn't hurt just to find out a little more? It was Grace's job to tear the newspaper into squares and skewer them onto the hook in the outside privy. It wouldn't matter if a piece was missing. And so, very carefully, she tore out the article, folded it and put it in the pocket of her apron.

* * *

'Oh.' Grace's voice landed with a thud of disappointment. It had been several days before she had found the chance to call into the wheelwrights' to speak to Martin, and now he wasn't there. Still, as she wanted to have a word with him in private, it was perhaps for the best. So she put a casual tone in her voice as she asked where he was.

'Skiving off somewhere as usual, I expect,' Larry grumbled. 'Why, did you want him for something?'

Grace hoped no one noticed the colour she felt tingling in her cheeks. 'No, not especially. I just wondered, that were all.'

'I thinks he were going up to the stables to mend that door what's rotted at the bottom,' John Sampson put in helpfully, and Grace knotted her lips. She didn't want to feel at all beholden to John, and was grateful when Larry spoke again.

'Was he? About time, too. I've been on at him for ages to do that.'

Grace was wondering what she could say next that would disguise the fact that she had indeed been looking for Martin, when a newly painted wagon wheel caught her eye. It had been decorated with an intricate design of small red and blue flowers, a typical example of a traditional farm wheel.

'Oh, that's beautiful, Mr Cowford!' she cried, taking a closer look. 'Excelled yourself again.'

'Proper pleased with it myself,' the elderly painter gloated proudly. 'I can see a time, mind, when folk won't bother with such things.'

'Well, they'll be missing out, truly they will. But I must be off. Just called in to say good day.'

'Bye, Gracie,' Larry called as she turned back out of the workshop and across the yard.

Grace hesitated as she came to the road. Would it look obvious if she turned left towards the field just outside the village where the Vencombes kept their three horses? But no one seemed to be watching her, and so she scudded past the inn and the school, following the road up the slight incline.

John Sampson waited just a few minutes before he announced that he was going to the timber yard to search for a suitable length of planking for the wooden chest he had been entrusted with repairing. But when he left the yard, he, too, turned left instead of right.

* * *

When Grace reached the field, the gate was padlocked. Typical of Martin, that would be, not bothering to bring the key but to drop his bag of tools over the top and then vault the gate himself. Grace had to hitch her skirt up to her knees to climb over. Not that it bothered her too much. There was nobody around to see, and if Martin caught a flash of her calves, it wouldn't count. They had all of them, Larry, Martin, Stephen and herself paddled in the Black Brook together all their lives. And if her legs were longer and more shapely now, it made no difference.

The two enormous carthorses and Sunny, the cob, were plodding contentedly about the field, their heads lowered as they went from one tasty mouthful of grass to the next. The large doors to the stable block were propped open so that the animals could take shelter if the weather suddenly changed, but there appeared to be no sign of Martin. He must be somewhere inside, then, since no one had mentioned exactly which door it was that needed attention. But when Grace checked each of the individual looseboxes inside, she found the place deserted.

'Martin?' she called in puzzlement, and turned to go back outside.

She almost collided with the short, stocky figure of John Sampson who had evidently come up behind her. She frowned, even more confused and not a little irritated that he had sent her on a wild goose-chase. 'You were wrong,' she said tartly. 'If you'm looking for Martin, he'm not here.'

She went to push past John's burly form, but he side-stepped into her path. 'I knows. He's gone up to Huckworthy Mill.'

'Huckworthy? Then why did you say—?'

The odd way he was looking at her made her pulse begin to throb. He had deliberately sent her up here, hadn't he, so that he could follow her? But . . . ?

'Been putting ideas in my Nan's head, haven't you?' he growled. 'Ideas above her station. Well, women's good for one thing only, and I's going to show you what!'

Before his words had sunk into Grace's shocked brain, he grasped her wrists in an iron grip and pushed her back against the stable wall with such force that a sharp pain shot down her back. For a few seconds it paralysed her so that when he released one of her wrists to rip open the front of her blouse, she was powerless to resist. It was only his hot breath in her face and his stubby, sweating hand reaching inside her camisole that brought her to her senses.

'Get off me!' she screamed, struggling to free herself. Panic seared through her veins, followed by a squall of white-hot rage. How dare he! But he only laughed, pressing his body so tightly against hers that she was completely trapped, no matter how desperately she tried to escape.

'Come now, it's what you wanted with young Martin, bain't it?'

'What!' Outrage burned inside her at the very idea. 'No, it most certainly weren't! However could you think—?'

'I've seen you, watching him across the yard with your big, yearning eyes!'

Oh, good God. Had he seen her looking at Martin when she had actually been thinking that she must persuade him not to encourage her brother to enlist? Her fury at once overtook her terror. 'Then you'm mistaken,' she grated with contempt, and hawking up a gobbet of saliva, she spat it full in his face. She held her breath, petrified lest it was entirely the wrong thing to do. But then as she saw the anger flare and then subside on his face, he suddenly stood back and gave a cruel, mocking laugh.

'You doesn't really think I'd want a scrawny vixen like you when I've got my lovely Nan waiting for me at home, does you? Just wanted to teach you a lesson for poking your nose into my affairs. And if you says ort, I'll deny it and say you was telling lies because I caught you trying to chase young Mr Martin.'

It was Grace's instinct to duck past him and run for her life, but his triumphant expression ignited her rage like a match to bone dry tinder. She drew herself up to her full height so that her eyes were on a level with his, and she glowered at him challengingly.

'No, I won't say anything,' she hissed back. 'But not because of that. Because I'm afeared you might take it out on Nan. Pity the poor woman, I do, married to a brute like you.'

'Huh!' John snorted, and then shaking his head with a derisive chuckle, he began to whistle as he sauntered out of the stables.

Grace stood, turned into a statue, until she heard the gate rattle as he climbed over it. And then, as her wildly beating heart slowed, she sank down on her knees, grasping her torn blouse across her chest. Dear Lord above, she could hardly believe what had happened. She would have to make some excuse as to why her clothes were in such a state. But for Nan's sake, she would never reveal what John had done. She couldn't, though, for ten minutes, bring her quaking limbs to move.

For his part, when he arrived back in the village, John Sampson hurried up to the timber yard to search for the required length of timber, a grimace of satisfaction on his lips.

CHAPTER THREE

'Going to join the Suffragettes, then, Gracie?'

Grace lifted her head and a surge of hot indignation swept through her at the man's teasing tone. She was crossing the small stone bridge over the brook, engrossed in the pamphlet she had received in the post that morning — and considering that while there were men like John Sampson in the world, it was imperative for women to fight for more than just the right to vote! So deep in thought had she been that she hadn't noticed the figure coming from the wheelwrights', and she was relieved to discover that it wasn't the bully she had just been thinking about.

'What's it to you if I am, Martin Vencombe?' she answered challengingly, though she quickly hid the front page with the title blazoned across it. 'Why shouldn't women have the vote? We'm just so good as men any day.'

'I'm sure you are.' Martin tipped his head in a jocular fashion, his eyes gleaming with mischief. 'You especially, Gracie. Hey, Larry!' he called over his shoulder. 'Gracie here's going to join the Suffragettes!'

Grace could have kicked herself. If she hadn't risen to Martin's teasing bait, this might have been the perfect opportunity to have that private word with him, for since the unpleasant encounter with John Sampson, she hadn't been able to bring herself to visit the wheelwrights' again. But now the moment was lost and Grace watched as another familiar figure came towards her, swaying with an odd, limping gait. The resemblance between the two brothers was uncanny, and yet it was Martin who bore the striking good looks. Larry's jaw was just a little too angular, his nose slightly too long, and of course he had been cursed since birth with the wretched wasted leg and club foot. He was just as strong as his brother, mind, and even though he had four years more experience than Martin, when Grace watched them at work, it seemed to her that Larry was the one who possessed a natural affinity with the wood and the tools with which he fashioned it.

Now his broad forehead dipped in a frown. 'Nothing wrong in that. Just mind you don't get arrested. And if you do, don't do anything stupid like going on hunger strike.'

Beside him, Martin at once cupped his own chin with one hand, holding his mouth open, and pretended to stick something down his throat with the other. 'Force feed you, they do!' he grated and proceeded to make a choking noise.

'Get away with you.' Grace dug him in the ribs, laughing as she saw the funny side of his antics. 'Don't you fret none. There's no rallies or ort like that going on around here, and I'm hardly likely to travel up to London or anywhere, am I?'

'You never know, there might be something nearer one day, in Plymouth or Exeter,' Larry said thoughtfully. 'Not that I'm advocating that you should go along. There was a rally in Tavistock once, about five years ago if I remember correctly. But it was a peaceful, non-militant branch of the movement. But shouldn't you be at work, Grace?'

'I'm just running an errand for Mrs Snell. Posting a couple of letters for her.'

'Going to the Post Office myself.' Larry waved the envelope in his hand. 'I'll come along of you. And you're supposed to be helping Reg,' he admonished, glaring at his brother.

'Hard taskmaster, you!' Martin grinned back. 'Only stepped outside for a few minutes' break.'

'Just because this is our family business doesn't mean any of us can slack off, you know.'

Martin pulled a face and then gave a broad grin as he strode round the corner of the house towards the mill and workshop behind. Grace wondered if she shouldn't go after him, but the time wasn't quite right, so she bounded forward a few paces to catch up with Larry.

'*You* don't think it's a silly idea, do you? Me joining the Suffragettes?' she asked.

'Not at all. But I know you, Grace. Too headstrong for your own good, and I wouldn't want you to get yourself hurt.'

'So you think I'm not capable of looking after myself?' she bristled. 'That just because I'm a girl—'

'No, that's not what I said. It's just that sometimes, well, you're inclined to jump in with both feet, and you might get into something deeper than you realize. Like when you insisted on copying us boys jumping off Huckworthy Bridge into the river when you can't swim. Fully clothed, and all. Could've drowned, you could.'

'But I didn't,' she pouted obstinately.

'Only because we rescued you. I hate to say it, but you need to grow up a bit, you do. But you know my opinion. I reckon the whole country will have some thinking to do soon, the way things are going.'

Grace had been about to retaliate, but Larry's change of subject altered the course of her thoughts. 'Do you think it'll affect us at all, then, if there *is* a war?' she asked instead. 'I mean, in wars in the past, it's just been going on in other countries and nort to do with us here.'

'But this time it's in Europe and right on our doorstep. And then there's all this Home Rule business in Ireland. They say the Unionists are smuggling arms from Germany, so it's all connected. But let's hope I'm wrong and nothing comes of it.'

So did Grace! And certainly not before she had a chance to have that conversation with Martin. Now she and Larry turned off to the grocer's which also served as the Sub-Post Office, and Larry held the door open for her.

'You first,' he said as they went inside. 'And I'd wait until this evening before you read that pamphlet again.'

Grace sucked in her cheeks. Yes, she supposed that, with her nose stuck in the pamphlet, she *had* taken too long walking into the village from the farm. But the passion burned inside her to do something *useful* with her life and joining the Suffragettes seemed to be the perfect first step. Besides, it would be one in the eye for John Sampson to see that she meant business!

So she smiled up at Larry, her eyes alight with enthusiasm. 'Yes. But I really think we should fight for what we believe in, don't you?'

'We may all have to do that sooner than you think,' Larry agreed under his breath.

'Grace dear, what can I get you?' Mr Trathern beamed at her.

'Mrs Snell asked me to post these letters for her, please,' she answered, and the sub postmaster walked over to the separate Post Office counter.

A few minutes later, Grace was striding back through the village and past the wheelwrights' again. When she thought about it, apart from Larry's words just now, there had not been so much talk of war recently, so perhaps her fears were unfounded and she need not speak to Martin after all. Not yet, anyway. The arrival of the pamphlet that morning was much more exciting, and Grace's head was buzzing with thoughts of joining the Suffragettes. She gave most of her meagre weekly wage to her mother, but Temperance always insisted she kept six pence for herself. Grace rarely spent any money except on little presents for her family for birthdays and Christmas, and so over the years had saved a tidy sum. Now she wondered if there was enough to buy a length of white calico to make herself a simple dress, and decorate it with green and purple ribbons. Those were the Suffragette colours: white for purity, green for hope and purple for dignity. She could see herself proudly wearing it to Chapel on Sundays during the summer to demonstrate her support for the cause. That would really give John Sampson something to think about!

Oh, she felt she was being borne along on a crest of inspiration, fired by this new passion in her life. What excitement it would bring! She couldn't wait for the evening to come and her chores to be completed so she could study the pamphlet in depth.

* * *

'My God, have you seen this?'

It was some weeks later and Grace looked up as Farmer Snell lifted his head from the newspaper as he ate his breakfast. At the opposite end of the kitchen table, his wife was making bread, up to her elbows in flour.

'What's that, my lover?' she asked, scarcely paying attention.

'It's happened, that's what,' her husband replied grimly, jabbing his head at the newspaper.

This time, his wife began to wipe her floury hands on her apron. 'What has, Mr Snell?'

Grace stood still, watching as an ominous silence settled about the table. It seemed that Farmer Snell had something very important to announce and he nodded, pushing his lips forward in a dramatic gesture.

'War,' he declared. 'Seems one Archduke Ferdinand of Austria and his wife were assassinated the day afore yesterday in a place called S-a-r-a-j-e-v-o,' he read, pronouncing the strange, foreign name with slow deliberation. 'Says here it was some young students sent by Serbia, like. After all what's been happening, it'll lead to general war within the month, I reckon.'

Grace's heart thumped in her chest. She had thought the situation had been settling down, and with the vision of John Sampson's livid face that day still fresh in her mind, she somehow still hadn't spoken to Martin. And now this. 'But the Prime Minister's been calming things down, hasn't he?' she protested, trying to dispel her own alarm. But it seemed that Larry had been right. War was creeping forward like some slithering evil, but Grace didn't *want* to believe it. 'And Lloyd George is firmly against war. It'll blow over in time, won't it?'

'I'm not sure, cheel.' Farmer Snell frowned. 'And what about that young devil, Winston Churchill? Forceful character, and he seems to *want* war.'

'Oh, let's not worry about that now. Safe as houses here, we are. Don't suppose it'll affect us here too much, will it? Now then, Grace, put this dough to rise, will you?'

A horrible coldness shivered through Grace's body. She was thinking of the other things Larry had said. It only needed a spark to set the whole thing off. And it would be like something the world had never known before. Could this assassination be that trigger? An excuse for Austria-Hungary to declare war on Serbia? Grace's energies had been focussed so intently on the Suffragettes that her mind had blocked out her fears about the consequences for her family if war indeed materialized. But this sudden news had brought her anxieties tumbling down about her once more.

'Well, I'm off to the village to see what others think about this,' Farmer Snell said gravely, getting to his feet. 'Your father has nipped home for his breakfast, too, and he'll likely not have heard about it yet. So I reckon we can spare you for half an hour, Grace, can't we, Mrs Snell, if you want to go and tell him.'

'Aw.' Grace saw the mistress purse her lips as if the gravity of the situation had just hit home. But then she nodded vigorously as she returned to her senses. 'Yes, of course you can go, maid. Try not to worry your poor mother too much, mind.'

'No, I won't, Mrs Snell. And thank you.'

Grace took off her apron and followed Farmer Snell out of the back door, not even bothering to put on the straw hat that she wore in summer. It was the very end of June, but Grace was scarcely aware of the early morning sunshine as her heart ticked nervously in her chest. She hesitated across from the front door of her family's cottage, remembering the mistress's words. Her mother would be alarmed to see her arrive home so unexpectedly, so perhaps it would be better to wait until her father came out again and give him the news first.

As if on cue, Ernest emerged from the cottage at that very moment. His expression showed that he was surprised to see her, and she drew him aside. But as she spoke, everything suddenly seemed macabre and unreal, and the enormity of what this war, if it indeed came, could mean suddenly pressed in on every side.

'Let's not jump to conclusions, Gracie,' Ernest said after a few moments' reflection, but she could see that he was deeply concerned. Her dear father, who always put everything to right, this time was being evasive.

'Shall I tell Mummy?'

'No. I'll explain to her later. No point worrying her too much. It might be a storm in a teacup.'

'Think so, do you?' Grace asked sceptically. 'When everyone else . . . ?'

She jerked her head towards the centre of the village. People were coming out of their homes and congregating on the bridge and on the road outside the Vencombes' residence. Ernest met his daughter's gaze from beneath dipped eyebrows and together they walked down in tense silence to join the other villagers.

People were talking in small groups, their voices low as if they were almost afraid to articulate their fears and yet craved the reassurance of discussing events with their friends and neighbours. Grace realized that her father had found Farmer Snell and the farmer from Gnatham Barton up the lane who had evidently ridden down on his horse. Mr and Mrs Nelson who ran the general store in the square were outside their shop deep in conversation with a very animated Martha. Just now, though, it wasn't Grace's garrulous friend she needed to talk to. It was Martin she must speak to, no matter what! And before he had a chance to influence Stephen in any way, since though she loved her brother dearly, Grace knew he wouldn't have the courage to back down once he had agreed to something. Fortunately Martha had her back to the road and Grace slipped past her unnoticed and scurried into Vencombe's Yard in a whirl of desperation.

She wasn't surprised to see the men standing about discussing the momentous news. Mr Vencombe was slowly shaking his head as if he couldn't contemplate what it would mean for them all, while John Sampson was declaring that he'd known all along that it would come to this. Grace shivered involuntarily, but her dislike of the man was of no importance now. Larry, Martin and Stephen stood together a little apart, and Grace hurried across to them, praying fervently that she hadn't arrived too late.

'Just a matter of time now,' Larry was saying with what seemed like wistful resignation as Grace came into earshot.

'Never mind, brother,' Martin grinned, boisterously clapping Larry on the shoulder. 'The army might not be able to take you, but I'll fight well enough for both of us. Enlist as soon as I can, I will. Soon teach the Hun a lesson! Probably be over by Christmas, more's the pity. Be a real opportunity to see a bit of the world!'

'And I'll come along of you!' Stephen told him, his eyes shining. 'Be a proper adventure, like! Always wanted to travel, me. Us can be in the engineers and mend broken wheels together.'

Grace's mouth dropped open in abject horror. The voices around her seemed to explode in a mingled, incomprehensible cacophony and all her eyes could focus on was Stephen's face alight with excitement. Oh, dear God. It was all her fault. All her fault for hesitating because of the fear John Sampson had instilled in her. She knew it now. She had been a coward and this was the result. Well, she would stand up to that fear now.

'But you could get hurt,' she blurted out, 'or even killed.'

She grasped hold of Stephen's arm, burning with guilt and with her eyes boring desperately into his. Surely he could see he couldn't do this to their mother? To any of them?

But before either of them could say a word, Martin went on exuberantly, 'Don't worry, Gracie. I'll take care of him. Come on now, Steve. Let's go into Tavistock and find out how we can join up.'

Grace glanced across at Larry, choking on her silent terror and willing him to put a stop to it all. But all he could do was narrow his eyes and say levelly, 'Don't you think you should wait until war is actually declared?'

But Martin only shrugged. 'You just said yourself it's only a matter of time. No, Steve and I want to be in on it from the start, don't we, Steve?' He took Stephen's other arm, propelling him forward. Stephen glanced over his shoulder at his sister, but his look said that he couldn't change his mind now, could he?

Grace's hand let go of Stephen's sleeve and fell to her side. Her stomach felt empty. Sick. She could have prevented this, if only she had faced up to reality and hadn't had her head in the clouds over the senseless campaign about votes for women. Perhaps John Sampson had been right after all. And suddenly the half-sewn white dress up in Grace's room filled her with anger and self-loathing.

CHAPTER FOUR

'You've done *what?*'

'I've joined the Battery,' Stephen declared, his chest swelling beneath its threadbare waistcoat.

'The . . . B-battery?' Grace stuttered. 'B-but—'

'The Third Devonshire Battery, Fourth Wessex Division of the Royal Field Artillery, Territorial Force. So what does you think of that, then?' came the proud reply.

Grace glared at him over the gate. She had been bringing in the dried laundry from Mrs Snell's washing line when he had suddenly appeared, beckoning her over to him. All day, she had been trapped in her own crucifying world of guilt, hardly able to concentrate on her chores. She prayed as she had never prayed before that Stephen and Martin would be told they would have to wait until war was declared before they could enlist. Or, even more passionately, she begged God not to allow any military conflict to materialize at all. But she hadn't thought of the Tavistock branch of the Territorial Army. Now, as she saw the grin spreading over her brother's face, she felt her knees begin to quake.

'Oh.' And then as the reality of his words kicked home, seething fury swept her guilt and horror aside. 'Oh, Steve, how could you?' she challenged him. 'You know how

Mummy still grieves over our lost little brothers and worries herself to death if one of the tackers so much as sneezes. And now you go and really give her summat to worry about!'

She watched the delight slide from her brother's expression and his brow lifted defensively. 'Well, that's the whole point, doesn't you see? I doesn't want to join the army proper, like. They'm the ones what'll be sent to do the proper dangerous fighting, and besides, I doesn't want to commit myself for years on end. But I does want to do my bit. Surely you sees that?' he questioned earnestly.

'No, I don't! You'd be doing your bit as you put it here in Walkhampton. The country still needs to be fed in times of war, and making farm-carts is an essential part of that without putting your life at risk!'

'Well, I thought you'd understand with all your talk of Suffragettes and doing summat useful with your life. And I won't be taking any risks,' Stephen insisted. 'The Territorials be just that. To defend England if the Hun try to invade us, and that'll never happen.'

'You don't *know* that!'

'And you doesn't know for sure that there'll even *be* a war. And if there is, it'll be across the Channel. It's highly unlikely us'll be invaded, but Mr Asquith wants us to be prepared just in case. So joining the Territorial Army is about the safest thing I could do. I thought you'd be pleased. I'll only see other parts of England, and that only if I'm lucky. I could've waited to join some volunteer force and go abroad, which is what I'd really like, but that'd be more dangerous.'

Grace drew in a harsh breath between her teeth, letting her anger subside. 'So, what happens next?' she asked, since she supposed — reluctantly — that what Stephen had said made sense.

'Aw, just a bit of training of an evening. We won't get our uniforms for a few weeks. Can't wait for that, I can't. Like a man in uniform, you girls, doesn't you?' he winked mischievously.

Grace did not return his jocularity. 'When you say *we*, I assume you mean you and Martin?'

'Yes and no.' Stephen pulled an awkward face. 'Proper interested in Martin, they was, him being quite educated, like. Shows at once, it does, by the way he speaks. Not like me. Never could cotton on to a better way of talking like you has, Gracie. Anyways, they said Martin would probably be officer material. They've taken all his details and he's going to come to the training sessions, but they advised him to wait and see what happens. Might be better for him to sign up to some other battalion when the time comes. Maybe some volunteer force or summat. He might be more use to the army like that.'

'Oh, he might, might he?'

'Yes. And he definitely wants to go abroad to fight, even if it'll be more dangerous, like, so he's going to wait.'

Grace closed her mouth into a knot. Well, she had to admit that the situation was not quite as bad as she feared. But if she had spoken to Martin in the first place as she should have done, Stephen probably wouldn't have been enlisting in any military group at all.

'So, you haven't told Mummy and Daddy yet?' Grace managed to contain her misgivings sufficiently to ask.

'Well, no,' Stephen faltered, and now he shifted his eyes evasively. 'I though as maybe *you* might—'

'No, I will not! If you think you'm brave enough to join *any* part of the army, then you'm brave enough to tell them yourself!' And with that, she spun on her heel and flounced away. But even as she picked up the full laundry basket and made for the house, she recognized that what she was really taking out on Stephen was her own anger at herself.

* * *

'War were declared overnight, Farmer Snell!' Grace heard the paperboy announce gleefully as he handed in the newspapers at the back door. It wasn't his custom to knock but today, Grace considered bitterly as his words percolated into her brain, was clearly different.

'Wish I were old enough to fight,' the boy persisted, his voice high with excitement.

'Thank the Lord you're not,' Farmer Snell replied gruffly.

Grace paused but momentarily as she kneaded the day's bread on the table. She felt as if her head was truncated from her hands which went on working apparently of their own accord. It had been reported the previous day that the Foreign Secretary, Edward Grey, had remarked while he watched the London gas lamps being lit at dusk that 'the lights were going out all over Europe'. That was exactly how Grace felt, as if a cold darkness had invaded her entire being. She had tried to ignore it, this sense of impending doom, even though they had all seen it coming for so long. After all the recent events — Austria-Hungary declaring war on Serbia, Russia mobilising its army, and in the last few days, Germany declaring war on both Russia and France — it was inevitable that Britain would become involved. And now it had happened.

It was the Fifth of August. Grace was sure she would remember that date for ever. And yet now it had come, she felt oddly calm. Relieved almost. As if the waiting, with its vain hope that the whole situation would just go away, was the hardest thing to bear. And yet the uncertainty was just as crushing. What would it mean for them all? For young men like Stephen and Martin? Would it all be solved by Christmas as so many believed? Or would people like Larry, who predicted it would explode into the biggest conflict man had ever seen, be proved right?

She glanced up as Farmer Snell entered the kitchen, already reading the headlines of the newspaper in his hands.

'This is it,' he said gravely. 'Germany invaded Belgium yesterday, and Asquith declared war at eleven o'clock last night.'

'Saints preserve us,' Mrs Snell murmured, and she solemnly crossed herself.

The gesture seared into Grace's mind, and she stopped in her work, absently observing her floury hands. 'We'm at war, then,' she stated quietly.

A thousand thoughts milled about in her brain. Up until then, she had mainly thought of the looming troubles as being between nations. Britain, the country, the government. But now, it truly was *we*. Not just the men who would be fighting on the battlefield, but everyone. And yet, Grace felt curiously detached, devoid of emotion. This had happened, and they must get on with it, whatever it might bring. And the deep emptiness of acceptance weighed heavily on her heart.

'They won't invade *us*, will they, Farmer Snell, like they have Belgium? We're an island, and the water'll protect us like it always has, won't it?'

'Don't you worry, Felicity dear. Britannia still rules the waves.' Farmer Snell gave his wife a comforting smile. 'Safe as houses here we'll be. It's those as go to fight that'll be facing the danger.'

'Well, I've always had a bone to pick with the Lord for not granting us any chiller. But now I thank Him for not giving us any sons to worry over,' Felicity sighed with vehemence. And then, as her eyes met Grace's across the kitchen table, they widened in horrified shame and her hand went over her mouth. 'Oh, Grace, dear, I'm so sorry. Your brother . . . Poor Temperance will be out of her mind.'

Grace pretended to be casual, although her insides were churning. 'Oh, he's only in the Territorials, so he's highly unlikely to be doing any fighting. Just being prepared. Just in case.'

Her mouth lifted in a half-hearted smile. That was what Stephen had said when he had told their parents that he had enlisted and their mother had almost fainted on the spot. And now Grace was saying the same thing, her words meant to reassure herself as much as Mrs Snell.

'Well, this won't get the bread baked,' she declared, wanting to blank the whole matter from her mind, and she directed all her misgivings into pummelling the dough.

* * *

They stood in the centre of the village's triangular-shaped 'square', the seven young men, sons of Walkhampton families, who had so far joined up to fight for their country — or to set off on a wondrous adventure, to judge by the glowing anticipation on their faces. Grace's brother, Stephen, and Joe Allawell from one of the cottages opposite the pub were off to rendezvous with the other members of the Tavistock Territorials that Joe had also signed up to before war had been declared. By coincidence, the five village lads who had answered the call to the new volunteer army were to leave for Exeter on the same day. Among them was Martin Vencombe whom the recruiting officer had said was bound to be taken off to train as a non-commissioned officer.

'I just wanted to slip away without any fuss,' Stephen had confessed to Grace. 'Would've been better for Mum, I reckons. But you knows the village folk wanted to make summat special of it, and it seemed ungrateful when they'd made such an effort.'

Certainly the whole village appeared to have turned out. Four members of the Tavistock band had offered to attend and were performing their military repertoire by the little bridge. Colourful bunting had been strung between the Vencombe residence and the house on the opposite side of the brook, and flapped patriotically in the August breeze. Although it was only mid-morning, Mr Brown had set up his trestle table in the square and had provided sandwiches, while women came out of their cottages carrying pots of hot tea. Uncomprehending children dashed about, happy not to be helping in the fields of fodder crops around the village, or whatever other tasks they were normally put to during the school holidays.

Grace fingered the buttons on Stephen's khaki jacket, in her nervousness unsure of what to say to the brother she had always been so close to. 'You'm proper handsome in your uniform, even if you'm an ugly old devil,' she tried to joke.

Stephen's eyes, the same cornflower blue as her own, smiled back. He grabbed the arm of their younger brother,

George, as he raced past them in some hare-brained game, swinging him round to face them. 'Hear that, did you? Grace has finally admitted that I's handsome!' he chortled.

'Oh, yes?'

George pulled a face and then broke away to chase after his friends. Faith and Maggie, though, were staring up at this big brother they hardly recognized in his strange attire, and little Maggie had her thumb firmly plugged in her rosebud mouth. Stephen knelt down and picked them up, one in each arm, laughing and jiggling them up and down in a pretence of jollity.

'I baked you a cake. In case they doesn't feed you proper like.' Temperance, her eyes red-rimmed, held out a package to her son. 'You . . . you will take care of yourself now,' she barely croaked.

'I's only going to Salisbury Plain!'

Stephen stood his little sisters back on their feet and gave a reassuring laugh. It was too much for Grace to see the anguish on her mother's face, and she had to move off into the crowd before the lump in her own throat became unbearable. She did feel proud of Stephen in an odd way, but she would miss him terribly. And if the worst came to the worst and Britain *was* invaded . . . But then they would all have something pretty serious to worry about, wouldn't they?

The sudden sight of Agatha Nonnacott, almost draped around Martin Vencombe, sickened Grace at such a time. The girl had one arm about Martin's neck, eyeing him coquettishly. It was lucky Aggie's strict, lay-preacher father was at work and not there to witness his daughter's behaviour, and her mother was a recluse who never left the house. But Martin seemed to be relishing Aggie's attention, his face burnished with excitement.

'My, won't you be mortal handsome when you get your uniform?' Grace heard Aggie's smooth, oily voice. 'You will let me see you in it when you come home on leave, won't you?'

'Of course, Aggie!' Martin grinned, placing his hand over his heart in a melodramatic gesture. And then he bent to whisper in her ear something that Grace was glad she didn't hear from the lascivious expression that came over the girl's face. And then, as Aggie threw up her head with a tittering laugh, she threw Grace a sneer and strutted over to the other volunteers.

Grace felt her blood boil and was overwhelmed with relief as Larry appeared behind her.

'This is it, then, brother,' he announced, jabbing his head towards where the vicar was holding up his arms to attract everyone's attention. 'Here, something for you. No drinking on duty, mind.'

Grace saw him slip a hip-flask into Martin's hand, but Martin only had the chance to nod his thanks before the crowd fell silent for the vicar to give a brief address followed by a short blessing. The tension was broken then by the clip-clop of horses' hoofs as Mr Vencombe senior drove a brand-new wagon across the bridge.

The gay frivolity faded from Martin's face. 'Time to go, then.' And his chest expanded in a sigh of sudden reluctance.

'Good luck, Martin.'

Grace felt her throat tighten and she stood on tiptoe to brush a kiss on his cheek before leaving him clapped in Larry's arms. Out of the corner of her eye, she saw Mrs Vencombe hurry forward. Grace turned away. She had her own sadness to deal with. She took a deep breath, steeling her nerves, and hurried back to where she had left her brother.

Stephen was locked in a crushing embrace between Ernest and Temperance, his head bent as he tried to comfort his mother who was now weeping openly. The little ones were standing in a bewildered huddle beside them, and Stephen broke away, relinquishing his distraught mother into his father's arms in order to give his young siblings a final hug. But Temperance at once dragged her firstborn to her bosom again, and Ernest had to use some force to peel her hands from their son's uniform. It was only as he picked up his army-issue haversack to join his comrades as they climbed onto the wagon, that Stephen met Grace's gaze.

They stared at each other in silence. No words. No time. Stephen glanced at the wagon. Everyone else was on board. A train to catch. Report for duty, must not be late.

'Grace,' she heard him murmur.

Then he was on the back of the wagon, legs dangling in a seemingly casual manner over the end, waving, as the vehicle he had helped to make began to trundle off up the hill. The villagers cheering and shouting, the little band playing, and everyone waving until the wagon moved out of sight.

The crowd turned away, slowly dispersing, wondering with trepidation how life would feel now and what the future might hold. The festive atmosphere had dissipated into thin air, and hearts were suddenly empty. There were audible sighs, mutterings. The musicians packed up their instruments, villagers cleared away the remains of the refreshments.

Grace watched her father comforting her mother as they made their way back towards their cottage. She saw Martha, bless her, run up and put her arms, too, about Temperance's frail shoulders, and they all disappeared inside, taking the younger children with them and leaving Grace feeling oddly alone. When she felt a hand on her shoulder, she was deeply grateful to find Larry there.

'Going to feel strange for a while, isn't it?' he said in his familiar frank but solid way. 'It'll be the same in towns and villages all over the country. All over Europe, in fact, whichever side you're on.'

Grace raised a surprised eyebrow. She had never thought of it like that. But then Larry always saw every side of an argument.

'You weren't going with them to the station, then?' she said limply.

'No. I thought I'd stay here to support Mother, but see, she's busied herself clearing away. Her way of coping, I suppose. A very practical woman, our mother.'

'I suppose we'll all find our own ways to cope.'

'Well, just you and me, now Martin and Stephen are gone. Till it's all over and they're back home again.'

Grace nodded. She knew what he meant. The clan — the three boys and her as their little sister — had somehow gravitated together since childhood, even though Larry and Martin were some years older. There were others of a similar age to Grace in the village, Aggie Nonnacott for instance, but she and Stephen had always preferred the company of the jocular Martin and the sombre Larry. And now . . .

'Back to work for me, I reckons.' Martha's Barry broke into her thoughts as he puffed past them.

'Martha's been so kind to Mummy these last weeks,' Grace answered. 'She really seems to understand.'

'Well, she would, wouldn't she, with our Horace always having been in the Navy and all?'

His words were spoken with quiet acceptance, yet they sliced into Grace's heart. Yes, of course. This horrible war was going to affect them all. No one knew to what extent as yet. Grace could only pray that the young men who had left the village on such a great adventure would return to it with equal celebration.

CHAPTER FIVE

'Morning, Grace. Haven't seen you here in a while.'

Larry was not alone in the workshop, but he was the only one who did more than nod his head in greeting. He was sitting astride the spoke horse, carefully finishing off a sturdy but handsomely shaped wheel spoke with a spoke-shave; he glanced up with a warm smile as Grace came towards him.

It was just what Grace needed to put her at ease. She had been actively avoiding the wheelwrights', or more precisely John Sampson. She could not shake from her memory the image of him up at the stables that day, and still blamed him to some extent for her not speaking to Martin. But time had allowed her to reason that Stephen might well have joined the Territorial Army anyway, and the way things were going in France, it was probably as well that his military service would be confined to England.

But she didn't want to arouse Larry's suspicions in any way, so she merely shrugged. 'Oh, I've been busy. You know, this and that.'

'So what brings you here today? A day off?'

'Not a whole day. I've been doing the laundry since six o'clock this morning and now it's all on the line. So Mrs

Snell's given me a few hours off as I'll be ironing all evening. And I've got a message for you from Farmer Snell. That spoke's coming loose on the dogcart again, he says, and please can you mend it for him.'

Larry puffed out his cheeks. 'I told him to let me mend it properly for him last time instead of doing a temporary repair. Or better still, have us make him a completely new wheel. It wasn't of our making in the first place, I hasten to add. Bought that cart from God knows where, he did. But now, well, we're rushed off our feet. You can see how busy we are with being three men down.'

'Three?'

'Yes. Reg has enlisted now as well. He'd have done so earlier, but when he heard about the send-off the village had planned, he didn't fancy being one of the objects of such attention. He went off quietly a few days ago.'

'Poor Sybil.' Grace's thoughts went immediately to Reg's young lady.

'Dad wasn't too pleased with it being one of our busiest times of year. Farmers finding their wagons aren't up to the harvest and needing them repaired immediately or wanting new ones almost straight away. You know how people come to us from far and wide. You don't mind if I get on?' He leant back, closing one eye to measure up expertly the shape of the spoke before drawing the spoke-shave along it again. 'Have you heard from Stephen?'

'Yes. He'm enjoying himself. Salisbury Plain's a bit like Dartmoor in a way, only not as dramatic, he says. He's been to Stonehenge. I remember learning about that at school. He says it's really impressive, far bigger than any of the old stone circles we have on the moor. Trekked over to watch the sunrise there, he and Joe did, when they had a twenty-four hour pass. He says it were amazing.'

'Everything all right with him, then.'

It was a statement rather than a question, so Grace felt no need to reply. But it was so easy to talk to Larry. He had such an unruffled attitude to everything. At least, he always saw the reality of every situation, even if Grace could see in his eyes if it was something that troubled him.

'What about Martin?' she asked eagerly. 'Has he written?'

A rueful smile twitched at Larry's mouth. 'Briefly,' he snorted. 'Not a great one for letter-writing is Martin, as you might expect. You know he's been creamed off to train as a non-commissioned officer? Well, seems he's a natural crack-shot with a pistol *and* a rifle. Quite proud of that, he is. Lucky to have the things to train with. By all accounts, the ordinary recruits hardly have any weapons, and nobody's got any uniforms yet at all. Can't tell us where he is for the sake of security, or so he says. Not that I believe that for a minute. Not while he's training, at least. That's just Martin wringing as much drama as he can from the situation.'

Grace gave a light chuckle. 'Yes, I can imagine. But does that mean you can't write back to him?'

'Oh, no. We've a central address, and then they forward post on.'

'Ah, yes.' Grace nodded pensively. 'Martha's always done that with Horace. You know, before now, I'd never really thought how it must be for her and Barry, having a son away in the Royal Navy. Martha's always so cheerful, but she must miss him terribly. And now she and Barry must be so worried about him and all.'

'I'm sure they are. I know they say that our navy's three or four times stronger than Germany's, especially now it's joined forces with the small fleet Russia has. But the Germans are bound to try and put it to the test.'

'Yes.' Grace released a heartfelt sigh. 'If things get worse—'

'Which they are.' Larry paused at the end of a stroke with the spoke-shave. 'You've read about the retreat at Mons, I suppose?'

'Yes. But hopefully as we send more soldiers over, we can attack again and drive the Germans back.' Grace's eyes travelled about the workshop and she was pleased to see that John Sampson was getting on with his work without so much as a glance in her direction. 'Everything's so normal and peaceful here, it's hard to imagine—'

Just as she spoke, Bob, the Vencombe's carpenter, released the lever on the mechanism that was driven by the waterwheel outside, and the machinery sprang into life. Cogs clunked and turned, drive belts began to whir and then came the high-pitched whistle of the circular saw as it powered through a hefty elm trunk that was being cut into lengths ready to be fashioned into cartwheel hubs.

'Peaceful, did you say?' Larry gave his rare grin. 'And what about you, Grace?' He raised his voice to make himself heard. 'Have you joined the Suffragettes yet?'

'The Suffragettes?' she repeated in surprise. She felt her cheeks colour slightly, since for all her heated indignation over the cause she had felt so strongly about, she had scarcely given it a thought since war had been declared. And it was partly because of her obsession over it that she had never had that all important conversation with Martin. It was water under the bridge now, but she still felt ashamed whenever the memory of it crossed her mind. 'Well, no,' she admitted. 'It doesn't seem so important now. Once the war's over, I'll join, mind. In the meantime, maybe there'll be summat I can do to help with the war instead. But it'd have to be something that weren't to do directly with killing Germans.'

'I don't think you'd ever be asked to do that,' Larry said quietly, and then casting his experienced eye along the spoke one last time, he went on, 'There, that's finished.'

He removed his foot from the treadle, thus releasing the spoke from its clamp, and stood up from the horse in order to stack the spoke with another finished one. Then he went to pick up another tenon, or length of oak that had already been given its basic spoke shape on the machine copier. Grace instinctively went to help him. She had spent so much of her young life in the workshop, that she knew exactly what was needed, and helped Larry position the piece of wood on the horse.

'Thanks, Grace,' Larry said, sitting back on the spoke horse. 'That's saved me a minute, and every second counts just now. Dad and I are having to work full-time in the workshop. I don't know how on earth we're going to keep up with all the paperwork and ordering supplies for the timber yard and everything else we have to do. Unless we can find another wheelwright from somewhere, we're just going to get further and further behind.'

He paused to flex his shoulders, working them round in circles, and then stretching his back. Grace took the opportunity to run her hand up and down the surface of the tenon, feeling the strength of the wood beneath her touch.

'Lovely, isn't it?' Larry said, his eyes sparkling with a gleam of appreciation, before he picked up the spoke-shave again and depressed the foot treadle to clamp the new tenon in place.

Grace knew, reluctantly, that she should leave Larry to get on with his work. Her eyes wandered around the workshop, all so familiar, so comforting, the scent of the freshly sawn wood wafting into her nostrils. She loved it here, and even with John's uneasy presence, she realized how she had been missing the place. It seemed strange, though, without Martin's constant banter, Stephen's quiet smile and now Reg . . .

The idea flashed across her brain with such force that she visibly jumped. Oh. Oh, of course!

'I could help,' she blurted out before she allowed herself time to ponder further. And even the fleeting consideration of John Sampson did not deter her. She must have spoken with considerable conviction as Larry stopped in mid-stroke and blinked up at her in astonishment.

'Bob, turn that off a minute, would you?' he called across to the older fellow working the saw. It ground to a stop, and in the ensuing quiet, Larry fixed Grace with a steady gaze. 'Go on,' he prompted.

'I could certainly help with the paperwork. I were really quick at picking things up at school, so I'm sure if you or your father were to show me what to do, I could do a lot

51

of it for you. And I know what timber you need for the yard. At least I would if I knew what orders were coming in. And I could do the wages and all. I mightn't have your skills in the workshop, but I know exactly what goes on in here,' she concluded breathlessly, astounding herself with her own ideas; it was as though someone else had taken over her brain.

She felt annoyed and embarrassed at herself as Larry frowned back at her. 'And when would you do all this?' he asked, though not unkindly.

'In my time off.' Grace bit her lip, since to be honest, Larry knew as well as she did that she didn't actually have that much leisure time. 'But,' she went on, her forehead wrinkling, 'I'm sure Mrs Snell could spare me more often than she does. The house doesn't *need* to be so clean as I keep it for her. Having me there all the time is a luxury, she often says so. *Your* mother manages without a maid, doesn't she? I'm sure Mrs Snell would agree, and I wouldn't mind if she paid me less.'

'Well, we'd make up your wages, of course.'

'Or if there were so much work that you needed me all the time, she could find someone to take my place altogether.'

Her tongue came to an abrupt halt as she realized Larry was staring at her, his head cocked to one side. Oh, Lord, had she made a complete fool of herself, jumping in with both feet, just as Larry had said of her not so long ago, she remembered? She realised that silence had fallen on the workshop and everyone, including John Sampson, was listening to her. Oh, wouldn't he love the fact that she had just made a complete and utter fool of herself?

'You know, that's not at all a bad idea,' Larry said slowly. 'It might just work. And it would all be for the war, really. The country still needs to eat, so farm-wagons are just as important as ever, and with us struggling to keep up with being three men down . . . Wouldn't hurt to have a word with Mrs Snell, would it? See if she'd agree. She's a good sort, after all. Hey, Dad, what do you think?'

Grace turned her head as Geoffrey Vencombe, having heard their conversation, came towards them, a thoughtful expression on his face. Grace's heart soared with pride. Perhaps she wasn't so silly after all.

'And I bet George would jump at the chance to help,' she announced, quite inspired now. 'He's always said he wants to do an apprenticeship with you when he's old enough. He could be an errand boy, sweep up the shavings and off-cuts, all that sort of thing. Term starts again next week, but he could come in for a few hours after school each day. He'd love it, and it would all help save time.'

She watched, holding her breath, as Larry and his father exchanged glances. And then a warm tide of happiness engulfed her as Larry laughed, 'Do you know, Gracie, you're a genius!'

* * *

'There you are, Mr Vencombe. All the invoices up to date. And I've checked what we have in the timber yard against all the orders, and that's a list of what I reckon we need to buy in, all ready for you to check.'

'I hardly think I need to check it,' Geoffrey Vencombe chuckled. 'You run everything as well as I ever did, only you're more methodical. I think you could put your hand on any piece of paper you wanted in seconds with that new filing system of yours.'

Grace was aware of a rosy hue flooding into her cheeks. 'But what I can't do is sign those cheques for our suppliers. If you sign them later, I'll post them tomorrow. Oh, yes, we had a letter from Symonds's today. They can't supply us with any more oak for about a month. At least, not sufficiently seasoned and we'm going to need it straight away. So I've made out an order to get it from Williams's instead. But we could get some from Symonds's and keep it ourselves until it's ready. There's room to store it, and it works out cheaper.'

'Good thinking, cheel. My, I have to say I never thought a maid could take on what you have and make such a success of it. We're having to work like slaves in the workshop, but we're just about keeping pace with everything, thanks to you.'

Grace felt herself glow with pride as she reached for her coat. It was beginning to turn chilly, and although it was not far to walk back to the farm, she needed the extra layer.

'See you tomorrow, then, nine o'clock sharp,' she said cheerfully. 'I reckon I need an hour or two here in the office, and then I'll help out in the workshop.'

'Larry says we'll make a carpenter of you yet. And you made a beautiful job of lining the coffin for Mrs Soakes, and varnishing it, too.'

Grace's basking pride fell somewhat at the mention of the old lady who had lived in one of the cottages adjoining the inn. Vencombes made coffins as well as gates and fences and almost anything made of wood, but being involved in local funerals brought its own sadness. 'Well, I wanted it to be nice for her,' she replied as Mr Vencombe followed her out into the workshop. 'I'll put the final coat of varnish on tomorrow, too.'

'You'd better watch out, John,' Mr Vencombe joked, addressing John Sampson who, as general labourer, would normally have done that particular task. 'She'll be doing you out of a job soon!'

Grace feigned a laugh, but secretly she was cringing. Although John had never made any allusion to the incident at the stables, Grace did not want to reignite his hostility towards her. She hastily made her way across the workshop where the men were hard at their various jobs. A half-made wheel, the spokes driven into the hub, was clamped sturdily in place, and Larry was carefully chiselling out an oval tang on the outer end of each spoke that would fit exactly into the hole he would drill in the corresponding felloe or section of the wheel's rim. It was exacting, precise work that required intense concentration, for unlike ordinary joiners, wheelwrights used no glue, a fact which always filled Grace with admiration.

As Grace drew level with Larry, she turned back round to call out her usual goodbye. A chorus of voices answered, and she stepped jauntily backwards. She didn't see the small toolbox that John Sampson had surreptitiously kicked behind her without anybody noticing, and she tripped over it, tumbling backwards and knocking Larry clean off his stool. A split second later, they landed together with a crash on the floor.

Grace was stunned for only an instant before she came to her wits and scrambled off Larry and onto her feet. 'Oh, Larry, I'm so sorry!' she cried in embarrassment.

Her first thought had been for the tang he had been working on. One blow in the wrong place could damage it sufficiently to ruin the entire spoke, and once a spoke had been driven into the hub, it was the devil's own job to remove it. Fortunately, one glance told her there was no damage done. But as she watched Larry picking himself up from the floor — wishing the ground would open up and swallow her — she realized with a shudder of horror that he was cradling his left hand and blood was dripping over his fingers. She looked down at the floor and knew instantly what had happened. As Larry had fallen, he must have put out his hand to save himself, and it had landed on a spare fret-saw blade that had also been knocked to the floor.

Grace's stomach cramped with guilt. 'Oh, Lord, Larry, let me see,' she groaned in disbelief.

Larry uncurled the fingers of his right hand, revealing a deep, ragged gash around the fleshy mound on the outer side of his left palm, and Grace had to gulp down her self-recrimination.

'Better let your mother bandage that up,' Geoffrey announced, appearing at Grace's elbow.

'It'll need more than that,' Grace dared to utter. 'It'll need stitching. Oh, Larry, I can't tell you how mortal sorry—'

'Huh! That's what comes of having women in the work-shop,' John Sampson grumbled loudly as he got on with his work. His words had certainly hit their intended target, cutting into Grace's heart.

'It's all right, Grace. It was an accident.'

'No, it were my fault, Larry—'

'Should've been looking where you was going. That's women for you.'

'That's enough, John.' Larry turned to Grace, the understanding expression in his eyes doing little to reassure her. 'You're not to blame. That toolbox shouldn't have been there.'

'Never mind about that, son,' Geoffrey said sharply. 'You'd better get yourself along to the doctor in Yelverton. Take the trap. It'll be quicker.'

'I'll bring Sunny in from the field and tack up for you,' Grace offered, desperate to make amends. 'It's the least I can do.'

'Thanks, Grace.' And for the first time, Larry winced as he glanced down at his hand. 'You do that while I get Mother to wrap something round this.'

'And I'll come along of you to the doctor's. Oh, I feel proper dreadful about this, really I do. And just when you need everyone working at full tilt.'

Her face was taut with remorse. She was supposed to be helping at Vencombes', and now she may well have put Larry out of commission for a few days at least! Oh, she felt sick with herself.

'You mustn't worry,' Larry insisted. 'It's only a scratch. If you can get the trap ready, that'll be a great help, but I think I can manage to get to the doctor's on my own. And Mrs Snell will be waiting for you.'

'Well . . . all right,' Grace submitted with reluctance. 'But . . . how can you ever forgive me?'

'There's nothing to forgive. Honestly.' And Larry's kind brown eyes smiled down at her.

CHAPTER SIX

Grace watched Larry urge Sunny into a trot and the trap bowled off through the village. How could she possibly face going back to the wheelwrights' after this? But she would have to. They really needed her.

She released a deep sigh, realizing that she was far more dejected than the incident in the workshop should have made her feel. She supposed it was because of the young men leaving the village and all the uncertainty of what the war would mean. But it wasn't only that. She had been pleased with what she had achieved at Vencombes'. She felt as if she was doing something really useful. Even though the opportunity had come about because of this awful conflict in Europe. The war wasn't her fault, but the pleasure her achievements had brought her almost made her feel guilty. And now this incident with poor Larry.

A gust of wind flapped at the hem of her coat as she crossed the little bridge, and she put up her hand to hold onto her hat. The village was its usual tranquil self and outwardly nothing appeared to have changed. But it had, and who knew if things would ever be the same again.

Stephen. Grace's stomach began to churn as her thoughts went to her dear brother. Their parents had received a letter from him the previous day, so they knew he was still training safely on Salisbury Plain. But that could easily change, the way things were going. What if he put in for a transfer to one of the Devonshire battalions that would surely be destined for the Western Front when it was fully trained? See the world? See hundreds of shell craters, the inside of deep, muddy trenches and miles of barbed wire, more like!

Heavy rain had battered from the sky earlier, but the brisk, early October wind had driven away the clouds and now brilliant sunshine was reflecting off the puddles and dazzling directly into Grace's eyes. She blinked as the sunlight played tricks on her vision. It must have been thinking so intensely about her brother that made her imagine she had seen him walking towards her. It was probably just a shadow, and Grace shook her head sadly. But when she squinted back into the brightness, she realized that there were two men in uniform coming down the hill. And, yes! One of them was indeed Stephen!

A fountain of joy erupted inside her as she catapulted forward. 'Steve!' she cried, and a second later, her feet left the ground as he swung her round in a circle. 'Oh, it's so good to see you!' Her hat had been jolted from her head and had landed on the wet road, but she didn't care. Stephen was back, and she gazed at him in breathless delight.

'Got a few days' leave, us has, Joe and me,' he grinned back. 'So us got ourselves back here as quick as us could.'

'Afternoon, Joe. You all right?'

'Proper clever, thanks, Grace. See you later, Steve.'

Joe began to whistle tunelessly as he sauntered on to his cottage in the centre of the village, and as Grace and Stephen stood outside their own family home, Grace paused to make sure her brother was real and not about to disappear into the ether. She put her hand on his arm and squeezed it tightly just to make sure.

'Mummy's going to be mortal happy to see you! We've all been so worried.'

'Told you I'd be all right, didn't I?'

Just for a moment Grace wasn't sure his voice was as casual as he meant it to be. But the doubt only lasted a split second, and in her jubilation, she thrust it aside. 'I can't wait to see Mummy's face!' she crowed instead.

* * *

'It were good of Mr Vencombe to let you have the morning off.'

'I'm a volunteer rather than an employee, even if he does pay me.' Grace linked her arm through Stephen's as they strode uphill. 'After what happened yesterday, mind, I were surprised he wanted me back at all.'

'I doesn't see why. You knows I met Larry in the trap as us was coming down the hill. He told us what had happened, but he didn't blame you at all.'

'But I blame myself, and Larry being so sweet about it almost makes it worse.'

'He's a good sort, is Larry. And his father. It don't surprise me he let you have some time off to spend with me.'

'I'd have taken it anyway,' Grace assured him. 'It's not every day my handsome soldier brother comes home on leave.'

Her remorse over the previous day's incident was fading, and for a while at least she was able to put thoughts of the war aside. She raised an impish eyebrow at Stephen, and he responded by pulling her hat down over her eyes.

'You rotter!' she laughed aloud, rescuing her vision. Then, already skipping ahead, she challenged him, 'Race you to the top. Bet you can't catch me!' she shouted over her shoulder as she streaked ahead.

They had walked up the steep, narrow lane passing the church on the left, and soon turned off right, clambering through the post and wire fencing to cross the single-track railway — not an easy operation for Grace in her ankle-length skirt and coat. Out on the open moor, they had crossed the Princetown to Yelverton road across the bleak, open upland.

Now they were heading even more steeply uphill towards one of Grace's favourite spots on the moor, the crest of Peek Hill. She raced ahead of Stephen, but the increasingly uneven terrain and the encumbrance of her long clothes slowed her down. Stephen, on the other hand, after weeks of vigorous training, was supremely fit and soon gained on her, scarcely out of breath.

'Thought as you'd beat me, eh?' he teased, grasping her about the waist.

She giggled back at him, and then drew in a huge breath before releasing it in a wistful sigh. She was so happy, but at the back of her mind niggled that lingering sadness. Stephen was only on leave.

'Come on, let's get to the top,' she said, pushing her unease aside.

They climbed to the very summit, and the magnificent vista opened up before them. Below them lay the glittering waters of Burrator reservoir surrounded by rolling hills. The azure blue sky of the previous afternoon had returned, illuminating the dying bracken and autumn leaves in brilliant shades of gold and cinnamon, while in the distance, the open sea beyond Plymouth shimmered like a flat lake. But — was that a warship Grace could see, sailing out from Devonport? She shuddered at the unwelcome reminder.

'Unbelievable, isn't it,' she said quietly, 'to think what's going on just across the Channel? Those two battles, the Marne and the Aisne. Everyone thought the BEF would give the Germans a bloody nose and send them packing, didn't they? And now look what's happened. Both sides dug into trenches and fighting over scraps of land with men getting killed and maimed . . . It were reported in the *Tavistock Gazette* last week. The first fellow from the town to die. A lieutenant, I think, in the regular army. What a waste of a life.'

'Not if you'm fighting for your country. And Britain might be next on the list for invasion.'

Grace's eyes shifted sideways, but she dared not voice the unspeakable. If Germany did try to invade Britain, Stephen might have to fight tooth and nail after all and his obituary might be in the paper before long, too. He must have read her thoughts.

'Grace,' he faltered, his voice unusually low and hesitant. 'I've got summat to tell you.'

'Oh.' Sweet Jesus, this was it, wasn't it? What she had always feared. This adventure-seeking brother of hers had indeed sought a transfer. Perhaps Martin had written to him and persuaded his young friend to join him. So it was still her fault, wasn't it? Grace's heart began to hammer in her chest.

'Us is being sent to India.'

'India?' Now this she wasn't expecting and her eyes bolted from her head.

'Yes. We'm leaving next week which is why us was given such a long leave. Only I haven't had the courage to tell Mum and Dad yet.'

'B-but why India?' Grace stammered. In her mind, India had never come into it. 'And I thought you said the Territorials were only to defend Britain itself?'

'They is. Officially, like. Only the government realized some weeks ago that things in Europe is going to be even bigger than they thought. So us was asked if us wanted to go to India to take over from our ordinary troops out there so as they can join the fighting in France. Us doesn't have to go, but Joe and me decided to volunteer.

'It'll be more a case of just being a presence rather than doing any proper fighting. So I thinks to myself, if I stays at home and things get even worse in France, then I could well be sent over there and that'd be far more dangerous. But if I goes to India, it'll be much safer, and think, Gracie, what an adventure! I'd never expected in all my born days to go to *India.*'

Grace nodded silently. She appreciated his reasoning, but India was so far away. On another planet. But at least he would be relatively safe.

'Oh,' was all she could say, and she opened her arms wide to hug him tightly, fighting the strangling lump in her throat. It was some minutes before she stood back. 'Well,' she croaked, 'it'll be some while afore you see this view again.'

In an effort to hide her tears, she gesticulated wildly about her. The view in every direction was spectacular, the bleak, windswept wastes of the moor with its dramatic granite tors, the tiny chapel of St Michael's crowning the steep pinnacle of Brentor far in the distance, while much nearer, the top of the church tower of St Mary's of Walkhampton was just visible. Usually from this amazing spot, Grace felt on top of the world, *her* world: Dartmoor. The cradle of her life, but just now that world was crumbling apart.

'Yes, I'll miss this place. But it'll be the opportunity of a lifetime, you does see that, doesn't you, Gracie?'

Oh, she could have wept. And God knew how their mother would take it. But yes, Grace did understand.

'And by the time I comes back, you'll be running the wheelwrights' the way I sees it!' Stephen joked.

'Well,' Grace laughed back, clinging onto any fragment of light-heartedness that she could, 'I reckon John's already worried I'll be taking over his job,' she told her brother. 'Always makes it quite clear what he thinks of women, he does. That we'm inferior beings.'

'Well, he'll have met his match in you, Gracie, I be certain!' But then Stephen's grin faded, and his eyes, too, misted with unshed tears. 'Not many cheels in the world like you, that's for sure. Be a lucky bugger that gets a ring on your finger one day.'

'Stephen Dannings!' Grace chided in mock horror. 'Not so sure about you being in the army if you'm going to learn that sort of language.'

And they fell about each other in forced, desperate laughter.

* * *

It had rained steadily all night, and being at the bottom of the mile-long hill, the road outside the cottage was a slippery quagmire. Fifty yards further down, the swollen brook had overflowed into the square. The Vencombes and the people who lived in the house next to the stream on the near side had put sandbags across their front doors, and Joe would have to splash through a couple of inches of water when he called for Stephen. With the rain had come a sharp fall in temperature and it really felt like autumn. George and Faith were in school, having already said their farewells to this brother who seemed god-like in their young eyes, leaving Ernest, Temperance, Grace and little Maggie to huddle with Stephen inside the open cottage door. The waiting was agony, and yet none of them wanted it to end.

'Joe's coming,' Stephen announced, and then turned back to his family. 'This is it, then. Goodbye, everyone. Wish me luck.'

He smiled at the beloved faces around him, but Grace could see that the light in his eyes was false. A terrible pain raked her throat, but she mustn't let it show, for her mother's sake especially. So she returned his smile, but it was all a game, wasn't it? A little like charades. Hiding the truth, the desperate sorrow that was breaking them all. For when were they likely to see Stephen again? It could be years.

He was half-hidden now in his parents' embrace, unshed tears glistening in Ernest's eyes and poor Temperance sobbing. Grace watched as her father peeled her mother's fingers from Stephen's lapels and held her against his chest. Grace took Stephen's hands. There were no more words, just a tightening of their fingers. Then Stephen bent to sweep Maggie into his arms, gave the bewildered child a hearty kiss on the cheek, and then handed her across to her big sister.

'Time to go, eh, Joe?' Stephen called as his comrade strode up to them. 'Goodbye, all. You all take care on yourselves, eh?' He sprang after Joe who had already begun the long haul up the hill. The Dannings family stepped out into the rain to wave them off, a little group of sadness. Like so many across the country.

'You will write, won't you?' Grace called to Stephen's back out of a desperate need to break the appalling tension.

'I promised I would!' He turned to give one ultimate wave, and then rounded the bend out of sight.

They all stood, staring at the empty road. Grace was hardly aware of her mother rushing past her and running up the lane after her son. Grace's own misery had paralysed her, and she could only watch as her father, still fit and athletic, dashed forward and caught up with his wife. He went down with her as she collapsed onto her knees in the mud, and Grace, unable to witness such grief, turned into the cottage with little Maggie still in her arms.

CHAPTER SEVEN

'No, Mr Vencombe, you can't possibly let them have Sunny!'

'Grace, my maid.' Geoffrey Vencombe looked at the distraught young girl with sympathy in his eyes. 'Sunny is just the sort of horse the army needs, as happy in harness as being ridden.'

'But those Canadian troops,' Grace protested, 'the ones who paraded through Plymouth last month, it were said they'd brought over eight thousand horses. Surely that's enough?'

Grace's gaze desperately sought Larry's agreement, but even he shook his head slowly. 'The army will need as many horses as it can get,' he answered. 'And look at it this way. Every horse that goes over to France will give a better chance for more of our troops to survive.'

Grace's eyebrows arched painfully. Oh, Larry. The sad resignation in his expression flowed into her, and she bowed her head in reluctant acceptance. Larry was right, as ever.

'I suppose so,' she muttered, though her heart groaned. 'But I can't bear to think of what might happen to him. He's master special—'

'Yes, he is. And he'll be doing a special job. So just be proud of him, and try not to think, well, of anything else.'

'Can I say goodbye to him?' Her lip was quivering now and she could feel the tightening at the back of her throat that was becoming all too familiar.

'Of course,' Geoffrey nodded. 'I'll be riding him to the collection point in Tavistock in the morning and coming back on the train.'

Grace gave a sniff and swallowed hard. 'I'll go up to the stables now, afore I go back to the farm.' She turned sadly away, her heart heavy as she went to cross the workshop. Oh, this war was becoming more horrible with every day.

'Huh, typical of a woman to be silly over a blooming horse!' she heard John Sampson comment. It was said out of the side of his mouth, but she was obviously meant to hear.

'For God's sake, have some compassion, man!' Larry grated between clenched teeth.

Grace hesitated for all of five seconds. She ought to ignore John's remark, but she still hadn't forgotten the episode in the stables. She had never said a word about it for Nan's sake, but she was sick to death of John's snide comments here and there. But now it was too much. Her sorrow over the kind and willing Sunny erupted in a shower of red-hot anger.

'And that's typical of *you*, isn't it?' she rounded on the culprit. 'A man who treats his wife the way you treat poor Nan is bound to have no soul. Women can do more than just sit at home cow-towing to their men-folk, you know! Look at all the women making shell-cases in the factories in Plymouth. Or the nurses and orderlies in the hospitals seeing *terrible* things and saving men's lives. Women might not be fighting on the battlefield, but this war will be won through their efforts just as much as men's, you know!'

She stopped, breathing heavily and her eyes flashing. All the men in the workshop had stopped working, staring at her in amazement, and silence crackled through the chilly air. Grace knew she was in the right and the colour that suffused into John's face proved it.

'I'm sure you're right.' Larry's voice was low and steady. 'But now I think we all need to get on with our work.'

Grace turned grateful eyes on him. Although pent-up fury sizzled in her breast, she was somewhat fearful of what John might say in retaliation. Her tongue had burned to proclaim that while he was happy enough to condemn Sunny to the battlefield, she noticed that he hadn't volunteered himself! But it would have been thoughtless to say that in front of either Larry who for obvious reasons couldn't enlist, or anyone else. Everyone had someone to fear for, a brother or a son. So Grace dipped her head graciously in Larry's direction and walked out of the workshop with as much dignity as she could muster.

Outside in the yard, she took a deep breath to calm the wave of nerves that washed through her. Damn John Sampson! But she supposed that, deep down, everyone was fraught. It was this wretched war. And maybe John was secretly afraid that one day he might be forced to go and fight, and who could blame him? Now that Turkey and the Ottoman Empire had entered the war, it put British troops in India in a whole new position, too, and Grace feared for Stephen. As far as she knew, he would only just have got there! So in a way, she could understand how John might feel.

'Penny for them, Grace Dannings.'

The smooth, slightly sarcastic voice brought Grace's head up. Aggie Nonnacott. Dressed in her good quality coat and matching hat against the November chill, and looking down her nose at Grace in that superior way of hers.

It didn't matter a jot to Grace that the Nonnacott family were better off than most in the village. It was common knowledge that Aggie's father had been exceptionally bright at school and upon leaving, had secured himself a job as a junior bank clerk in Tavistock, to which he travelled every day from Horrabridge Station. He worked there still, although now as manager. He was also a Methodist lay preacher, but whenever it was his turn to give the sermon, it was so full of hell fire and brimstone that the congregation was left feeling utterly depressed and guilt-ridden. The family occupied one of the few larger houses in the village, and as Mrs Nonnacott had only produced the one child, there had never been any need for Aggie herself to find employment. The only people Aggie considered to be on an acceptable social standing with her were the Vencombes, and even then, it was mainly Martin she liked to associate with.

The altercation with John just now, her heightened anxiety over Stephen and now the thought of the mild-mannered Sunny being ridden into battle, had put Grace just in the right frame of mind to face Aggie's goading. For goading it was, at least in Grace's eyes, not so much the words themselves as the way they were spoken, as if any thought Grace might have would be inferior to Aggie's own. And when Grace recalled Aggie's behaviour on the day Walkhampton had sent its initial volunteers off to war, it made her seethe, even if Martin had appeared to welcome Aggie's attentions that day.

'I don't think you'd want to know any thoughts of mine, Aggie,' she retorted. 'And I doubt you'd have the wit to follow them anyway.'

She knew it was an unkind thing to say as Aggie was actually quite intelligent, but she wasn't going to let the sneering remark go unchallenged. Aggie had no need to suppress any surprise. She and Grace had known each other since childhood, and the antagonism that had developed between them was only to be expected nowadays. It had come to be a game of words that Aggie, at least, relished.

'You'd be surprised,' she answered with a curl of her lip, and walked away with a toss of her head.

Grace watched her go, nostrils flaring. But she had more serious matters to concern her than Aggie's jibing. Having a few moments alone with dear Sunny was the first she had to deal with. And when she arrived at the stables and the affectionate animal trotted up the sloping field to greet her, Grace was helpless against the torrent of tears that poured down her cheeks.

* * *

'You look bright and perky,' Larry commented. 'Is it that hint of spring in the air that's cheered you up?'

'No,' Grace grinned back. 'We've just had a letter from Stephen.'

'And how is he?'

'Proper clever, I'm pleased to say. Still training somewhere five hundred miles away from Calcutta.'

'Not seen anything of the Turks yet, then?'

'No, thank goodness. And I hope it stays that way. But even if he hadn't volunteered to go to India, he might've seen some action here at home. Look at those awful zeppelin raids over London. Maybe we'm going to be invaded after all,' she concluded glumly.

Larry's face, too, clouded. 'Let's hope not. With winter coming to an end, the fighting's bound to start again in earnest over in France, so the Boche will probably put all their efforts in over there. I don't suppose it'll be too long before Martin's battalion is sent there, too.'

'Perhaps it'll all be settled afore then,' Grace said with false optimism.

'Thanks, Grace, but we all know it won't.'

Grace's mouth firmed to a fine line. 'No, I suppose not. Well, I'd better see what needs doing in the office.'

'Not a great deal. Or so Dad says from the look of things, the way you have it running so efficiently. So we wondered if you'd like to help out in the workshop a bit more. Maybe we could train you up on the machine-copier. For the lighter stuff anyway.'

'The machine-copier?'

'You've watched us using it often enough. And I reckon you could manage some initial chiselling as well.'

'What?'

'You've a feel for the wood. I've often seen you, running your fingers along the grain. Following its twists. Dad and I reckon we can make a carpenter of you. No harm trying you out on a few things, anyway.'

Grace bit her lip and glanced around the workshop. Everyone was busy and she was sure no one had overheard their conversation. Nevertheless, she felt nervous when she spied John Sampson hauling in some heavy timber with the help of Derek Gammet, the other general labourer. Grace hadn't had any more run-ins with John recently, and didn't want to antagonize him in any way again.

'What about John or Derek? Surely they'd know more about it than me?'

'Derek wouldn't want to touch it. He's said so before. And John, well, to be honest, when he has done small jobs for us, he's a bit ham-fisted. Besides, we need his brawn around the place. So,' Larry ended with an encouraging smile, 'let us know when you've finished in the office, and if there's time, we'll get you working on something. Dad wants a word with you, too. He's thinking of installing one of those bonding plates that drops the wheel into a trough of water when you've got the tyre fitted. It would really save time, and that's of the essence now we're so short-staffed.'

'Bonding day wouldn't be the same, though, would it?'

'No. But things have to change, Grace. And there's a war on, you know.'

Larry's attempt at wry humour brought a wan, reluctant smile to Grace's lips. Yes, everything was changing, and she wondered if life in Walkhampton would ever return to how it was before the war began. But, on the bright side, though it filled her with trepidation, she couldn't wait to try her hand at some of the skills in the workshop. She just hoped she could live up to Larry's expectations of her!

* * *

'Do you remember that bonding day about a year ago? When we were all wondering if war would really come?'

'When you had that argument with John about the Suffragettes? Yes, I remember it.'

Grace sucked in her bottom lip at Larry's reply and gazed wistfully over the gushing waters of the Walkham. It was a Sunday afternoon towards the end of May, the only time of the week when everyone seemed to take a few hours off to recuperate from their strenuous labours. Larry had noticed Grace with her younger brother, George, and their two little sisters sauntering along the village street. Without Martin and Stephen to make up the old foursome, it might have appeared inappropriate for Larry to ask Grace if she would like to go for a walk. But with her siblings in tow, it was perfectly acceptable.

They had wandered together down to the beautiful old stone bridge that spanned the Walkham at Huckworthy, and Larry and Grace were standing in one of the passing places in the parapet. Immediately below them, the clear water was deep, the very spot where the boys used to jump off the bridge and Grace, though she would never admit it, had nearly drowned when she had leapt in after them. Just below the bridge, the river widened, thus becoming shallower, the water splashing and gurgling over large boulders. On one side, a grassy bank dipped to a tiny gravel beach where George, Faith and Maggie were paddling safely in a few inches of water. It was such a tranquil, peaceful scene, and Grace's heart lurched ruefully.

'Seems hard to imagine now, doesn't it,' she sighed, 'a time when this war weren't constantly gnawing away at the back of our minds? They said, if it came, it'd be over by Christmas, and now look at it.'

'Yes.' Larry nodded gravely. 'Neuve Chapelle, they called it, and now another battle at Ypres already this year. So many lives lost, and all the Allies have done is halt the Germans, not driven them back.'

'I know. It's all so horrible. And have you heard about that awful poisoned gas the Germans have started using? It's unimaginable. I keep thinking what it were like—'

'Then don't. And no doubt we'll invent something equally horrible.'

Grace blinked at the cynicism in his voice. She could see the muscles of his lean jaw working furiously as he stared out across the water.

'You'm thinking of Martin, aren't you? Going out there afore too long?' And then she ventured, 'Does it upset you, not being able to go and fight yourself?'

A short silence passed before she heard Larry release a torn sigh. 'I don't know really. I hate the Germans for what they've done, and I know there's no choice but to fight back. But war is . . . so wrong. Such an appalling waste of life. I'm glad for moral reasons that I can't actually be part of it. But, yes, if it weren't for this bloody leg, I'd have been one of the first to volunteer.'

He flashed Grace a look of remorse, but didn't apologize for his language. There was no need. They were so close, they both understood the world was different from how it had been a year before. Grace squeezed his hand, and he glanced wryly at her with his brown eyes. 'Come on. I should be getting the tackers home for their tea. You three!' she called over the parapet. 'Out of the water and let your feet dry off.'

Ten minutes later, they were slowly climbing the steep hill up from the river. The lane was shady, bordered by high banks on either side that at this time of year were at their most beautiful, bedecked with bourgeoning red and white campion while the occasional clump of bluebells still nodded their gracious heads. If only . . . But then Grace's mood changed completely as she noticed a lone figure coming towards them, impeccably dressed, as always, in a fine outfit to match the season. It was lucky that hemlines no longer quite swept the ground, but Grace's nose wrinkled scornfully at the fashionable boots with their small heels that had evidently collected mud from the road.

'Afternoon, Aggie,' Grace greeted her stiffly. 'Does your father know you're out on your own?'

'He's gone to a Methodist conference. Besides, no harm'll come to me just walking down to the bridge and back,' Aggie told her, lifting her head snootily. 'And I'm safer on my own than in the company of some people I could mention. I'd prefer to be with a *real* man. Oh, I wonder where *that* came from?'

She halted in front of Larry and looked in mock surprise at a white feather that suddenly floated down and landed at Larry's feet. Grace stared at her in disbelief. Good God, how cruel could Aggie be? And if she had her sights set on Martin, she was going the wrong way about it, seeing as the two brothers were so close. Black anger flared in Grace's breast in a storm of rage.

'How dare you!' she fumed. 'It isn't Larry's fault he can't enlist. He's working like a slave in the yard to keep up with demand to help keep the country fed. Just as important as going to fight. And I don't see *you* doing much to help the war!'

'Huh!' Aggie sneered back. 'There's other ways than putting on trousers and pretending you can do the same work as a man, you know. I've knitted dozens of socks for the troops, doing my patriotic duty without losing my dignity.'

'Socks!' Grace scorned. 'Faith here is knitting socks at school and she's but six years old.'

'Come on, Grace.' Larry's voice was utterly calm as his fingers closed on her elbow. 'Leave it. She's not worth getting yourself in a lather over.'

'No, I won't leave it!' Grace shook herself free. 'How can you stand back and let her insult you like that? She—'

'Because I pity her.'

'Pity her?' Grace was almost as outraged at Larry as she was at Aggie.

'Shush. Yes. Look at her.' Larry bounced his head towards where Aggie was strutting triumphantly down the lane. 'Can you imagine having a father like hers? It must affect you. It's no wonder she has no friends. And as for Martin, well, I can tell you he doesn't really see anything in her.' He bent to pick up the feather and then hopped down the hill after the retreating figure. 'Miss Agatha!' he called deferentially.

73

'Yes, Larry?'

The girl turned, a smirk on her face at his respectful tone. And then Larry suddenly produced the feather which he had kept hidden behind his back.

'I think you forgot something,' he said with the most charming smile.

Grace watched the satisfaction slide from Aggie's face which proceeded to turn scarlet from the neck upwards. It was so comical that Grace burst out laughing, joined at once by George who, at a wise eleven years old, understood perfectly. Their merriment was so raucous that Aggie stomped off down the hill, and even Larry couldn't help breaking into a grin.

'Oh, Larry, that were priceless!' Grace crowed.

'Well, there's usually some way to get back at people like that. And if anyone wants to jeer at me, then let them. I've had so much of it all my life that it really doesn't bother me any more.'

Grace's laughter was spent now as they turned back up the hill. Larry was always so clever at managing people, wasn't he? She wished she could think of what to say in such situations as he did. Poor Larry. It wasn't fair that such a good person should have been cursed with that wretched infirmity. But . . . perhaps it wasn't such a curse. It would keep him safely out of the war, even if he had to endure the ignorant jibing of the likes of Agatha Nonnacott. And, as they traipsed back to the village, Grace fell silently pensive.

CHAPTER EIGHT

'Nan, let me take that!'

Grace sprang forward to relieve Nan Sampson of her heavy shopping basket as the young mother struggled across the road. Little Sally was walking independently, but Nan was carrying Billy who at thirteen months was a solid and heavy-looking child.

'Thanks, Gracie.' Nan's haggard face drooped with relief. 'Would you mind bringing it inside?'

'Course not. I were just on my way to work at the yard, but a minute or two won't make any difference.'

'Yes, I sees.' Nan nodded her head towards Grace's legs. 'Don't it feel queer like, wearing men's clothes? John'd never let me.'

Grace grinned as she followed Nan inside the cottage. 'I felt a bit self-conscious at first, but trousers are far more practical and, well, quite liberating,' she declared, remembering the word from an article about the Suffragettes she had read what seemed a lifetime ago now. 'You can move about much easier in them. Women are wearing them in the munitions factories, so I thought why shouldn't I? Only when I'm working at the yard, mind.'

Grace didn't add that the sheer horror on John's face the first day she had worn them had almost made her choke as she stifled a roar of laughter. It was a pity, though, that she couldn't really relate the funny moment to Nan. Poor thing looked as if she could do with cheering up.

'Well, you looks master grand in them, being so tall and slim.' Nan set Billy on his feet and he toddled across the flagstone floor only to wobble and sit down on his bottom. 'I'd look like a lump o' lard in them, especially with another one on the way.'

Grace's jaw dropped as she noticed Nan's thickening waistline for the first time. 'What, another one? So soon? Oh, Nan!'

'As John says, I must be made for having babbies. I doesn't mind at all, but I does get so tired sometimes. This place were a mess while I were going through the sickness, but I's over that now and I's gradually licking everything back into shape.'

'Yes, but . . .' Grace bit her lip. Should she dare . . . ? But she hated to see Nan so worn out. It was too late this time, but perhaps in the future? 'You do know there are things called condoms the man can wear when . . . you know . . .' She felt herself colour as the words slipped out of her mouth as if on their own, as if someone else was speaking. After all, she had no experience herself whatsoever of such matters.

To her surprise, Nan nodded in a down-to-earth way. 'Yes, I did mention it. But John said it were interfering with God's will.'

'God's will? Since when were John religious? He never goes to chapel. No, you really ought to persuade him, Nan.'

Nan sucked in her cheeks thoughtfully. 'Maybe I'll try working on him while this one's growing.' She patted her stomach with an affectionate smile. 'But he's a good man, my John. Provides well for us, he does. Works hard, and don't spend his wages on drink like some do, as I've heard tell. I's not pretty like you. So when John asked me, I weren't going to give up the chance. And him being older and settled like, with a cottage all to himself. Gave me . . .' Nan frowned, searching for the right word. 'A safe future I reckons you'd say.'

A safe future? Grace wanted to scoff. With a man who would corner another young woman in a stable? But had John really only meant to frighten her, even though he had gone quite far with it? Grace shuddered at the memory of his hand on her flesh. But did he lust after other women when he had his meek and trusting wife at home? Grace had to admit that she doubted it. The village was so close-knit that it would surely be noticed. But whatever the case, she mustn't let on to Nan what had happened, and so she forced onto her face what she hoped appeared as a genuine smile.

'You'm very lucky,' she heard herself say. 'But think about what we've just been talking about. Only probably best not to mention it were me you were discussing it with. Anyway.' She turned swiftly to the door, feeling heat prickling around her neck at the thought of what John might do if he knew she had been 'interfering' again. 'I must get to work afore they start wondering where I've got to.'

'Thanks for your help, Grace,' Nan called at her back.

Grace felt uneasy all morning, first attending to the paperwork in the office and then in the workshop. John was in and out, bringing in some heavy timber, and Grace felt his eyes were on her even if they weren't. She couldn't wait to get away, and decided to call in to see her mother at dinner time.

'Aw, it's you, my flower!' Temperance beamed as Grace opened the door. The children were squeezed around the table having a meagre meal, little Maggie, of course, and George and Faith home from school for dinner.

Grace immediately felt a quiet contentment soothe her troubled soul. 'You look happy, Mummy,' she greeted her mother with a questioning smile.

'Had a letter from Stephen this morning, us has,' Temperance answered brightly, withdrawing an envelope from her apron pocket. 'Mortal clever, he be.'

'Oh, that's grand!' Grace cried back, for indeed it was a huge relief to have good news about her brother. She perched on the end of the bench and for a few minutes was immersed in Stephen's untidy scrawl. He had been back in Barrackpore since March, she already knew, of course. The monsoon season had begun soon afterwards with unbelievably draining heat and humidity. But as Stephen was writing, the battery was on one of its short, recuperative visits up in the hills of Darjeeling where it was cooler and more comfortable. The area was beautiful, he wrote. He could not describe how lovely it was, but he was in fine fettle and the best of health.

Grace sniffed, somewhat disappointed that Stephen hadn't made more of an effort to tell them about the far-away land. But he was well and in good heart, and had not mentioned anything about fighting of any sort, and that was the most important thing. Grace was overcome with relief. News had been filtering through of bloody battles in a place called Gallipoli and the Dardenelles where thousands of Australian and New Zealand troops had joined forces with the British against the Turkish Army, and of course, desperate fighting was continuing along the Western Front. At least Stephen wasn't involved in anything like that. Not yet, anyway.

'Sounds in good spirits.' For the second time that day, Grace arranged her face into a smile that didn't quite reach her eyes. 'Perhaps he'll have seen enough of the world by the time the war's over.'

'Well, so long as he keeps himself safe,' Temperance nodded, although Grace knew she was being brave about it. 'I'd far sooner he'd have stayed here, but there us is. Now, will you have summat to eat, Gracie?'

'No, thanks. Mrs Snell let me make some sandwiches. They wanted me to stay on at the yard another couple of hours this afternoon. But I'd love a cup of tea.'

'She'm good to you is Mrs Snell.'

'All part of helping with the war, she says. When it's over, it'll all go back to normal.'

'And that day can't come quick enough for me. Your brother gallivanting to some heathen country and you, a maid, making wheels. Whatever next?'

Grace lifted her eyes ruefully over the rim of the cup as she sipped at the tea her mother had handed her. She loved working at the wheelwrights' even more than at the farm, although she would have preferred it if John Sampson wasn't there, too. Like everyone, Grace prayed the war would end as soon as possible, but her heart flickered at the thought of how her life would change once the conflict was over and something tightened inside her chest like a clenched fist, for she had the unnerving feeling that the war and her part in it had a long way to go yet.

* * *

'Martin!'

Grace couldn't believe her eyes when a few weeks later she arrived at the workshop and there appeared to be an extra member of staff. It might be the beginning of July, but rain had fallen steadily all night and still had not let up. Grace had hurried along the lane from the farm, navigating gigantic puddles and huddling beneath her umbrella. But closing it down distracted her from looking directly at the stranger — who turned out not to be a stranger at all!

Grace's heart lifted with joy, and she cast herself head-long into Martin's arms. 'Oh, it's proper grand to see you!' she exclaimed as he hugged her tightly. 'When did you get back?'

'Hadn't you heard? We all got back last night — Reg, Bob's son and the rest of us.' Martin held her at arms' length, his eyes bright with teasing. 'If I'd known I'd get such a warm welcome from my pretty maid, I'd have come up to the farm directly.'

'Oh, you!' Grace grinned back, and heard a chorus of amused chuckles behind her.

There was one muttering voice, though, that spoilt the moment. 'Anyone'd think you was family, taking liberties like that.'

Irritation rasped in Grace's throat and she was about to reply with a sharp riposte, when Larry said mildly, 'She's as good as family is our Gracie. But we've work to get on with, Second Lieutenant Vencombe, so you can make yourself useful while you're here and talk as you work.'

Grace's momentary frustration at Larry's answer when she would have gloried in rebuffing John herself was soon lost as Martin tutted in an exaggerated manner and rolled his eyes. 'Slave driver! Hasn't changed any, has he? Does he boss *you* around like that, Grace?'

'Hmm,' Grace considered with a frown. 'Sometimes, but not always.' She gave a light giggle and tossed her head. 'But he'll be chasing me if I don't get into the office. I'll be out in the workshop later, mind.'

'Yes, I've heard what you've been up to since I've been away. And I must say how fetching you look in trousers.'

Grace snorted wryly to hide her embarrassment. Martin had always enjoyed a little flirtation, she knew only too well, but she had never been on the receiving end of his complimentary remarks. It was so good to have him back to liven the place up, and she danced over to the office past a smiling Geoffrey Vencombe who was delighted to have his younger son home again.

'Will Mrs Snell give you some time off, do you think, so the three of us can walk up onto the moor?' Martin asked.

'I'm certain she will,' Grace replied, opening the office door. 'She'm such a good sort and I'll work twice as hard for her to make up for it.'

* * *

'Just like old times, isn't it?' Grace breathed in blissful contentment.

'What, having a picnic in the rain?'

'You old kill-joy, brother!' Martin laughed as they sought shelter in the lee of some rocks up on the open moor. 'It's only drizzle, and this *is* Dartmoor if I remember rightly. I do hope it clears, though, before I go back. I'd like to see the moor in sunshine one last time.'

His boisterous tone tapered off in a wistful trail as he unwrapped some sandwiches from their greaseproof paper, and Grace's buoyant mood slipped away.

'How much leave have you got?' she asked. With Stephen thousands of miles away, the importance of Martin's presence was somehow intensified. It was as if they were venerating his absence and the lifetime of friendship the four of them had enjoyed together.

'Six days. And then the battalion's off to France. At long last. Can't wait to put some of this training into practice.'

'Aren't you,' Grace faltered, 'a bit scared?'

Martin shrugged. 'I wouldn't be human if I said no. But I'm looking forward to seeing a foreign country. Wish I'd gone with Stephen, mind. India must be so much more exotic.'

'Hot and sticky and alive with mosquitoes according to his letters,' Grace assured him. 'But parts are really beautiful, and he says the young women are stunning. The rich ones dress in brightly coloured clothes called saris, and they're often embroidered with gold thread.'

'I bet most of them are peasants dressed in rags, poor sods.'

'I expect you're right, Larry. But it's made me determined to visit India myself once the war's over.'

'I don't see that happening any time soon, the rate things are going.'

'No, probably not,' Martin admitted dejectedly. 'If the Americans were to join in, it might hasten matters. I'd have thought the sinking of the *Lusitania* would have persuaded them, but it hasn't.'

'Not yet, maybe, but it'll all go into the melting pot, I'm sure. But I reckon we should eat our sandwiches before they're completely soggy from the rain.'

And then Grace was jolted from listening to the brothers' conversation when Martin muttered under his breath, 'Soggy sandwiches will be the least of our worries once we're over in France.'

* * *

'Grace, cheel, would you go out on the down and drive in they three bullocks?' Farmer Snell asked a couple of days later. 'I want to take them to market tomorrow, only my hip's giving me jip and your father's out checking the meadows for me. Seeing if the grass has dried out enough to start hay-making.'

'Yes, of course. If that's all right with you, Mrs Snell?' Grace added, turning to her mistress.

'Whatever Farmer Snell wants, my flower,' Felicity Snell beamed back.

'You'll probably find them down by the ford. Like it there, they do. And with the weather having turned so hot this afternoon like, after all that rain.'

'Righty-ho,' Grace called as she waltzed out into the rear passageway of the farmhouse, her heart still resounding with the happy morning she had spent at the wheelwrights' listening to the banter between the Vencombe brothers. They were so different, and yet when they were together, lively conversation seemed to bounce naturally between them.

Grace rammed her straw boater on her head. It was strange the way that when she wore her trousers to go to the workshop, she didn't feel the need for a hat. Indeed, the thought of a hat seemed faintly ridiculous. Instead, she tied her golden curls up into a knot beneath a scarf. She had wondered about cutting her hair off short as many women were doing, especially in the factories, but when she had mentioned it, Larry had been aghast.

'Don't you dare!' he had cried so adamantly that Grace had recoiled. 'Just make sure it's tied back safely when you're working here.'

Grace was glad now that his reaction had swayed her decision. As she stepped out into the July sunshine, so different from the afternoon of the picnic only a few days earlier, she felt distinctly feminine, back in her plain blouse and skirt and with her long tresses rippling down her back. She was eighteen years old, a young woman with growing feelings towards the opposite sex, although such matters hadn't really come into her life just yet. How could they when niggling at the back of her mind was always the war. Time to go in search of love when the fighting was over.

The farmhouse backed directly onto Knowle Down on the fringe of Dartmoor. Farmer Snell had adjacent fields where he kept his animals and grew hay and other fodder crops. But he also enjoyed grazing rights on parts of the moor and on the down that stretched as far as the next village of Horrabridge. Indeed, part of the down that dipped steeply to the Black Brook as it plunged its way downhill from the centre of Walkhampton, actually belonged to the farm.

Grace scrambled down the track through the tall bracken that cloaked the dizzy incline. Her heart was light, burying her qualms deep in her soul. Martin had two more days of leave, it was a beautiful day and the sun was scorching down from a clear, gentian sky.

Sure enough, Grace found the three bullocks grazing on the flat area of grass beside the stream. It was probably Grace's favourite spot around the village, tucked away, idyllic. The clear, sparkling water tumbled over a shallow cascade beneath the shade of low, gnarled trees. Their ancient branches hung in full leaf out over the bank as if dipping their fingertips into the flow and forming an emerald canopy. A few feet further down, just before the stream opened out into a shallow ford, stepping stones spanned its gushing eddies. And on the opposite bank, half hidden among the stunted trees and other vegetation, a stone wall that enclosed some of Farmer Snell's fields lent some privacy from the outside world, like a little hide-away.

To Grace, this had always been a special place, magical and enchanted. She had spent such wondrous times there throughout her life, playing hide-and-seek, paddling in the ford, or scooping up a handful of water and launching it into the air in a glittering arc. Surely it wouldn't matter if she spent just a couple of minutes enjoying its peace and beauty on this lovely afternoon, and reaching the bank, she hopped across the stepping stones to the other side.

It was then that she saw them, the man and the woman lying together, nestled against the wall and hidden by the trees — or so they thought. The man was on top of the woman, half-kneeling, his under-drawers and khaki trousers around his thighs so that his rump was exposed to the air, and the woman's spread legs were also bare.

Grace's heart began to pound sickeningly. Shock, disgust, *outrage* stung into the very core of her, and though she yearned desperately to turn and flee, her feet were rooted to the ground. An involuntary gasp crackled in her throat, making a blackbird on one of the branches take flight. The man reacted by glancing over his shoulder, the dread of discovery on his face, and the woman sat up, wide-eyed, as she pulled down the hem of her skirt. Aggie, and . . . and Martin.

In that instant, the gentle innocence that was Grace Dannings was lost for ever. She knew what the act of love-making entailed, but it was something pure, meant for two people whose souls were entwined in eternal love vowed at the altar. To discover that Aggie . . . Well, she didn't care about *her*, but *Martin*, whom she had grown up with, worshipped for the fun he constantly brought to her life, *loved* as a brother. It was just too much, and all Grace could do was stare at them through eyes blurred with disillusionment.

She suddenly became aware that Martin was coming towards her, tucking his shirt into his trousers that were now back about his waist. His expression was tense and mortified, but when he put his hand out to her, Grace shrank away. Martin let his hand fall to his side. 'Oh, Gracie, I'm so sorry. I never wanted—'

Before he could finish, Aggie sprang up behind him, her eyes wild and begging in a face contorted with terror. 'Grace, for God's sake, please don't tell anyone!' she squealed desperately. 'If my father found out, he'd kill me. You don't know what he's like. No one does. Oh, Grace, *please*!'

Grace blinked at their pleading, horrified expressions, and the sense slowly trickled back into her shocked brain. She couldn't believe what she had just seen. She felt betrayed, let down, and the bitterness of it finally spurred her tongue into action.

'You should've thought of that afore, don't you think? And what if you get pregnant?' she demanded, her eyes stabbing into Aggie's. 'Your father'd know about it then, wouldn't he?'

'I was making sure she wouldn't,' Martin admitted, lamely it seemed to Grace. Like a naughty boy being reprimanded by his teacher. 'I was just putting on . . .'

'You mean you hadn't actually . . . ? Well, it's lucky I came along when I did, isn't it? And as for you, Martin Vencombe, well, I'm proper ashamed of you.'

'But, Grace, please, I beg you!' Aggie wailed again. 'I'll do anything . . .'

But Grace didn't want to hear another word. All she wanted was to escape this horrible, unforgivable thing she had just witnessed. Spinning on her heel, she sprang back across the stepping stones. As the bullocks, startled by her haste, backed nervously away, she heard footfall on the grass behind her.

'Grace, I need to explain.' Martin's voice was low and husky. 'This time next week probably, I'll be in France. Sent up to the front line. And I might . . .' He paused. Gulped. 'There's a strong possibility I may never come back. And I don't want to die not knowing what it's like to . . . to . . . And Aggie . . . was willing. So, please, Grace, don't judge me too harshly. Try to understand.'

His words clawed at Grace's heart, breaking her. This appalling war, wrecking people's lives in more ways than one. But she couldn't turn back to face him, and spreading her arms wide, began to herd the three bullocks up the steep slope, her vision blinded by angry, bitter tears.

CHAPTER NINE

'Well done, George, lad,' Geoffrey Vencombe chuckled, ruf-fling the boy's fair curls. 'You keep this place clean as a new pin. And all the little carpentry jobs we've given you, well, you've done them perfectly. We'll make a wheelwright of you in no time. It must run in the family, first Stephen, then Grace, and now you.'

Larry glanced up from his work on the spoke-horse. 'What do you think, Dad, about offering the lad an appren-ticeship when he finishes school next year?' He kept a straight face as his eyes held George's astounded expression — after giving his father a surreptitious wink since the two of them had already discussed the matter.

'Well . . .' Geoffrey frowned, rubbing his hand thought-fully along his chin before grinning from ear to ear. 'It's yours, laddie, if your father agrees.'

George's young face was a study of delighted incredulity. 'D-does you mean it?' he finally stammered. 'And . . . and does you think,' he went on, growing in confidence, 'that I could have Stephen's old room over the workshop? Until he comes back from India, anyways, like?' he added, glancing across at Grace's equally astounded face.

'I don't see why not,' Geoffrey considered. 'And even when he does come back, there's room enough for two.'

'Only I's getting a bit too old to be sharing a bed with the tackers much longer, and them being maids and all, bain't I, Gracie?'

His smooth skin creased into a questioning frown as he studied his elder sister. Proper maudlin she'd been ever since Martin had gone back to the army. Well, he knew she and Stephen had always been really close to the Vencombe brothers, but she'd gone master quiet since Martin had gone over to France. Aw, she weren't soft on Martin, were she? George's chest inflated with wonderment. He could imagine Stephen wanting to have a girl in his life, but Gracie? In *love*? The idea was inconceivable. Anyway, all George was interested in was this new adventure that had so suddenly opened up before him.

But George's euphoria was quickly deflated by Grace's stern look. 'Don't you think you should be thanking Mr Vencombe before you start making sleeping arrangements?' she said tartly. 'And don't forget you need Daddy's permission, too.'

George went to pull a face, but stopped himself. Poor Gracie. Her uncharacteristic shortness of temper was just further proof of her secret feelings for Martin and her fear for him. After all, soldiers were being killed right, left and centre in France, whereas in India where their Stephen was, there had hardly been any fighting at all.

'Aw, he's bound to agree.' Joy exploded onto George's face as he ignored his sister and instead bobbed his head vigorously in Geoffrey's direction. 'And thanks ever so much. I can't wait to leave school now. And I'll work harder for you than anyone else ever has, I promises!'

Geoffrey gave a throaty chuckle. 'Well, you get on with your work, and I'll have a word with your father this evening. Doesn't mean you can slack off at school next year, mind. In fact, you need to work really hard, particularly with your reckoning. Need to be good up here,' he stated, tapping the side of his head, 'as well as with your hands to make a good carpenter or wheelwright.'

'Yes, Mr Vencombe. And thanks again!'

'It'll be a pleasure to train you up.' And Geoffrey turned back to the workbench.

Grace had been marking the screw-holes for the hinges on a farm-gate she had helped to make, and put down the bradawl she had been using.

'Thank you very much, Mr Vencombe,' she repeated George's words. 'But . . . you don't see George as a replacement for Stephen, do you? I mean, Stephen *will* be coming back.'

Geoffrey blinked his cinnamon brown eyes at her. The same steady eyes that Larry had inherited. Could Grace detect a shining trace of moisture in them?

'I'm planning for a future with a full house again, maid,' he answered huskily. And then the hint of a smile coloured his expression. 'You, too, if you want to stay on after the war and some lucky young fellow hasn't whisked you away.'

He was curious to see Grace's face stiffen. 'You won't find me tied to a kitchen table with half a dozen chiller under my feet, I can assure you!'

Geoffrey was somewhat taken aback and Larry, who had heard the brief conversation, drew his head back on his neck. Grace hadn't been the same since Martin had left. They were all worried sick about him, himself and his parents, just as Bob feared for his son and Sybil for Reg. And almost everyone in the parish, which extended to remote farmsteads right up on the moor, was in the same boat for more young men had joined up since the initial wave of enlistment. But worrying didn't get you anywhere, and Larry was both surprised and concerned that Grace had taken Martin's departure so hard. Although come to think of it, she had been behaving strangely since a couple of days before Martin had left. They hadn't had some sort of argument, had they?

But Larry never found an answer to his ponderings for just then he spied two small figures nervously holding hands as they inched onto the threshold, eyes wide and like shiny pebbles in their little faces.

'Good day to you, young maids.' Larry got to his feet and made towards the open workshop doors. Faith and Maggie clung onto each other even more tightly. They were well acquainted with the tall man with the funny walk who was coming towards them. He had played with them often enough, and he was Stephen and Grace's friend. But they had never entered the busy workshop before, and everything was strange and overwhelming. The elder of them, Faith, had the wit to lift her hand and point at her big sister.

'Grace,' she whispered. 'Gracie, you'd better come. A boy came to the door. And now Mummy's gone . . . proper crazy, like. And us was afeared . . .'

'What?' Grace's eyebrows swooped downwards. Entangled in her own jumble of emotions, she hadn't caught all of Faith's muddled words, but she had heard enough to know that something was amiss. 'Do you mind if I pop home for a minute?' she asked, sorry that she was having to take advantage of Mr Vencombe's generosity.

'Of course not, cheel.'

'Do you want me to come?'

'No thanks, Larry. It's probably nort.'

'I'll come,' George put in. 'I can tell Mummy the good news, and that'll cheer her up a bit.'

'Off you go, then.'

Grace's expression was set as the four of them traipsed out through the yard. She knew her mother sometimes still became upset if the memory of her two dead children chanced to sear into her mind. Grace herself had vague rec- ollections of her lost siblings which saddened her at times. But the double tragedy had occurred years before, and surely Temperance could contain her grief in front of little Maggie and Faith who was at home because school was still closed for the long summer holiday.

'So what did you say happened?' Grace questioned Faith who was trotting along behind her.

'A boy came,' Faith faltered, somewhat perturbed by the sharp attitude of her big sister who was usually so loving. 'He gave Mummy a letter. And when he'd gone, Mummy opened it and she went master quiet, like, and then she started screaming.'

A sudden iciness crept through Grace's flesh. Was it . . . a telegram? Her thoughts flew at once to Stephen. No, it couldn't be. To her knowledge, there had been little if any fighting in India, despite the close proximity of the Ottoman forces. But that wasn't to say . . . And news didn't always travel fast.

Oh, God. She forgot George and her little sisters, her mind closed to everything but the dread that rampaged through her body. Oh, *please* . . . But as she ran up to the front door, she could hear the blood-curdling shrieks from inside. She paused for just an instant, scraping up her courage.

'You stay here,' she instructed, but from George's suddenly white face and the way the girls were cowering together, it was hardly necessary.

Grace pushed the door open just a fraction, and her mother's hysterical wails spilled out into the August air. Panic locked Grace's heart in fear, but she had to do this, and gulping hard, she slipped inside this loving home that had suddenly become cold and hostile.

Temperance stood at the far side of the table, her eyes wild and bolting. Her expression seemed to register the fact that Grace was there. But then, with some crazed voracity, she filled her lungs to let out another ear-splitting screech, all the while staring into her eldest daughter's face.

Grace had to claw her way through a fog of shock. On the table was a crumpled scrap of paper. A telegram. Her pulse crashed at her temples as she slowly moved her trembling fingers towards it while keeping her eyes on Temperance who continued to stand there, just screaming and screaming as if every fibre of her being was directed into that and nothing else. And then the moment came when Grace must read the print that wavered in her hand as she smoothed out the paper.

DEEPEST SYMPATHIES STOP PRIVATE STEPHEN DANNINGS DIED PEACEFULLY OF

MALARIA ON 20 AUGUST STOP FULL CHRISTIAN BURIAL IN THE CEMETERY AT BARRACKPORE.

So, that was it. At first, Grace felt nothing at all. Stephen, her beloved brother, was no more. His life, in a little box, put to one side. Fact. And life would go on. It just would. Another fact. And then, as Grace lifted her eyes, here was this raving, deranged woman whom she alone must cope with in the next few moments. No space for her own fractured emotions. Her own grief. And she watched in appalled horror as the lunatic hurled a cup across the room. Grace ducked out of its path and the missile crashed against the wall where it smashed into a thousand pieces. Grace stared as her mother snatched up a second cup, and then she was aware of George creeping into the room behind her.

'Take the girls next door to Martha,' she ordered over her shoulder. 'Then get Mr Vencombe to send for the doctor, and then go and find Daddy.'

Out of the corner of her eye, she saw George back out of the door just as the second cup landed by the first with the unmistakable tinkling of shattering china. Good Lord, what should she do? Desperation scored into her heart as Temperance went to one end of the table, arm outstretched, and swept everything off the opposite end with an almost triumphant cry. Grace seized the opportunity to skate round behind her and snap her arms round her mother's form, pinning hers to her sides. Temperance struggled like a thing possessed, kicking and screaming, but Grace gritted her teeth, ignoring the pain of her mother's booted heels against her shins and hanging on determinedly. Slowly, very slowly, Temperance's rigid stance softened, her shouts lessened to a howl and finally to racking sobs as mother and daughter sank onto their knees together.

'There, there, Mummy,' Grace soothed. 'See what it says. Peaceful. No wounds or pain. Just slipped away. He always wanted to travel, and he did. And India, well, you couldn't get more exotic than that. He . . . he went happy, like.'

She could croak no more, her throat closing painfully. And she knew no words could help. It was like a lie, trying to find ways to ease her mother's misery — and her own. Stephen was dead, and nothing she could think or do or say could ever bring him back.

* * *

Grace sat, immobile as the granite rock on which she perched, watching the August sun float down and paint the wispy ribbons of cloud a flushed apricot. Less than a year it was since she and Stephen had stood on this very spot on the crest of Peek Hill, admiring the familiar, spectacular view before Stephen had revealed his decision to go to India. It seemed a lifetime ago and yet it might have been yesterday. She could still see his anxious, pleading face, hear his voice. And now he was lost for ever.

It felt so strange. Her poor mother had been so steeped in misery that Grace's concern had been for her suffering alone, and her own grief had needed to be locked away. Now, though, Ernest had persuaded his wife to take the sleeping draught the doctor had prescribed and the younger children were staying with Martha, so that Grace was free to deal with her own black sorrow. And yet she was dry-eyed. There was just a terrible, hollow emptiness inside her that refused to allow anything to enter it, not even sadness or tears.

And so she sat as the great, flaming disc slid majestically below the horizon, robbing the surface of the reservoir of its brilliance and cloaking the moor in shadow. But nothing would ever change. It had been the same for thousands, millions of years, and would go on being the same until eternity. Sunrise, sunset. Whether Stephen was alive or not. Long after Grace herself, her family and everyone she knew had gone. So should it matter that one person, her dear brother, no longer walked the earth? But it did matter. To her. Although exactly how it mattered to her, her grieving soul was as yet unable to fathom.

The shiver that suddenly quivered through her body brought Grace to her senses, and she pulled her cardigan across her chest. The air was turning chilly, and though she felt she could stay there all night, saturating herself in calming peace, she knew that she should go home. She hadn't told anyone where she was going and someone might be worried. And so, with reluctant heart, she began walking down off the moor, one foot placing itself mechanically in front of the other, her mind faded and sterile of thought. Even when she came to the railway line and clambered through the post-and-wire fencing, her limbs moved of their own accord since it was something she had done a thousand times.

'Grace, look out!'

The familiar voice brought her back to reality as she stepped onto the track. There, chugging towards her, was the evening train, clattering its way down to Yelverton. She stared at it, fascinated somehow as it rattled forward. And then the voice, yelling at her now, made her consider that she should get out of the train's path, and she leisurely finished crossing the line, climbing through the fence on the far side and turning to watch the engine and its two carriages trundle past.

'Grace, for God's sake, what were you thinking of?' Larry limped up behind her in as close to a run as his leg allowed. 'Didn't you see the train? Didn't you *look*?'

His face was creased in desperation, anger, *horror* even as he shook her by the shoulders. Grace glared back at him, hot with defensive disdain.

'Of course I did! There were plenty of time.'

'No there bloody well wasn't! You were that close—'

'No I weren't. And don't swear. And kindly take your hands off me.'

Larry blinked at her, and as soon as he let his hands fall to his sides, Grace stomped off past him downhill so that he had to struggle to catch up with her. She sniffed in irritation and her eyes flashed at him accusingly.

'So what were you doing following me?' she demanded.

'I wasn't following you. Not exactly. We all know what's happened and we're all really sorry, but then we realized you'd disappeared. It's getting late and your poor father's worried. I guessed where you'd gone. It was always a favourite spot for . . . the four of us. And so I said I'd come up here to look for you.'

'Well, as you can see, there were no need. I were coming home—'

'But if I hadn't called out to you . . . And, although we all do it, we're not supposed to cross the line anyway. Oh, Grace, look at me!' Larry grasped her by the arm and turned her towards him, his eyes deepening to mahogany as he fixed her reluctant gaze. 'Stephen is dead. He was my friend, but he was your brother. You are allowed to grieve for him, you know. Don't bottle it up.'

'But you don't understand!' Grace rounded on him as her anguish suddenly exploded. 'It were my fault!'

'What?' Larry was incredulous. 'How could it be your fault?'

'I should've persuaded him not to join up. I were going to. At least, I were going to tell Martin not to encourage him. But I were so wrapped up in stupid ideas about the Suffragettes and . . . and . . . other things that I never did.'

Larry's face stilled. And then his eyebrows arched in pity. 'Oh, Grace, you're not to blame. Don't you ever think that. Steve was the sort . . . He'd have volunteered sooner or later. At least he died being cared for in a hospital bed and not in agony on the battlefield. And he'd seen a corner of the world that none of us ever has. So don't you dare go blaming yourself.'

Grace screwed her lips rebelliously. It *was* her fault. But much as she wanted to drag her gaze away from Larry's face, she somehow couldn't. He was too familiar, his presence too strong a reminder of the happy foursome she had been part of all her life. All her tamped down emotions suddenly rushed at her and her face crumpled. Something inside her snapped and, as a brutal sob broke from her lungs, she found herself wrapped in Larry's embrace, weeping against his chest.

How long they stood there, alone on the moor as dusk closed in, she wasn't sure. All she knew was that Larry held her in silence, pouring his own strength into her and taking away the burden of her guilt. Her tears finally ran dry, though her heart still ached. Would ache for ever. But reality had crept into her soul, and now she could face the truth, that Stephen was dead and somehow she must cope with the future.

* * *

Grace made her halting way across the yard. Everything looked the same. Nothing changed. And it hadn't, had it? Stephen hadn't been at the workshop for over a year. When she walked through the doors, the same people would be there as always. Yet it was the *knowing* that was breaking her. The knowing that she would never see her brother at the lathe or the workbench again.

They had received the official letter now, praising Private Dannings for being such a willing and dedicated soldier. It was Joe's barely legible scribble that had brought the family a trace of comfort. He had been at Stephen's bedside, holding his hand, at the end. He had been delirious for some while, but had spoken to Joe quite lucidly before lapsing into the peace in which he had drifted away. Grace's bottom lip had quivered as she read it. Her mother had started howling again and Grace had cajoled her into taking another draught.

Grace set her jaw and walked boldly into the workshop. Every head turned towards her and she felt a crimson flush warm her cheeks. She didn't want any attention. She just wanted to get on quietly with her work. But she couldn't be cross as Larry, dear Larry who had been so kind to her, came towards her.

'Are you sure you're ready to come back? You don't have to.'

'No, I want to,' she told him firmly. 'But I'm not working for Farmer and Mrs Snell any more. They've let me keep my room there, bless them, but they'm going to find some-one else from the village to take my place. Mummy can't be left alone, you see. She'm still crying all the time, and she can't do ort in the house. Just sits there. George and Faith are back at school, of course, so Daddy's taking Mummy and Maggie next door to Martha afore he goes to work. And then I'll be there in the afternoon to take care of them and do the cooking and cleaning and washing and everything. So I'm afeared I can only be here until dinnertime in future, if that's all right.'

Larry's eyes closed for a second in his sombre face as he nodded. 'Of course. It'll be good to have you back if only for half the day. And do let us know if there's anything we can do.'

'That goes for all of us, maid,' Geoffrey echoed.

'Thank you. Now what would you like me to do?' Grace enquired as she glanced about her. 'Oh, isn't Bob in today?'

'Oh.' Larry's voice dropped and Grace saw his promi-nent Adam's apple rise and fall as he swallowed hard. 'No. He . . . er . . . he's not coming in today. He . . . Grace, there's only one way to tell you this. He and his wife, they got a telegram this morning. Their son . . .'

Grace felt her heart clench in horror. Oh, no. Not some-one else from the village?

'B-but he'm in the same company as Martin, isn't he?' she managed to croak, watching Larry's face blanch.

'Was. There's been heavy fighting at a place called Loos.'

'And . . . and Martin?'

'We don't know,' Geoffrey broke in. 'But until we hear otherwise, he's still alive. But hanging about gossiping won't help. Work to do.'

Grace met Larry's gaze and a bitter stone settled in her chest. This war, that should have been over by Christmas. This was just the beginning, wasn't it?

CHAPTER TEN

'Let's have a pot of tea ready for when Faith gets home from school,' Grace said purposefully as she folded the last of the ironing. 'George is going straight to the yard. So, will you set the mugs out, Mummy?'

She raised a desperate eyebrow at the gaunt figure that sat inert in the rocking-chair beside the range. It was the first comfortable piece of furniture in the Danningses' home, made as a present by Mr Vencombe and Larry to help ease Temperance's sorrow — but also as a sort of thanksgiving that Martin had survived the terrible battle at Loos almost unscathed while others in his company had perished. The whole parish was in mourning, having lost three young men in France, besides a much loved son who had succumbed to illness in far-away India. Temperance had shrivelled to a wizened old woman, or so she appeared to her eldest daughter who observed her with reckless hope across the small room.

But the movement Temperance made was merely to set herself rocking back and forth as she did for hours on end, staring sightlessly at the range. A disappointed sigh escaped from Grace's lungs. Oh, well. She had tried. For the umpteenth time. It seemed nothing could shake her mother from the bottomless torpor she had toppled into since Stephen's death.

'I'll do it, Grace,' little Maggie piped up, and Grace nodded at the child who seemed to have blossomed since their mother had slid over the brink into some silent world of her own. Maggie fussed over her constantly, as if their roles in life had been reversed — even though Maggie was somewhat confused as to why her mother was so sad just because Stephen had gone to help baby Jesus look after his little brothers who had already gone to heaven.

Grace made the tea, knowing how much painstaking encouragement it would take to persuade Temperance to drink it. Eating was even more of a challenge, and the flesh had fallen from her bones. Grace tried to tempt her with whatever tasty morsels she could lay her hands on. But they weren't exactly rich and it wasn't always easy to obtain something out of the ordinary, especially with the war on.

'Oh, I forgot to tell you. Nan Simpson had another little boy last night,' she announced, forcing some brightness into her voice. 'Healthy little chap. John's as proud as punch.'

Much as she disliked John, Grace had congratulated him, and had even experienced some part in his evident joy. Now she hoped the news might rouse Temperance from her inertia. Her heart leapt as she detected a flicker of recognition in her mother's eyes, but almost at once, it was extinguished. Grace gave up. For now. It was . . . just so draining, having to prop Temperance up like this and keep her own grief under control. She was almost angry with her mother for doing this to her, and yet guilt ripped her apart for allowing herself to feel like that. And her poor father was out of his mind with worry when he was deep in his own misery, too. At least Grace had released some of her agony when she had wept in Larry's arms, and the memory of those snatched moments sometimes brought her a little comfort.

'Shall I pour you some tea, Mummy?' she suggested lamely, returning her attention to the present. And her heart sank for she knew it would be the devil's own job to persuade Temperance to drink even half a cup.

* * *

Grace held her hands towards the heat that emitted from the small forge. The first heavy frost of winter had turned the muddy puddles in the rough road through the village into icy patches between ruts that were frozen solid. Inside the workshop though, the forge kept the place relatively warm and it was only Grace's hands that tingled with cold as she worked at the machine-copier. John was hauling in some lengths of wood and Bob was busy cutting them into the required lengths. Geoffrey and Larry, however, and Edward — the other wheelwright they employed — were poring over some plans. They had been sub-contracted to make a number of wagon-wheels for the military. Heavy metal hubs, each consisting of a pair of flanges and a pipe-box, together with special triangular-shaped bolts had all been supplied, but the wooden parts had to be fashioned to an exact specification.

Grace understood that the wheels would be for supply wagons, and in some strange way, that knowledge brought her some relief. Hopefully they would be used for carrying some sort of comfort to the troops, food and blankets, perhaps even medical supplies for the field hospitals. She closed her mind to the fact that the wagons could well be transporting munitions, and forced herself to consider that at least these were not gun-carriage wheels, helping to deliver death to the young men fighting for the other side.

It was odd that, she mused pensively as she set up the machine-copier to turn twenty-eight tenons into their basic spoke shape for a pair of rear wheels. She wanted the war to end, of course she did, so the quicker the Allies killed off so many of the enemy or that they surrendered, the better. But Larry had made her consider the fate of the Germans and Turks and everyone else on the other side, too. They were the aggressors, of course, but they had probably been brought up to believe that they were in the right. It was hard to consider the enemy's feelings when Grace's family had been shattered by a loss caused, when all was said and done, by the outbreak of war, and when so many other families in the parish were also suffering the same wrenching emptiness.

Grace was suddenly aware that she had been staring at the machine in front of her. It was ready to go, following the pattern she had set for the lathe. She glanced round to see if anyone had noticed her lapse of concentration, but apparently not. Only John was stacking wood behind her.

'How's Nan coping with the new baby?' she asked, as much to cover up her moment of daydreaming.

'She'm doing very well,' John smirked after the initial surprise had slid from his face. Since the long-ago but not forgotten incident in the stables, he was aware that Grace ignored him as much as possible, although not his wife. Now he could see a chance to satisfy his need for retaliation. 'She'm made for having babbies, despite what some folk thinks. And as for not having no more, well, whoever's been talking to her should be shot for interfering. And I has a sneaking suspicion I knows who it be.'

He glared meaningfully at Grace, eyes gleaming maliciously, before turning back to his work. Grace snatched in her breath. Poor Nan. She had obviously tried, without success, to broach the delicate subject they had discussed, and John had guessed the source of his wife's argument. Oh, well, Grace sighed. She had tried for her friend, but now she had greater worries to occupy her mind. Her mother still hadn't rallied from the dreadful chasm she had fallen into since Stephen's death. The future looked bleak for the entire family, for how could any of them return to any semblance of normality when Temperance could not be left alone, and her state of mind was drowning them all in sorrow and depression?

Grace lifted her chin. She wasn't going to let John's remarks upset her. But she was saved by a commotion out in the yard which drew Geoffrey and Larry to the workshop doors. A moment earlier, Grace had caught the gentle clip-clop of horses' hoofs. She presumed that Derek had returned from collecting a large consignment of timber that was being delivered to Dousland Station. Some of it was due to be unloaded directly at the workshop, while the rest would be stored up at the timber-yard. But now the distinctly distressed neighing of the horses and Derek's agitated shouts drew them all outside.

The sight that met her eyes drew a shocked gasp from Grace's throat. She wasn't sure exactly what had happened, but it looked as if one of the carthorses had slipped on a pocket of ice and had gone down on its knees, falling sideways between the shafts and pulling its companion in the same direction. Their combined massive weight had tipped the wagon sufficiently for its heavy load to be dislodged, and the top timbers were sliding off the far side. Slipping sideways in the driving-seat, Derek was trying to correct the situation by urging the horses forward and hoping they could thus manage to right themselves and the wagon. But the thunderous boom as the lengths of wood landed on the ground was frightening them further, their hoofs scrabbling on the ground and their eyes rolling in terror. The two normally docile giants had suddenly become dangerous beasts, one kicking out as it tried to keep its footing, and the one down on its knees throwing its head about in panic as it pawed frantically at the slippery patch it still failed to get a grip on.

Grace looked on, rooted to the spot, as Larry darted forward between the dangerously swaying shafts. Pulling off his jacket, he threw it over the head of the first horse which at once began to calm down. Then, with apparently no thought for his own safety, Larry grasped the other animal's bridle. He managed to steady the flailing head by brute force and began encouraging the creature with a smooth and steady voice to get back on its legs.

It was still struggling, and Larry instinctively ducked under its huge hairy chest to use his shoulder to assist its attempts. Before she knew it, Grace found herself taking his place by the horse's head. Working together and dodging the flying hoofs, their efforts finally allowed the mighty beast to heave itself into a standing position, righting the wagon so that both equine companions stood together, quivering and nervous but upright at last.

The humans stepped back, panting with relief, and Grace saw Larry puff out his cheeks before turning to her with anger blazing in his eyes.

'Why the hell did you do that? You could've been hurt!'

Indignation flared in Grace's nostrils. 'So could you!'

'But they're *our* horses. *Our* responsibility.'

'But you needed help—'

'I was right behind you, cheel,' Geoffrey put in. 'But you beat me to it. Now, everyone's all right, aren't they? So let's get back to work.'

Larry threw Grace a reproachful glance and she set her chin stubbornly. Was she supposed to have stood back when her instincts told her to go to Larry's aid? The poor horses were terrified, and she couldn't bear to watch them suffering. She didn't dare imagine what poor Sunny was going through. The poor thing might well have met a gruesome death by now for all anyone knew. Grace hadn't been able to protect Sunny, but she had been able to help the two carthorses that were gradually settling down under Derek's soothing ministrations. And if Larry didn't appreciate her efforts, well . . . well, sod him, she swore silently, even though she cringed at the thought that such a word had entered her head.

She pushed waspishly past John who had only just appeared in the doorway to see what the rumpus was about in the yard. Frustration circled about Grace's heart as she set the machine-copier in motion. It was all just because she was a girl, wasn't it? But women were doing dangerous work in the munitions factories, and what she had done was nothing compared to the risks they faced every day.

The first tenon had now been turned into a spoke ready to be finished by hand. Grace removed it from the machine and replaced it with a new length of oak. Everyone else, too, had returned to their various tasks and Grace felt her resentment subside. At least she was competent in the job she was entrusted with, and couldn't be criticized for that!

'Grace, what on earth are you doing? They're all too short! You must have put the wrong pattern in the machine.'

'What? No, I haven't.'

'You have. Look!'

Grace's senses reeled as Larry held two spokes together, showing clearly the difference in their lengths. Oh, no! How many had she already run off? How could she possibly have made such a mistake? She looked up at Larry, and the unusual anger in his expression frightened her. It was too much. Her resolve suddenly failed, and she burst into tears.

She didn't see the spasm of remorse that at once twitched at Larry's face. 'It doesn't matter,' he said, returning to his normal level tone. 'It's a bit of a waste, but we can keep them for next time we're making a smaller wheel. You'll just have to make some new ones, that's all.'

'Of course it matters!' Grace protested, smarting under the degradation — and the great, suppressed emotion that was her grief over Stephen, her mother and everything the war meant for her. And as Larry stepped towards her, arms outstretched and his face alight with concern, she slipped past him and ran outside, to the astonishment of everyone else.

John Sampson turned his face away to hide his satisfaction.

CHAPTER ELEVEN

It had snowed on Dartmoor during the winter. It always did to a greater or lesser extent. But now, well into the new year of 1916, the snow had virtually gone especially lower down on the edge of the moor. There could well be more snow to come, blanketing the wilderness in pure, crystal brilliance that would twinkle in the weak winter sun. But for now, Grace was enjoying the respite in the weather. Having cooked the family Sunday lunch, she had been ushered out of the cottage by her father who insisted the children get some fresh air while he kept an eye on Temperance. They had started up the steep road towards the church, but had soon turned off right, cutting obliquely through fields and thus arriving at the tiny, picturesque hamlet of Welltown. Grace didn't go there often as she preferred the open freedom of the high moorland, but a wicked wind was biting into their faces and it would be more sheltered down in the valley.

The younger girls were trotting along beside George who had developed a talent for making up spine-chilling stories about dastardly tree-spirits and beautiful water-nymphs who always won the day with their superior good magic. Grace was grateful as, while Faith and Maggie squealed with the glee all children seem to derive from gory tales, it left her mind free to wander, something she had little opportunity for these days.

The afternoon sunlight caught the brooch she kept pinned to her coat, and her thoughts travelled back to when Larry had given it to her at Christmas.

'It's not much,' he had said as she gasped at the piece of costume jewellery in its velvet-lined box. 'It's from Martin as well. He asked me to get something for you in his last letter. I hope you like it.'

Tears welled in Grace's eyes. She was somehow deeply touched by the lovely gift when there was so much sadness in the world. 'It's beautiful,' she choked. 'I've never owned ort like it afore. We only ever give each other practical things as presents.'

'They're not real gemstones,' Larry went on apologetically. 'We couldn't afford those. I wish we could, though. And we *are* truly friends again, aren't we?'

Grace knew instantly what he was referring to, and her chest squeezed with mortification. 'Yes, of course we are. It's just, well, that day, everything seemed to get on top of me.'

'I was just as much to blame. I just couldn't bear to see you hurt. Ever.'

His eyes had softened as he smiled at her, and she had felt a warm tenderness seep into her body. She could feel it now, and she was so glad that she had such a good friend as Larry. The day nearly three months ago now, when she had made the costly mistake in the workshop, was well and truly forgotten.

They were coming back into the village, having made a loop back up past the church. George had just taken from his pocket the precious halfpenny bar of chocolate their father had given them to share. He was holding it aloft out of his younger sisters' reach, claiming that he was going to consume it all himself. Faith was jumping up at his raised arm, shouting at him, while Maggie had burst into tears. Irritation spurred Grace from her reverie and she swiped the treat out of George's hand.

'Don't be so horrible, George!'

'Aw, Gracie, I were only teasing,' the boy pouted in reply. 'You knows I didn't mean it.'

'But you've made Maggie cry. I've a good mind to let the girls have your bit and all.'

'You wouldn't be so mean . . .'

'Oh, yes, I would. And you should be more grateful! Just think of the sailors who've risked their lives to bring us the cocoa or whatever else is needed to make the chocolate in the first place. You know how German U-boats are attacking the merchant ships. You should be ashamed of yourself for . . . for . . .'

Grace lost her train of thought as her attention was drawn by the raised voices of a couple standing opposite the inn. She immediately recognized Aggie Nonnacott and John Sampson who appeared to have just emerged from his cottage. Aggie had adopted her usual superior pose while something small and white was fluttering down from her hand to land at John's feet.

Grace's heart gave a painful thump as the day Aggie had done the self-same thing to Larry sprang into her mind. The other girl had been behaving unobtrusively since Grace had discovered her with Martin down by the stepping stones, and now the memory of both incidents grasped Grace by the throat. It seemed that Aggie was up to her old tricks, but Grace knew it didn't do to get on the wrong side of John Sampson! Now, however, he bent to retrieve the white feather, gazing at it in mock surprise before he exploded in a guffaw of laughter.

'You doesn't expect us to be afeared of *that*, does you?' Grace heard him chortle, and she held her breath as, before Aggie had a chance to move, John stroked the feather along the suddenly slack-jawed girl's cheek. 'And surely you doesn't think I can be intimidated by a stuck-up tart like you?'

Oh, Lord, what would happen next? Grace turned protectively towards her squabbling siblings, wanting to shield them from whatever unpleasantness was about to occur, but she couldn't help but glance over her shoulder in fearful fascination. Having taken a step backwards, Aggie had quickly regained her normal composure and was sneering back at her victim.

'Well, I'd be afeared if I were you,' she snorted. 'Be called up soon, you will, with that new conscription law. Men up to forty-one, and I don't think even you can get away with claiming you're older than that.'

'Huh! Not so clever as you thinks.' John poked his head forward so that his nose was almost touching Aggie's. 'Haven't read about it proper like, have we? If you had, you'd know it's only for unmarried men or widows with no chiller. It might've escaped your notice, but Nan be alive and kicking, and us had three tackers last time I counted them.'

Aggie was not to be thwarted. 'Oh, so that's why you've given the poor woman so many children, is it? To hide behind?'

'We had the first two afore the war started, if my memory serves me rightly. So, young Aggie.' Grace saw John take Aggie's hand, place the feather in her palm and close her fingers around it. 'You'd better look after that for when you needs it again. Only next time, make certain of your facts.'

He gave a short laugh before striding off down the road leaving Aggie staring, dumbfounded, after him. It was some moments before she noticed Grace and the children watching her.

'What you looking at?' she barked before spinning on her heel and marching away.

Grace lifted her eyebrows in genuine surprise, since the ugly scene had prompted a reaction inside her that both astonished and confused her. She actually felt *sorry* for Aggie. It was quite gratifying to see someone trying to get the better of John Sampson, but she had been shot down in flames in much the same way as Grace had been when she failed to influence John over his treatment of his wife. So, in some peculiar and oblique manner, it put them on the same side. On the other hand, John had been quite right in all he had said, and after all, it would be appalling for Nan if he had to go and fight — and maybe never return. Grace knew only too well what it was to lose someone, and John was also the breadwinner for the young family.

'Come on, you lot,' she ordered, shoving George forward and attempting — unsuccessfully — to cast her unsettled emotions to the back of her mind.

* * *

'This certainly puts a different complexion on the matter,' Grace heard Geoffrey comment as she arrived at work.

She guessed what they were discussing. She had seen what was in the morning paper — at least, Farmer Snell had read it aloud at the breakfast table. The new maid, who had come to work for them the previous September, had only just turned thirteen and didn't realize the far reaching consequences of the news. But everyone else did.

'Married, widowed, with or without chiller,' Bob summarized, nodding his head gravely, 'all men between eighteen and forty-one it is, now. As if it baint bad enough already for those of us what's lost a son, it's to be husbands and fathers as well now.'

Geoffrey clapped the carpenter sympathetically on the shoulder. 'I know. The first conscription act only came into effect a couple of months ago, and already the government's decided it's not enough. Makes you wonder if they're not planning some big offensive on the Western Front. This war's already dragged on nearly two years, and if something radical isn't done soon, it'll carry on in stalemate another two from what I can gather.'

'But it'll take months to train up all these new conscripts,' Larry reasoned, 'even if we have got this new daylight saving British Summer Time arrangement. Look how long Martin's battalion was training before they went to France. It wasn't far off a year.'

'Desperate situations call for desperate measures, lad,' Edward grimaced. 'They might not plan on training them to such a high standard. And at the start of the war, there were hardly any weapons to train with. Now we're churning out shells and machine-guns like nobody's business. That must make a difference.'

'Possibly,' Larry conceded. 'Oh, morning, Grace,' he said as he caught sight of her. 'You've heard this new announcement, I assume. Won't affect your father, will it? He's older than that, isn't he?'

Grace had been listening to the conversation with the dull numbness that comes from being forced to accept something dreadful. A similar discussion had gone on around the farmhouse table, Farmer Snell voicing the same opinion as Geoffrey Vencombe. Now Grace puffed out her cheeks in a wistful sigh.

'Yes, Daddy's forty-three, thank goodness. Can you imagine what it'd do to Mummy if he had to go off to fight as well? As it is, if she didn't have us all to muddle through the day with her, she'd have to go into an asylum or summat.'

'She's no better then?' Geoffrey asked in his usual kindly fashion, and Grace shook her head. 'Ah, well, I reckon we'll just have to see what this'll mean for us. The only person we could lose is you, John, as far as I can make out.'

Grace noticed that John had been getting on with his work without entering the conversation, almost as if he were trying to block it from his ears. Now, though, he was forced to lift his head and talk to his workmates.

'Looks like,' he answered gruffly. 'If I has to go, then I has to go. I'd prefer not, but I never said I wouldn't. My poor Nan's not going to be too happy about it, mind, not with the three tackers to take care on.'

At least he wouldn't be there to make it four, Grace considered grimly to herself. But then she bit her lip. That was unkind. Cannon fodder was the term Farmer Snell had employed that morning, sending recruits to the Front with so much less training than they had at the start of the war and relying on higher numbers of troops and more powerful weaponry instead. And John was right. It really would be hard on Nan.

'Well, let's hope for all our sakes you don't get your call-up papers too soon. It won't be easy to manage here without you, either,' Grace said, astonishing herself — and John, too, judging by the sudden change of expression on his face.

'Maybe we could argue that we really need John here,' Larry put in. 'I know even being a skilled wheelwright wasn't officially a reserved occupation in the first wave of conscription. But with all these attacks on merchant-ships bringing our imported food and farmers being told to increase production as a result, well, we all know our books are full for months ahead. It's as much for the war effort as working in a munitions factory. And don't forget, we've been sub-contracted a couple of times to make a consignment of wagon-wheels for the military.'

Geoffrey raised a thoughtful eyebrow. 'No harm in trying, I suppose. But I doubt it'll wash. The rules will probably be even stricter this time round. Even in farming, only the farmers proper were protected, not farm-labourers. Farmers have been drafting in women to take the place of the conscripts who've been called up, and we'll have to do the same. After all, we have Grace already, and look how successful that's been.'

Grace was aware of the scarlet that flared into her cheeks. Bar the odd costly mistake, she reminded herself ruefully. But it might be pleasant to have some female company at the wheelwrights', much as she got on well with the men. Excepting John, of course. But as he continued with his work, quietly for once as if locked in his own thoughts, Grace felt a twinge of pity. It must be unimaginable for any man, whoever he might be, to contemplate staring death in the face on the battlefield. She shuddered, and thanked the Lord that Larry was at least one young man in the village who would be spared that horror.

* * *

'I really mustn't be late,' Grace proclaimed, putting away the tools she was using. 'It's amazing that Martha insisted on carrying on looking after Mummy and Maggie for us, but I feel I must get back on time.'

'She's a rare soul is Martha. But that's perhaps how she's coping, throwing herself more than ever into helping others.'

'I think she's still in shock. Fancy reading in the paper that your son's ship has been blown to kingdom come in a big sea battle . . .'

'The *Defence*, wasn't it?'

'Yes, at what they're calling the Battle of Jutland. But I don't think she'll believe that Horace has been killed until she gets official notification.'

'Poor soul.'

'I know. She'd do anything for anybody, and doesn't deserve this. But I really must go. See you all tomorrow.'

Grace hurried out of the yard. It was only days into June and the weather was being kind, but this new tragedy in the village was weighing heavily on everyone's heart. Temperance had seemed more relaxed of late, even the faintest memory of a smile lifting the corners of her mouth on occasion, so they had been careful to keep the news from her. It had, however, reignited Grace's own smouldering grief over Stephen, and she kept imagining poor Horace drowning, the panic as his mouth and nose and then his lungs filled with water. Perhaps he had been screaming in agony from an injury, the sea all around on fire from burning engine fuel. Oh, good God, it was no wonder poor Martha was blanking it from her mind.

'I'll believe it when they tells us official, like,' the poor woman had told her with an emphatic nod of her head. 'In the meantime, us doesn't want to upset Temperance now, does us? Us must get on with our work. I mean, it don't make no difference to our lives here, do it? Horace has been away for years, and he don't have no missus or tackers. Not like our Jim or our Stanley. Both got families, but they'm only labourers, so they'm likely to be called up any time now.'

Grace's forehead had ruched into a frown of sympathy. She knew from her own experience that it didn't matter what anyone said, or how kind people were. You just had to deal with it in your own way. Inside yourself. On your own. And so she had kept her thoughts to herself. Time enough for her to support Martha when the official letter came.

Now she pushed open the door of the Wedlake cottage, her disquiet deepened by the beaming smile on Martha's face. Dear Lord, the truth was going to hit her so hard when it came. But then, to her astonishment, the woman thrust a telegram into her hand.

'Just arrived it has. Barry don't even know yet.'

Bewildered, Grace took the paper from her good friend's trembling hand, and her jaw dropped a mile as her gaze took in the words at a glance.

NOT ON DEFENCE STOP ALIVE AND WELL STOP HORACE.

Oh. Grace snatched in her breath. Oh, God, it was a miracle!

'Oh, Martha, that's . . . wonderful!' she squealed in delight, and wrapped her arms around the other woman's rotund form. They danced about in a circle, tears of joy coursing down both their cheeks. Grace glanced over her shoulder at her mother and little Maggie who were both smiling at their antics, but thankfully neither of them understood the reason for their elation. For if they could, wouldn't they have wanted Stephen to come back from the dead as well?

CHAPTER TWELVE

Grace hurried into the village, anxious to arrive promptly at the wheelwright's yard. It was a pleasant September morning, overcast but warm and still, with a promise of the cloud breaking later. There should have been a spring in Grace's step as she breathed in the sweet fragrance of the countryside. But like everyone who kept abreast of events, an insidious grey fog dampened her every thought.

Since the beginning of July, the country had been receiving news of a massive attempt by the Allies to break the deadlock in France in an area along the River Somme. So Geoffrey and Farmer Snell's conjecture had been proved correct. But things weren't going to plan. Published casualty lists were growing longer and longer, running into hundreds of thousands now, Larry had reported gloomily. Grace knew what was gnawing at the back of his mind — because it was gnawing at hers, too. Martin.

Somewhere, out in the terrifying mayhem of the battlefield, was Martin. Perhaps, at any instant, while Grace was drinking a cup of tea, chasing timber suppliers or soothing her mother as she caught up with the neglected household chores, Martin had just been blown to smithereens, was choking to death on poisoned gas, or was lying, riddled with bullets, as he breathed his last.

If there was bad news, would Grace try to work out what she had been doing when it had happened? She somehow had a feeling that she would. A morbid despondency seemed to pervade everything she did, however hard she tried to throw it off. It wasn't as if there was anything more between them than Martin being like another brother to her. But if the worst happened, it would be like losing Stephen all over again, and she wasn't sure she could bear that. She even wondered wryly if she had been wrong to interrupt Martin and Aggie down by the stepping stones after all. Or whether Stephen had ever succumbed to the dusky charms of some beautiful maiden out in India before he had died. She almost hoped that he had.

Oh, she must stop thinking as if she were the only person in the world who was suffering this agony. God alone knew how many soldiers and their worried relatives were involved. The fighting wasn't confined to France. There were theatres of war also playing out in Egypt and Palestine, Salonika and Mesopotamia where the fall of Kut to the Turks back in the spring had been an appalling blow. With Larry's help and the aid of an old atlas, Grace had followed it all, but lately she hadn't been so keen to do so. There was clearly no end in sight, and the more she knew, the more depressed she became.

'Morning, all,' she called with false brightness as she entered the workshop. And seeing that not everyone was there, she enquired, 'Where are Gladys and Elsie?' Certainly the two young women who had been employed to take John's place were nowhere to be seen. To Nan's dismay, John had been called up only weeks after the second conscription act had come into force, and Geoffrey had needed to fill the gap pretty quickly. He sometimes wondered if he had made too hasty a decision and taken on the wrong applicants!

'Hurrump,' he answered Grace's question, the twist of his mouth portraying his displeasure. 'Gone up to the field with Derek to catch the horses and tack them up. You'd have thought they could manage on their own by now.'

'Oh, come on, Dad. Neither of them had been near a horse before. And they're mighty willing and able about the place. And they brighten things up a bit.'

Geoffrey threw his son a grudging glance, making Grace smile to herself. Gladys and Elsie were indeed a pair, having worked in service together in Tavistock. Higher wages and a sense of freedom had drawn them to apply for the advertised posts, and both being strapping young girls, their combined strength made up for the loss of John's brawn. Between them, they managed to lug heavy timber to wherever it was needed, and their antics brought some amusement to the hardworking atmosphere in the yard and workshop.

'Talk of the devil,' Bob put in, jabbing his head towards the open doors.

'Aw, stop, you bloody girt animal!' Gladys's strident voice jangled from outside. 'Just missed my foot, you did! An' now you've got to go a few steps assards!'

'I told you to give 'em a wider turning circle,' Derek corrected her. 'Anyways, now you two can bring the wagon up an' see if you can get the horses to back up to the shafts.'

Grace chuckled as she walked over to the office, hearing the disgruntled snorting of the horses as the two girls tried to persuade them to step backwards up to the wagon. Grace knew a line of wheelbarrows was waiting to be taken for despatch up at Dousland Station, and she could imagine the colourful language Gladys in particular would use as they pushed the heavy handcarts up the ramp and into the wagon. Geoffrey would frown in disapproval but the rest of them would hide a smile. It was yet another way the war had changed their lives, Grace mused as she closed the office door. Two years ago, she would have been disgusted at the swearing that tripped so easily from Gladys's tongue. But now she wondered with amusement how the girl had managed to contain her natural means of expression while she was in service. No wonder she had jumped at the chance of employment in what she had imagined would be an entirely male workplace!

With the trace of a smile lingering on her lips, Grace got on with the business's paperwork. She finished it in record time and was about to go and lend a hand in the workshop when she heard Verity Vencombe's raised voice through the door. It was rare that the good lady did more than provide mugs of tea and plates of biscuits for their employees, although she was always ready with her kind smile to administer to their needs if anyone cut a finger or had any other mishap. So it seemed to Grace that something must be amiss, and she popped her head around the door. Verity was waving a sheet of paper in the air, her drained face taut with some unfathomable emotion. Grace was aware of her own pulse speeding up as she stared at the agitated woman, and a sudden fear stung into her mind, too.

'It's from Martin,' Verity babbled, her voice almost a squeal. 'He's been wounded. He's in a field hospital, but . . . they might be sending him home to recover.'

Numbed shock sizzled about the workshop, followed by a chorus of voices as everyone tried to make sense of the news, bombarding poor Verity with questions.

'What sort of wounds?'

'Coming home? When? Home here? To a hospital?'

'I-I don't know,' Verity stammered, 'He doesn't say.'

'Well, he's alive, thank God.' Geoffrey stepped forward and took his wife's trembling hands. 'And he'll be out of the fighting for a while, at least.'

'It must be a relatively serious wound if they're sending him home,' Larry frowned, taking the letter from his mother. 'More minor wounds they patch up somewhere behind the lines before sending them back to the Front. On the other hand, he's well enough to travel.'

'Does he not say ort more?' Grace eagerly grasped Larry's arm and leant over it so that she could read the letter in his hand for herself. She felt strange, torn in two. Of course, it was dreadful that Martin had been hurt, but he had survived and might soon be safely home in England. Possibly for good. Oh, it would be so marvellous to see him! And the excitement flared inside her like a torch of flame, burning away the horror of what Martin might be suffering. They would find out the nature of his wounds soon enough. For now, she would bask in the knowledge that he was alive and safe, and the smile that crept onto her face was slowly echoed by those who stood around her.

* * *

'Nan?'

The front door to the cottage hadn't been shut properly which was how Grace had caught the faint sobs coming from within. Her heart at once constricted with sympathy since poor Nan had been so distressed when John had been called up.

Grace's gaze travelled about the usually tidy room, for John was right in that Nan was a born home-maker. But the sight that met her eyes was one of chaos and disorder.

'Give it me!' little Billy was bawling at his big sister who, at just turned four years old, was fiercely clutching a worn and pathetic rag doll to her chest.

'No, it's mine! Aw, now look what you've done!' Sally screamed and burst into passionate tears as she stared at the detached leg.

Grace saw the fleeting horror on Billy's face that was at once replaced by an obstinate pout. 'Sally's fault!' he retorted, and promptly tripped backwards over the baby who was crawling on the floor and began howling when his older brother landed on top of him.

Grace raised her concerned eyes to her friend. Nan was completely ignoring her off-spring as she knuckled the tears from her eyes. Grace stepped forward to lift Billy onto his feet and, sweeping the crying baby into one arm, retrieved the dismembered doll's leg from the floor where Billy had now abandoned it.

'Oh, we can soon sew dolly's leg back on,' she soothed, smiling down at Sally. 'Now, why don't you two go and play out the back while I talk to your mummy?'

'So . . . will you mend it for me, Grace?'

'Of course, I will. Now off you go, and play nicely.' Grace watched with relief as the two little souls went out through the back door, evidently friends again. The infant in her arms was also calming down, deciding that pulling Grace's hair from its neat bun was much more interesting than crying, and Grace turned her attention to Nan.

'What's the matter, Nan?' she asked tentatively, and her heart swayed as Nan turned her tear-stained face to her. She was a picture of misery, her eyes red and swollen.

'John . . . be on his way to France,' the poor girl choked. 'To the Front.'

'Oh.' A lead weight sank in Grace's stomach. Of course. It was what every parent, spouse and child dreaded. To have a loved one in such terrible danger hundreds of miles away and there was nothing anyone could do about it. Just the awful sterility of waiting for news — one way or the other. What Grace couldn't voice was the thought that, like all conscripts nowadays, John had been sent to the battlefield with so little training.

'They gave him just enough time to come home for a few hours to say goodbye. Didn't you see him yesterday afternoon?'

Nan's eyebrows knitted as if, in some obscure way, it might have helped her if Grace had. But Grace had to shake her head.

'Worst of it is,' Nan faltered as if she were about to break into tears again, 'I's pregnant again, and I had to hide it from him. I didn't want him thinking that he could die and never see his next child!'

Her homely figure trembled as she broke down once more and Grace put her free arm about the young woman's shoulders, pain scratching at her own throat. She must be strong for poor Nan. Whatever she herself thought of John, he was Nan's husband and she loved him. She was devastated without him. Grace bit her lip, and a curious sensation came over her. There was no one she loved as a woman loved a man, not in that sense. It was something she had mentally put out of her mind, concentrating on her work and her family until this horrific conflict was over.

And she thanked God that she had.

* * *

'Now, remember what Mum and Dad said after their visit yesterday,' Larry warned. 'He's not quite his old self.'

After some weeks of silence, Martin's parents had been informed that their injured officer son had been returned not only to Devon, but to his nearest home town of Tavistock just outside of which Mount Tavy House had only recently been turned into an auxiliary military hospital. It was to receive injured soldiers mainly from the Devonshire Regiment whenever possible, and specializing in neurosis patients. Grace had read in the *Gazette* that the substantial residence had been left in trust to a local doctor and his wife to be used for the good of the community, and what better way could there be than to help the poor devils who had been wounded in defence of their country?

And so, one early October afternoon, Grace and Larry had taken the train into Tavistock together. Grace had thought that she couldn't possibly leave her mother for the afternoon as well, but dear Martha had insisted that she could take care of Temperance for the whole day. Grace was so pleased that she was able to accompany Larry that only now was she beginning to consider what the hospital visit might hold.

Larry had seemed disinclined to talk during the short train journey and instead, Grace had enjoyed the magnificent views over the western edge of the moor. When they arrived in Tavistock, Grace had been surprised to see so many soldiers in the town, even though she had read how heavily garrisoned the area had become. Now, as she and Larry climbed the steep hill to the grand house on the way up onto the moor, Grace's heart began to gallop. And it wasn't just the exertion of conquering the soaring incline that was making her breathless. They couldn't go so terribly fast anyway because of Larry's leg. No. It was his subdued words that had set her mind, and consequently her pulse, racing.

Grace gulped, her mouth suddenly as dry as desert sand. 'Yes, I know,' she replied, trying to make herself sound more confident than she felt. 'But your parents said that he were really looking forward to seeing us both, so we must do our best to cheer him up.'

'Exactly,' Larry said forcefully, but the sombre expression on his face hardly looked encouraging.

They turned in at the gates where the young lad who was manning the entrance asked their business and then directed them across a stone bridge and up the sweeping driveway. The house sat atop a hill, surrounded by stunning grounds whose grassy banks were dotted carefully with specimen trees so as not to spoil the glorious view over Tavistock and the green hills on the far side of the valley. Where the ground was not so steep, vegetables had been planted as part of the campaign, Grace surmised, to grow as much non-imported food as possible. She was enchanted. She had never seen anything so grandiose as the house and its grounds, but her rapture vanished as the reality of the situation struck home.

The mild autumn afternoon had drawn the inhabitants of the house outdoors to sit on benches or wander across the grass. It was these people that made Grace falter in her steps, and beside her, she felt Larry hesitate as if he, too, were enveloped in the same tearing sensibility as she was.

The grounds were wreathed in tranquillity, hardly a breath of breeze stirring the turning leaves on the trees or the autumn flowers in the neat borders. All was so calm, like a silent paradise, figures floating like gentle spirits in a sea of green. Yet there *was* sound, far away and muffled. Soothing voices, quiet laughter even. Women in white, ankle-length pinafores and head-dresses like starched scarves tied in intricate folds at the back so that they resembled angels' wings. Each beside a man, bent over in an attitude of caring, holding a hand, helping the lame to limp forward. The men in shapeless, saxe-blue suits with wide lapels and finished with a scarlet tie. Bandages covered an eye, swathed an arm. An empty trouser-leg, a vacant sleeve pinned to the chest. The crunch of gravel as one of the angels pushed a bath-chair past the young couple on the driveway. A blanket where there should have been two legs. The angel smiled at Grace so serenely as they passed. And Grace turned to watch, and felt her heart rupture.

'Can I help you?'

The kind, compassionate voice enlivened Grace's senses, and the scene about her sprang back to reality, the players no longer moving in slow motion, sounds returning to normal levels. Grace blinked, aware suddenly of the moisture that was pooling in her eyes. Dear God. These poor, broken souls. Young lads turned into old men, their lives in tatters.

'We've come to visit my brother, Second Lieutenant Vencombe,' Grace heard Larry reply to the tall, slender figure in a scarlet nurse's uniform who stood before them, a woman in her late forties, Grace would have guessed. 'The boy on the gate directed us this way,' Larry concluded by way of explanation.

'Ah, Liam.' The lady smiled affectionately. 'A good lad. His mother's a VAD nurse here.' She lifted a wistful eyebrow. 'We'll be losing young Liam to the army, too, though, in a year or so if this dreadful business isn't over by then. He already has two elder brothers out in France, poor devils. But, do come this way.' She shook her head as if throwing her melancholy thoughts aside. 'Your brother's a little brighter this afternoon. The visit from his parents yesterday cheered him up no end.'

'You know him personally, then?' Larry sounded surprised.

'We've only just opened so we're not up to capacity yet, so I've learnt everyone's name so far. But I intend to make it my business to know all of my patients individually.' The woman turned her confident, sincere smile on them again. 'I'm Ling Franfield, by the way. Officially the VAD Commandant, but I prefer to be called Matron. It were to me that dear Agnes left this place, and with so many poor souls returning from the Front with their nerves in pieces, well, my husband suggested we opened it as a sort of sanctuary for them. We couldn't think of a better way to carry out Agnes's wishes to do something for the town. Not that we'd turn any poor fellow away, but we do try to give priority to anyone from the Devonshire Regiment.'

They were approaching the portico at the entrance to the house when a most curious sight drew Grace's attention. She tried not to stare, but a strange fascination dragged her gaze towards two patients coming towards them. She couldn't say they were walking, because they weren't. Making their way — or struggling their way would be a better way to describe it.

Grace was used to Larry's strange gait, but one of these poor fellows was twisted from his head to his feet, tottering precariously. The other stopped every couple of strides while his head and shoulders twitched violently and an odd, guttural cry emerged from his suddenly flapping mouth. These two shattered souls resembled severely mentally and physically disabled invalids, yet they were attired in the military patient uniform, and so only recently must have been fit and healthy young men.

Grace had imagined all kinds of horrific physical injuries that killed or maimed, but never anything like this. What she instinctively knew must be a brain injury of some sort. A helpless sense of futility choked her appalled mind, for what on earth could be done to help such damaged wretches? She averted her eyes as she and Larry followed Mrs Franfield into a vestibule twice the size of the downstairs room of her family home.

'Unbelievable, isn't it?' the matron said in a voice that resonated with sympathy. 'There's nothing physically wrong with them. That's what we're mainly going to deal with here, the mental trauma of receiving some permanent physical injury, or of just being in the trenches. Some simply can't take it. Their nerves are so deeply affected that it produces the sort of physical effects you saw there. In the early stages, sufferers can appear crazed. They can cower, or freeze with fear. We talk openly about it here. It's part of the therapy. And we want the world to know about it. At first, it was labelled cowardice. Sometimes soldiers suffering from it were physically pushed "over the top", as they call it. Others have even been shot for cowardice because they ran away. But at least, the army has finally recognized that it's a true mental condition.'

Grace had been listening intently, wondering why Martin had ended up at this place, wonderful as it seemed to her. They passed through the doors in a skilfully crafted glass wall into a massive double-height hall. At one end, a grand staircase led up to a galleried landing around the inner walls of the upper storey, above which a magnificent stained-glass atrium roof in shades of yellow and amber allowed light to flood into the hall below. Indeed, there was a further, slightly smaller such atrium roof over the stairwell itself.

Grace could never have envisaged such beauty. The building itself would be instrumental in lifting one's sorely tried spirits, she considered, and it was a moment before her attention was drawn back to the occupants of the enormous room. At the opposite end to the staircase, it opened into a wide bay with a broad, almost full-length arched window overlooking the grounds. Nurses were tending a good number of patients resting in chairs, and tea was being served from a trolley. Grace noticed a piano to one side, the lid open and sheet music on the stand as if someone would be playing later. And all the time while she spoke to the visitors, Ling Franfield was nodding her head and smiling at patients here, patting a shoulder there.

'I expect you know we've only been open a week,' Ling continued, leading them towards a doorway. 'The idea is to offer our patients as much peace and quiet as we can, so we're taking on as many volunteers as come forward, many of them VADs. I expect you know the Devon 10 opened a small hospital for the physically wounded in Bedford Villas, and they also take some at the town's cottage hospital. But as I say, what we're aiming to do here is to treat the mind. Some of our volunteers just listen or chat. Or just sit quietly, showing that they care. We're planning on giving some of our patients little jobs, to relax them and get them to concentrate on other things besides their fears. Gardening, or in the kitchen. And we'll encourage hobbies, anything from stamp collecting to painting or basket weaving.'

She paused, her fingers closed about the door handle, and her chestnut eyes danced with inspired enthusiasm. 'There's a man called Arthur Hurst,' she went on. 'A doctor with the military at a place called Netley near Southampton. He's helping victims like our acute patients you saw just now by using hypnosis. Getting magnificent results. Elliott, my husband, has gone there for a few weeks to study under him. Obviously he doesn't expect to learn everything about it in so short a time. But if he can learn some techniques to help his patients relax their minds, empty out some of their terrors, it must surely help.'

Grace felt herself mesmerized by the passion that shone from Mrs Franfield's face. The woman was still very attractive, but with a strength of character that reflected through her beauty. Grace was in awe of her and was sure she would offer amazing comfort to those who would pass through her care.

'Now then, I'm certain you can't wait to see your brother. He's here, in Sunshine Ward. It's really for amputees, for us to assess their mental ability to cope with their loss as well as to convalesce physically. Your brother was brought here because his commanding officer considered his behaviour had been a little erratic of late.'

She opened the door to a spacious room that was indeed bathed in the afternoon sunlight blazing through another arched window that matched the one in the main hall. The ward smelt faintly of disinfectant and was home to two neat rows of beds, four on either side. In the centre was a desk where sat a corpulent woman in a dark blue uniform and a white pinafore, but without the red cross Grace had noticed on so many of the other nurses.

'Visitors for Martin Vencombe, Sister,' Ling announced.

The sister beamed at them and rose to her feet. 'This way, my dears.'

Grace's heart jerked. She had been so appalled and yet intrigued by what she had seen and by Mrs Franfield's explanations that she had allowed herself to blank out the reason for their visit. Trepidation rushed back at her, and she felt herself break out in a cold sweat. Martin. Dear, jovial, devil-may-care Martin. Would he be the same? How could he after what he had been through? And what was it the matron had said about erratic behaviour? And . . . and amputees?

Grace was suddenly terrified, and was grateful when Larry squeezed her hand.

CHAPTER THIRTEEN

Martin was lying in the furthest bed in the corner. Grace wouldn't have recognized him so pale and skeletal was his face, so it was as well that the homely nursing sister had shown them the way. His eyes were closed, his cheeks as white as the crisp sheet that covered him.

Grace slid behind Larry so that he went to the bedside first. Verity had been so upset the previous day that she had apparently gone straight to bed and Geoffrey had gone up to take care of her. In the morning, Grace had merely over-heard him saying to Larry that Martin's main injuries were to his legs, and Grace had not wanted to pry further. Now she stared at the bedclothes resting on a cage over Martin's legs, and horror took her by the throat as Matron Franfield's words reverberated in her skull. Oh, dear God. They hadn't needed to . . . to . . . ?

Her own legs began to wobble and she was relieved when a nurse brought up two chairs for them. She sank gratefully onto hers, dissolving like a puppet. Larry, though, leant over the inert form in the bed, and watching him, Grace dreaded the moment when it would be her turn to speak to this life-long friend who suddenly seemed like a stranger.

'Martin?'

The heavy eyelids flickered upwards and his eyes wandered for an instant before focusing on his brother's face. It was difficult to tell through such weariness, but Grace believed she detected a spark in Martin's dulled expression.

'Larry,' he answered simply, and then a hand appeared from beneath the covers and grasped Larry's, fingers tightly entwined.

Grace saw the infinite compassion on Larry's face. The slightest twitch at the corner of his mouth. It was almost unbearable, and she wondered how it would have been for her if it had been Stephen lying there instead of Martin. For one brief, shattering moment, her own grief broke to the surface again, and she balled her fists as she brought it under control.

She saw Martin's hand drop back onto the bed. 'I feel better already,' he said, 'seeing you two again. Well, not you so much, you ugly bugger, but Gracie . . . My, what a sight for sore eyes! You didn't tell me in your letters — or those that got to me — what a beauty she's grown into. Saving her for yourself, were you, you crafty old devil?'

His voice appeared to gather strength as he spoke and Grace thought she noticed the familiar teasing light returning to his eyes. She thanked God, and when he opened his arms and said, 'Come on, Gracie, give an old crock a hug,' she went to him without a thought, and even kissed him on the cheek.

'You don't have to be gentle with me,' he told her gruffly as she sat down again, and Larry, too, made use of the chair that had been brought for him. 'I won't break. If a Boche shell can't kill me off, *you* certainly won't.'

'Is that what happened? A shell?' Larry asked.

'Got a bit too close to the damned thing. Not close enough to blow my legs off, thank God, but I caught some of the shrapnel from it. A couple of small bits in my arm, but a large piece in my calf, and a bullet in my thigh. No smashed bones, miraculously. And missed all major arteries, or I wouldn't be here. And certainly not with both legs intact. At least they will be when they're healed. So, brother, you won't be the only Vencombe with a limp. For a while, at least. But they tell me I'll live to fight another day. Literally. I should be fit enough to go back to the Front in a couple of months.'

Grace had almost collapsed with relief to know her worst fears were unfounded. But Martin had seemed to need to talk without stopping, as if it were some sort of release. But his final words had been laced with such grating sarcasm that Grace was shocked to the core. It was so unlike him. She felt split in two. Over the moon that he had survived his injuries and would recover, but filled with anger that he might well have to return to the maelstrom of the battlefield.

'Is it . . . terribly painful?' she ventured to ask.

'Sorry, you'll have to speak up.' Martin's tone was sharp now. 'That's the other thing. The constant noise. Shells and heavy guns. It's affected my hearing. I've got this ringing in the ears. The medics give it some fancy name. Tin-something. They say it'll lessen in time. But it might never go away completely. And going back won't exactly help, either.'

Grace felt a little piece more of her heart shear off. Poor Martin. That sounded appalling. She didn't know what to say. Should she repeat her question in a raised voice? But Larry saved her from having to make the decision.

'So, how long will they keep you here, do you think?'

Martin shrugged. 'A few weeks, maybe. Depends how quickly the wounds heal. They were a bit infected. Gave me a slight fever, but I'm over that now. They wash out deep wounds with something called Carrel-Dakin solution. It's brand new, apparently. Supposed to stop gangrene setting in. Bloody agony each time they do it, mind. But if it saves your leg . . . I'm well past that stage now. Wouldn't have minded if I *had* lost my leg, though. It would have saved me from having to go back.'

Grace had to stifle a gasp. She could tell he really meant it. Dear Lord, he was so changed from the bright young man who had champed at the bit to give the Boche a bloody nose, as he himself had put it. There were moments when Grace glimpsed Martin's old sharp wit, but it was so tainted with rancour that she doubted he would ever be the same again.

'We could certainly do with you back in the workshop,' Larry was telling him, clearly trying to divert the course of the conversation, and Grace realized it was easier for Martin to hear a deeper, male voice than her own. 'Grace here's a marvel, but she only works mornings. Young George has left school now and started his apprenticeship with us.'

'Yes. Like Steve did.' Martin's words were flat now. 'I'm really sorry about what happened to him, Gracie. We'll all miss him. But at least he had it relatively easy in India. Not like at the Front.'

It was as if a spike twisted in Grace's side. She saw Larry glance at her warily and was grateful when he went on, 'Well, George is a fast learner, just like Steve was. But he is only twelve years old, so he can hardly take the place of a fully trained wheelwright. Oh, John's been called up, did you know that?'

'John Sampson?'

'Yes. Sent to France some time ago. Your paths might have crossed if it hadn't been for this. He's in the Eighth Devons, too, apparently. But Dad's taken on two brawny wenches to take his place. Bit of a laugh, they are.' Larry gave a forced chuckle. 'You should hear them. One of them in particular, Gladys, swears like a trooper.'

'Sounds like I should look forward to meeting her.' And Grace rejoiced to see a smile break onto Martin's face for the first time.

* * *

'So where's that handsome brother of yourn, then, Larry?' Gladys dug Elsie in the ribs one morning a few weeks later, and her friend failed to conceal a giggle. 'Like to get to know him better, us would, while he's at home.'

Larry exchanged glances with Grace and threw a dark look at the two heftily built girls. 'He's still in bed, if you must know. He's here to recoup his strength now he's been discharged from hospital. And I'm sure he'd appreciate being left in peace to do so.'

'Aw, keep your hair on. I were only asking.'

Grace frowned. Gladys had meant well, she knew, but Larry did seem a little touchy. 'I expect Martin were relieved not be woken up at the crack of dawn for his breakfast,' she put in, trying to keep the peace. 'He says they wake you up so early in hospital when all you really want is rest.'

'Well, us won't disturb him,' Gladys answered haughtily. 'But when he *is* better, us'll have a bit of a laugh with him. And maybies cheer him up. Enough to kill a dead man, *you* are, you'm so serious.'

She spun on her heel and Larry returned to his work with a heavenwards roll of his eyes. Grace chewed on her lip as she came up beside him.

'She's right, you know,' she said softly. 'I'm certain Martin would love their company when he's feeling better.'

Larry turned his head sharply towards her, but then released a ponderous sigh through pursed lips. 'Yes, you're probably right. But . . . last night wasn't too grand.' He lowered his voice so that no one else could hear. 'It was a lot for him, emotionally, coming home after what he's been through. His first night. He said it was too quiet. He couldn't sleep. So he came into my room. Can you imagine, the two of us squeezed into one bed? It was like when we were children. Me, looking after my little brother.' He paused, and Grace heard the catch it his voice. 'Do you remember what Mrs Franfield said about the nightmares?'

'Yes, I do.' On the few occasions when Grace had managed to accompany Larry to the hospital, the matron had always found time to exchange a compassionate word with them. She was not allowed to say too much about a patient's condition, of course, but she had warned them that, like so many soldiers from the trenches, Martin suffered from terrible nightmares.

Grace put a hand on Larry's arm. 'Did he keep you awake, then?'

'I didn't get much sleep, no,' Larry admitted. 'But that's nothing to what the poor devils out in France go through night after night. And I know Martin's been discharged from the hospital, but I am still worried about his state of mind.'

'Oh, I'm sure after a few weeks peace and quiet, he'll be fine.'

Grace tried to sound reassuring, but Larry didn't seem convinced. 'Well, I hope you're right. But there's no obvious reason why he shouldn't be returned to the Front when his leg's fully healed, and I really don't think he should be. But, Grace, keep this under your hat about the nightmares, won't you? I don't think Mum and Dad heard him in the night. He eventually went back to his own room and was sleeping like a baby this morning. I don't want them having anything more to worry about than they already have.'

Grace saw the lines deepen about his mouth. Dear Larry. He always took the weight of the world on his shoulders — always had done ever since she could remember.

'Of course.' She nodded, her lips compressing into a wry, understanding smile. She experienced a sudden, overpowering desire to brush a kiss on his cheek to show how much she cared. But then it was gone, and she merely tightened her grip on his arm for a second before she made off to the office.

Grace knew, though, that her mind wasn't on her work and had to force herself to concentrate. Despite her attempt to reassure Larry, she, too, was concerned for Martin, not so much his physical injuries which were healing well as his uncharacteristic behaviour. For someone who had always been so relaxed and jocular, he seemed tense, like a coiled spring, his normal sense of humour turned to laconic irony. Grace wished Dr Franfield had returned from studying under this Arthur Hurst before Martin had been discharged from Mount Tavy and had been able to assess his mental state. But at least Grace could draw comfort from the fact that Martin wasn't like the poor fellows she had seen at the hospital whose mental terrors had been translated into physical disabilities.

Grace wished that she herself could do something to help the patients at Mount Tavy. The atmosphere under Mrs Franfield's direction was so efficient and yet infinitely tranquil that she envied the VADs who worked there. Helping to make wagon wheels to keep the country fed when imports were so impeded was all very well, but what she had seen on her few visits to the hospital had inspired her heart to higher aspirations. Ah, well.

It was when she had the business's paperwork up to date and went back out into the workshop that a familiar figure appeared in the doorway. No longer in 'hospital blues', Martin was dressed in his civilian clothes rather than his uniform which had been damaged beyond repair when he was wounded. His health regained, the only difference in his appearance from pre-war days was the walking stick he was using. Grace's heart gave a little leap. Perhaps with a good long rest in the harmonious peace of the village, his good spirits would be restored as well.

'Good morning, Martin!' she called cheerfully as she sprang across to him, spreading her face into a welcoming smile. 'It must feel good to be home again.'

He gave an indulgent nod almost as if he considered her a child still. But Grace didn't feel piqued. He hadn't been there for two years apart from that short leave, and perhaps didn't realize how she had matured in that time.

'You can make yourself useful if you want,' Larry told him. 'Not that I imagine you do. Always a bit work-shy if I remember.'

Grace noticed Martin pull a wry face. But then his features hardened as his gaze took in the all so familiar scene. He appeared to hesitate, but as if steeling himself, he then limped over to where Bob was chiselling out some joints on a farm gate. Grace turned away. Better to let Martin take things at his own pace, but she couldn't help keeping an ear open for any conversation.

'Bob,' she heard him say, his voice expressionless.

'Martin,' the older man acknowledged him. 'It's good to see you recovering.'

'Thank you.' Martin paused as if he were summoning up supreme courage before he continued. 'I was so sorry about Paul. You know I was with him when he was killed. He died bravely. And . . . if it's any comfort, it was quick.'

Every muscle in Grace's body locked rigid. Sweet Jesus, of course. Bob's son would have been in the same company, possibly the same platoon even as Martin and Reg and all those from the village who had signed up at the same time. Nowadays, with the desperate necessity to replace the thousands of casualties as swiftly as possible, the system of keeping local 'pals' together was breaking down somewhat. But it meant that, for Martin, being back home was a cruel reminder of horrific events on the battlefield.

'Thank you, son,' Grace heard Bob reply, and she saw Martin continue to stand there as if he wanted to say something else, but couldn't bring himself to do so.

'I-I . . .' he stammered, and Grace was aware of an electric tension quivering from Martin's hunched shoulders.

'Aw, there you are, Martin, bain't it?' Gladys burst in through the open doors with Elsie in her wake.

'Remember us from yesterday afternoon, does you?' the other girl chimed in.

Martin appeared to draw back, half reluctant and half relieved, it seemed to Grace, before he turned round to face the two broad-shouldered lasses with a sensuous lift of one eyebrow. 'How could I forget such apparitions of beauty?' he replied.

For an instant or two, not even the irrepressible Gladys was sure if he was being sarcastic or flattering. But her natural ebullience immediately came to her aid. 'Aw, you'm a proper tease, you are!' she guffawed. 'So what you'm doing tonight, then? Good looking soldier like you shouldn't be on your own in a quiet place like this.'

'Doesn't look as if I will be, does it, ladies?' Martin answered with all his inherent charm.

Grace glanced across at Larry and he met her gaze, neither of them knowing if this could be a good or a bad thing. Time alone would tell, and Grace was only pleased that Geoffrey happened to be inside the house.

* * *

'Are you sure, Daddy?'

'Of course I am, cheel. You gets little enough time to enjoy yourself.'

'But it's your only time off, Sunday afternoon.'

'But you'm young, and you takes care on your mother so much. If you've been invited to tea at the Vencombes', then you must go. Besides, look at your mother,' Ernest instructed, glancing over his shoulder. 'She'm quite calm this afternoon.'

Grace sucked in her cheeks. Since he had started his apprenticeship, George had taken over Stephen's room over the workshop, but he always went home on Sundays. Now he was sitting up at the table, very much playing the big brother as he oversaw Faith and Maggie's artistic attempts with a box of crayons on scraps of waste paper Grace had rescued from the office. George was growing taller by the day, aided perhaps by the good dinners Verity provided. He was looking more like Stephen than ever, and Grace wondered if somewhere in her mind, her mother believed it was her elder son who sat before her. Temperance certainly appeared content, neither in a state of agitation nor enshrouded in silent misery, and so Grace shrugged into her coat.

'Thank you, Daddy,' she said, kissing him on the cheek.

Outside, a keen November wind blustered about her, and Grace was glad it was such a short walk to the Vencombes'. As she crossed the village triangle, a strong gust snatched the little hat from her head, and she only just managed to retrieve it before it was blown into the stream. Stupid thing, she tutted to herself as she hurried the last few yards, and almost collided with Larry as she rounded the corner of the house. He was coming out of the back door, pulling on his jacket over his collar and tie and the grey jersey Grace knew that Verity had knitted for him. His face was set and Grace frowned since this should be a happy afternoon for them all.

'Hello, Gracie,' he greeted her. 'Haven't seen Martin anywhere, have you? We all thought he was in his bedroom, but he's not. Mum and Dad haven't realized he's gone missing, so I thought I'd try and find him before they do. Mind you, I saw Aggie loitering around earlier, so you never know what they might be up to.'

Grace gulped hard, and the vision of Martin and Aggie down by the stepping stones on that distant summer's day slashed across her memory. She had never breathed a word about it to a living soul, and the idea that Larry knew there could be something between the pair of them brought colour into her cheeks.

'Do you . . . want me to help you look for him?' she stammered, deliberately ignoring Larry's mention of Aggie.

'If you wouldn't mind. Look. George remembered to lock the workshop, good lad.' Larry nodded towards the giant padlock. 'Can't risk any tools going missing these days. Anyway, it means Martin's not in there. Maybe the store room? Ah.' His voice tumbled as he glanced towards the barn-like building at the far end of the yard where, among other large items, the wheelwrights' own wagon was kept. The single door to one side was slightly ajar and Larry cocked an eyebrow towards it. 'I bet they're in there,' he said, suppressing a sigh, and then raised his eyes to where a sheet of the corrugated iron roof was suddenly lifted by the wind and banged back down again with an echoing crash. 'Must remember to get up there tomorrow and nail it back down. Wouldn't need a much stronger wind than this to tear it right off, and that could be dangerous.'

He seemed to hesitate, and Grace guessed he was about to tell her to go into the house — while he extracted Martin from whatever embarrassing situation he had got himself into. But in that moment of stillness, their startled eyes met.

A piercing, petrified scream reached them from inside the building. They both hesitated only as long as it took the sound to register in their brains before springing forward. Larry hurled himself towards the door and Grace followed, her heartbeat accelerating wildly.

She almost crashed into Larry's back as he halted just inside. The light was dim, and but for the booming clatter as the loose roofing sheet was rattled by the wind again, there was no sound to indicate where the human shriek had come from. But just then, another gasping cry squealed from the further corner and Larry shot forward.

What Grace saw was Martin towering over a shorter figure forced back against the wall, a choked hiss wheezing from its mouth. Grace's heart caught in her throat as she realized what was happening. For some inexplicable reason, Martin had his hands about Aggie's neck and was throttling the life out of her.

'You bloody Hun,' he was grating between clenched teeth. 'I'll kill you for what you've done.'

Horror streamed through Grace's veins, rooting her to the spot. Dear God Almighty. As the roof above them slammed down again, thundering like the explosion of a shell in the contained space, Grace knew that the sound had transported Martin's tortured mind back to the battlefield. And in the absence of a weapon, he was using his hands instead.

'Let go of her!' Larry was shouting as he tried to drag his brother away, but Martin's terror had given him a super-human hold on Aggie's throat. Grace leapt forward. Aggie's lips were turning blue, her eyes bulging. Instinctively, Grace grasped hold of the little finger of Martin's right hand and pulled it backwards. He let go with that one hand with a yelp of pain. It was just enough for Larry to be able to wrench him free.

Aggie collapsed into Grace's arms, spluttering and fighting for breath. They sank on the floor together, Grace protecting the limp form while Martin lashed out at Larry with demented force. Grace's stomach knotted in fear as the brothers fought tooth and nail, crashing about the barn, punches flying, until Larry, with his surprising upper strength and slightly heavier weight, finally pinned Martin to the floor.

'Wake up, Martin!' he panted desperately, shaking his brother with restrained force. 'It's me, Larry! And you're safe at home.'

Even in the murky light, Grace saw Martin's eyes flash savagely, but then they seemed to focus on Larry's face. His jaw slackened and he gazed about the barn in utter bewilderment.

'W-what happened?' he mumbled as his heavy breathing slowed.

'I reckon you thought you were under attack in the trenches,' Larry gulped, breathless himself from the struggle. 'You tried to strangle poor Aggie here.'

'What?' Martin's eyes stretched wide as he looked at the two girls huddled by the wall. 'Bloody hell. Oh, Aggie, I'm *so* sorry.'

'It's . . . all right,' Aggie croaked, rubbing her neck as Grace helped her stagger to her feet. 'I understand.'

'You'd better take her home,' Larry ordered brusquely, dipping his head at Grace. 'And we'd better calm down before we go back inside. I don't want Mum and Dad knowing anything about this. I just hope neither of us develops a black eye.' And then frowning at Aggie, he said pointedly, 'I trust I can rely on you not to say anything to anyone. People might want to know what you were doing here alone with Martin.'

Aggie nodded silently, not taking any umbrage, Grace noted, as she led the trembling girl towards the door. She would need to sit her down quietly somewhere, perhaps on the low wall of the little bridge, until she was recovered enough to go home without arousing any suspicion. After all, it wouldn't look out of place for them to be sitting there chatting. Grace shook her head as she hurried Aggie forward, hoping that neither Geoffrey nor Verity would spot them out of a window. Poor Aggie. Whatever Grace thought of her, it must have been terrifying. And poor Martin. They would all of them need to keep this secret buried, but Grace was sure it would fester in her own mind, at least, for ever.

CHAPTER FOURTEEN

'My last afternoon back at the homestead,' Martin declared in a partly jocular, partly wistful tone as they walked up the steep lane towards the open moorland. 'I can't think of a better way to spend it than with you two. Pity it's such rotten weather, though. But that's Dartmoor for you. And I guess that's the way I'll always remember it.'

Grace bit her lip. The way Martin had spoken was as if he would never be coming back — which of course was a strong possibility. She must drive the thought to the back of her mind and not let it spoil her last few hours with this life-long friend.

But, she pondered sadly, this wasn't the same Martin she had grown up with. He had changed. He still had that air of flamboyance about him, but it was tainted with sarcasm and bitterness. Grace felt awkward in his company and hated to admit even to herself that she would be relieved when he left in the morning to rejoin his battalion. When this dreadful war was over and he came home for good — *if* he came home — she prayed that he would eventually return to the likeable, devil-may-care young man he always used to be.

'Mum's preparing the best meal she can for tonight in your honour,' Grace heard Larry reminding him. 'It's her way of coping, keeping busy with domestic chores. I'm sure she and Dad were secretly hoping you wouldn't make such a good recovery and be invalided out of the army.'

'What, you don't think one lame son is enough for them?' Martin joked, clapping his brother boisterously on the shoulder.

Grace cringed. In the 'old' days, Larry's disability would never have been mentioned. It was just accepted, part of life. Now Larry exchanged a swift glance with her, and from his expression, she knew exactly what he was thinking. *Better two lame sons than two dead ones.*

'We've started using armoured tanks since you were wounded, haven't we?' Grace tried to bend the conversation in a more optimistic direction. 'Maybe that'll give us the upper hand and bring the war to an end afore too long.'

'I doubt it,' Martin scoffed. 'From what I've heard, it's been so bloody wet out there, the damned things keep getting stuck in the mud. You haven't the faintest idea what it's like as soon as there's a hint of rain,' he went on scathingly. 'The shells have destroyed everything, trees, grass. There's nothing left to hold the soil together. I can imagine what it must be like with all the rain there's been. Just a bloody great sea of mud.'

The rancour in his words seemed to kill all conversation. Even Larry couldn't think of any comments to ease the tension, and as they reached the open moorland, they all retreated into silence. As Martin had observed, it was hardly the kindest late November day. Fine, icy drizzle topped the hills in mist, and the unusual calm meant that it was unlikely to be driven away any time soon. There was little point in climbing to their favourite spot on Peek Hill as the view would be obliterated by the low cloud. Instead, they followed the course of the railway before branching off to skirt the farm at Routrundle. From there, they picked up the track that would provide a complete turn back along the Walkham Valley and hence eventually take them home.

It was as they were descending the hill that they came to a natural halt as if of a single mind. Given the weather conditions, it was the best view they would have, with the wooded valley stretching below them, while the higher ground on the far side vanished eerily into a bank of grey obscurity. The scene nevertheless held them spellbound, a murky blur without colour or life, and the still, heavy dampness deadening all sound.

'You'll miss all this, won't you?' Larry whispered at length. 'The quiet. It's almost mystical on a day like this.'

'Like hell I will,' Martin snorted, the force of his sudden outburst astounding his companions. 'All I can hear when it's as quiet as this is the damnable ringing in my ears. I'll never hear silence again. So you can keep it. The sooner I get back to the noise of the trenches, the better.'

His vehement words turned Grace's blood to water and she wanted to rear away from them. Pretend this wasn't real. They weren't standing there in the drizzle, gazing out over the valley. It was just a dream. A nightmare. And then Larry spoke, echoing her own thoughts.

'You don't mean that,' he said gravely. 'You can't possibly *want* to go back. In time, your—'

'Oh, yes, I do.' Martin cut him short. 'It's not just the quiet that makes my stomach churn. It's knowing that I should be out there, leading the men in my platoon. You haven't been there, so I can't expect you to understand.' He turned to Larry, and Grace saw his eyes, burning and yet steady as rocks. 'While this bloody war goes on, my place is out there. On the Front. I don't belong here any more. I-I don't deserve it.'

His mouth compressed into a thin, challenging line, and he turned away as if the conversation was finished. But Larry caught his arm, spinning him back to face him. 'Of course you deserve it. You've done your bit. Fought in two of the biggest battles mankind has ever seen. Been wounded so seriously you were brought back home. You deserve *not* to be ordered to go back. In my opinion, you're not in a fit state—'

'Oh, yes, I am. And I'm not going to let myself off the hook until I've done my duty. Atoned—'

'Atoned?' Larry was angry now, frightening Grace as she witnessed the heated argument. 'What the hell for?'

'For . . .' Martin seemed to stumble, mentally as well as physically as he took a step backwards. 'For killing a man, if you must know.'

'Killing a man? Well, of course you killed a man. Lots of men. It's in the nature of war. You can't be blamed for that.'

'No, you don't understand.' Martin rolled his head agonisingly, eyes shut as he strained away from some terrible, vicious truth. 'One particular man. I-I killed Paul. Bob's son, Paul.'

Grace felt herself sway, trying, in the most appalling silence of her life, to stay upright. She glanced instinctively at Larry. His eyes had darkened to mahogany, his square jaw set like granite as he stared at his brother.

'What? You mean . . . ?' It was his turn to stammer. 'You mean, enemy fire? But . . . it happens sometimes. Mistakes. We're all of us human.'

'No. Not that. He was caught on the wire.' Martin's voice was hoarse. Dry. The words scraped from his throat. 'Tried to free himself, but the more he struggled, the more entangled he got. Sitting target for the Boche. Only they didn't kill him. He was hanging there, riddled with bullets. Screaming in agony. But there was nothing we could do. We were in the middle of a battle, for God's sake. We'd never have got him out, and every one of us would have been killed as well. And Paul looked at me. There was blood coming from his mouth. He knew he was a goner. And then he looked at the revolver in my hand. And he said, quite calmly, *Do it, Martin. Do it.* So I . . . I'll never forget his eyes. Looking straight at me.'

His voice had hardened, devoid of emotion. As if the horror of it was so deep that his mind had shut down to it. Grace stared at his ashen face, motionless, thundering waves swamping her brain until she sank beneath them and slithered to the ground. Larry was at once beside her, arm around her, supporting her, and she slumped against him while her swimming head slowed.

'You should have told me before, Martin,' Larry's quiet voice seeped into her consciousness. 'And not in front of Grace.'

'But, you *see*? She blames me as much as I do myself.'

His mangled tone made Grace force open her eyes and she peered at him from the protection of Larry's shoulder as Martin, too, dropped onto his knees.

'No, I don't blame you,' she heard a voice — her own voice — assure him. 'It's just so *horrible*. I think . . . you were both so brave. You and Paul, both.'

'She's right. It must have taken immeasurable courage to do what you did. And it *was* the right thing to do.'

'But you understand why I need to go back? To make up for my guilt, or whatever it is.'

'Yes. Of course.'

Larry stretched his other arm wide, and his younger brother came into his embrace. Larry held them both close, in the circle of his strong, stalwart arms. And he stared over their heads out over the misted valley, his face like hewn stone.

The telegram came just in time for Christmas, the same day that Nan Sampson gave birth six weeks early to her fourth child who, by some miracle, managed to survive.

'Grace?'

She looked up as Larry quietly entered the office. For the past few months, an unspoken grief had pervaded the wheelwrights', oozing malignly into every nook and cranny. Smothering and inescapable. Even though spring was not so far away, its approach had done nothing to lift anyone's spirits. For never again would the teasing, jocular younger son of the establishment lighten the long working day. It was Vencombe and Son now, not *Sons*, Grace reflected morosely, although she would never suggest blanking out the 's' on the firm's stationery. It was too final.

'Yes?'

'Have you got a minute?' Larry's taut expression told her it was something serious.

'For you, always.' Grace gave a subdued smile, since the time for anything happier hadn't yet come.

'I wanted a word while Dad's not around. In fact . . .' Larry paused, clicking the door shut behind him. 'To be honest, I'm not sure I should be telling you, either. But . . . Well, only you and I know what Martin told us up on the moor that day. And I thought, in an odd sort of way, it might help. To know that Martin achieved what he wanted.'

Grace frowned, and her heart began to beat nervously. 'I don't understand.'

'You will, when you read this. You know Sybil called in earlier to tell us Reg has been wounded? Well, he'd sent her a letter for me. You'll see why when you read it.'

He held out a flimsy piece of paper, and Grace took it from him in a hand that shook slightly. 'Are you sure I should read it?'

'Not entirely. It's going to upset you, but I think you should know. Only please forgive me if I'm wrong.'

'Of course—'

Larry held up his hand in protest. 'Not until you've read it.'

Grace blinked at him, a hesitant swoop of her lashes, before she placed the letter on the desk and smoothed it out. Larry's face was a picture of consternation as she turned her eyes away from him and began to read.

Dear Larry

I'm writing to you from a clearing hospital. I only have a minor injury and I don't suppose it will be many days before I'm sent back to my unit. So I'm taking the opportunity to let you know exactly how Martin died. I'm sure they told you it was rescuing another soldier, but I feel you should know the details leading up to it. I thought you should be the one to know, and can decide whether or not to tell your parents.

I was with Martin from the beginning, as you know. There was a terrible event at the Battle of Loos not that long after we came out here. He kept it to himself, but I reckon that Martin was understandably very upset by it. He became generally bitter, and his personality seemed to change. He'd been trained to lead us, and he was good at it. He made sound decisions on the battlefield, given the circumstances and also orders from above. We trusted him, but I think being in charge of the fate of friends was hard. Harder than if we were strangers. So sometimes the 'pals' system has its draw-backs, although it has to be said that since last summer, we've been getting in drafts from all over the place. But Martin was just as scared as the rest of us. He tried not to show it, but I could tell that he was.

By the time he came back after recovering from his wounds, the months of bitter fighting that they're now calling the Battle of the Somme had died down. The weather had got so bad and it's been a fight for both sides just to survive the cold. But there were still small skirmishes, sniper fire and the like. Martin volunteered for every dangerous mission there was, as if he was trying to make up for something. I don't know how to describe it exactly. He became reckless. Not where others were concerned, but for himself. Almost as if he was deliberately playing with death. And that was how he died. Trying to rescue a wounded man when it was obvious that if anyone tried, they'd get killed, too. We tried to stop him, but he got away from us, and thirty seconds later, he was dead.

They could only let me have this one sheet of paper so I can't write more. I hope none of what I've put will get censored out. Look after yourself and say a prayer for me that I will survive this mayhem.

Your friend,

Reg

A heavy, sinking sensation had tightened Grace's stomach as she read the letter. Now she folded it carefully which seemed somewhat ludicrous as it was already so crumpled, and then she handed it back to Larry.

'So,' she faltered, her voice tiny. 'You think he almost wanted to die? To make amends for what happened at Loos?'

Larry lowered his eyes. 'Yes. At least, I reckon he felt that if he was risking his life, it was saving someone else from risking theirs. And at the same time, he was challenging fate. Defying the devil, but knowing the devil would win eventually.' Larry paused, sucking a sharp breath in between his teeth. 'God, he should never have gone back, the state his nerves were in.'

'But . . . it were what he wanted.'

'Yes. I know. And what Reg says confirms it. I-I did do right to show you the letter?'

Grace nodded slowly. 'Yes. But I'm not sure your parents should know ort about it. They don't know about Paul, do they? No one does. Just us.'

'And Reg. He was there. That's what he means by the event at Loos, I'm sure of it. But he can be trusted never to say anything.'

'Yes, I'm sure.' Grace sighed, closing her eyes. 'It's just all so horrible. Such a mess, isn't it?'

'All such a bloody mess, war, yes,' Larry murmured half under his breath, though the bitterness of his meaning was all too clear. 'But what choice have we ever had but to fight back? I just wonder how many more men we're going to lose from the village before it all stops. You and I, we've both lost both a brother and someone who was like a brother. Or . . . I mean . . .' He hesitated only a moment, as if the time for utter frankness had come. 'You didn't have stronger feelings for Martin, did you? You're a grown woman, and Martin was so likable — even if he did drive me to distraction at times.'

His question was so direct that it sent a flush of heat through Grace's body, although she couldn't have said precisely why. She experienced a stab of unwanted confusion as she answered truthfully, 'No. Nothing like that. I know Martin were very attractive to women. I could see that myself. But I only ever loved him in the same way as I love you. As a brother.'

She glanced away, and didn't see the momentary spasm that flitted across Larry's face. 'Ah,' he said softly. 'That's good. In a way, I suppose. That might have made it even more painful. To lose a brother is devastating enough, but someone . . .' He broke off, wet his lips in a nervous gesture. 'If only we had bodies to bury. Graves to focus our grief on, rather than all that sadness and anger just going nowhere.'

Grace closed her lips wryly. As ever, Larry had put his finger spot on it, expressing perfectly the frustrated emotions she shared with him. 'If only that army doctor hadn't passed Martin as fit to return to duty,' she muttered miserably.

146

'Yes. It would almost have been better if his nerves had been affected in the same way as some of those poor devils we saw at the hospital, and then he'd never have been sent back. You know, I read in one of the national newspapers the other day that the army doctors have coined a phrase for it at last. They're starting to call it shell-shock.'

'Shell-shock? I guess that's a good name for it. You know, I've often thought about them. The men we saw at the hospital. I've not said ort before, but what with them and the state Martin were in, well, that's what I'd really like to be doing. Helping the soldiers directly. I'd like to train as a VAD nurse.'

'Really?'

She met the surprise on Larry's face with a positive nod of her head. 'Yes. I know my work here is really important. More so now the U-boats have recently doubled the amount of shipping they've been sinking, and our farmers are under greater pressure than ever before and needing new carts and wheels as fast as we can make them. But I feel I'd be more use at a hospital like the one in Tavistock. I've had enough experience dealing with Mummy, and I think I could really do some good. A silly idea, I know.' She shrugged, pulling a rueful face. 'And I've still got Mummy to look after every afternoon. I couldn't expect Martha to look after her all day, and who'd do all the chores around the house? All the cooking and washing and ironing? Faith helps as much as she can, and Maggie, but they're both at school all day, and they're too young to do most things. And you know I've been helping Nan as well since she had the last baby. And anyway,' Grace sighed, 'only women from wealthier families can become VADs. You have to be rich enough to be able to support yourself, and I can't do that. No.' She gave a half smile. 'I'll content myself with my job here. Talking of which, both you and I need to get back to work.'

Larry returned her smile. 'Yes, we do. And thanks, Gracie. I don't know what I'd do without you to talk to. But we are agreed that we keep this to ourselves?'

'Definitely. But thank you for sharing it with me. Poor Martin.'

'Yes, poor Martin.'

Larry lingered for a moment with his hand on the door handle before going back out into the workshop, leaving Grace to turn her attention back to the paperwork on the desk. But the figures and letters on the pages blurred in front of her eyes, transforming themselves instead into an image of two young boys playing by the river: the older, dark-haired one, laughing and teasing, while the younger, fair-headed lad followed him with shining, happy admiration in his corn-flower blue eyes. And then the picture faded and was gone.

Grace felt her empty heart tear.

CHAPTER FIFTEEN

'Miss said today that now America's joined in the war, the Germans need to watch out!' Faith announced knowledge-ably after school one afternoon. 'She said they was taking a huge risk sinking so many more American ships bringing us food, and now they'll never stand up to the Americans.'

'Well, I hope she's right,' Grace answered sceptically.

'Of course she is,' Faith went on in a matter-of-fact tone. 'There's lots of them, the Americans. And they has lots of money so they can afford lots of guns and things. So Miss says that with them on our side, we should be able to beat the Germans and the rest proper quick, like. That's mortal good news, bain't it, Mummy?'

Temperance turned her head from her usual place in the rocking chair, and Grace caught her disconsolate gaze across the room. She knew exactly what her mother was thinking. The end of the war, whenever it came, wouldn't bring back her beloved eldest son. Nothing could do that.

Besides, Grace considered bitterly, the Americans had taken their time. If they'd supported the Allies a deal earlier, the war might have been over by now. As it was, over the winter, the Germans had constructed a formidably strong position miles to the rear of the Front, and had withdrawn behind its impenetrable defences. This new Hindenburg Line, as the British had christened it, was going to cause the Allies even more problems than ever — as if the prolonged, bitter fighting at the Somme hadn't been cataclysmic enough already.

Then there had been the uprising in Russia a month previously that some were calling a revolution and that had caused the Czar to abdicate. Who knew what that might mean to Russia's role as an ally? And as well as the Western Front, there was everything that was going on in the Middle East. The assault on Gaza had only narrowly failed, and the recent defeat of the Turks at Baghdad and with it, the capture of the Berlin to Baghdad railway, had boosted morale. But as far as Grace could see, the conflict in all its locations in the world was far from over. And in her opinion, it would be a long time before America's belated pledge could have any effect whatsoever!

'Well, let's hope it does some good,' she said to Faith. 'Now, why don't you and Maggie tell Mummy what else you did at school today?'

Before the little girls had a chance to open their mouths, however, the front door burst open, banging back on its hinges. Four astounded pairs of eyes swivelled to the forlorn figure that wavered on the threshold, looking like some demented apparition, hair awry around a face crumpled with tears. Three small children clung about the young woman's skirt, while an infant bawled in her arms.

Grace was filled with alarm as she stepped forward. 'Nan, whatever's the matter?' she cried, and then her heart crashed to her feet as she spied the unmistakable paper screwed in Nan's fist. Oh, no. A telegram. For a few seconds, Grace felt numbed. She had been there herself, first with Stephen and more recently with Martin. She knew what it was to be shocked with grief. But while she had her family with whom to share her bereavement, poor Nan was alone in the world and had no one else to turn to.

'I-I didn't know where else to go,' Nan faltered, her words a forced squeal as she squeezed them from her throat.

'Oh, Nan, come here.' Grace put her arm around the other girl's trembling shoulders. 'Come and sit down. Faith, do some bread and dripping for the tackers, only mind your fingers on the knife.'

Faith leapt at once to the task, enjoying the responsibility and pulling Maggie from the bench to make room for the three children. The two elder ones sidled onto the rough wooden seat, their eyes wide in bewilderment, and Maggie hoisted up the youngest to join his siblings.

'What wrong with Mummy?' Billy asked, his little face screwed up in confusion as he nevertheless crammed into his mouth the bread Faith had given him.

'She'm not feeling very well,' Grace answered quickly, sitting Nan down in Ernest's chair. 'Oh, Nan, I'm so very sorry,' she said to the young mother who sobbed broken-heartedly while the baby struggled and yelled on her lap.

'M-missing, pre-sumed dead,' Nan spluttered.

'Oh, dear Lord.' Grace gave a heartfelt sigh as she still cradled Nan against her shoulder. 'But . . . missing isn't the same as . . . well, you know. So there's still hope,' she attempted to encourage her.

'No. He'm dead, I's certain of it. Oh, Gracie, what am I to do without him?" Nan rasped as her tears, calmed for a moment, broke out afresh. 'I thought . . . as I could manage . . . for a bit,' she wheezed, 'until he comes home again. And you've been so good to me. But . . . I doesn't think I can go on without him anymore!' Her voice rose on a crescendo, a wail of misery, and she seemed unaware of the infant who was now screaming against her chest, not understanding why his violent demands to be fed were not being answered.

'Oh, er, let me have the baby,' Grace offered, although when Nan gratefully relinquished the wriggling bundle into her arms, she didn't have a clue what she was to do with it, either. 'Er, pour yourself some tea. There's some left in the pot. It's a bit weak, mind. Like everyone, we'm having to use the leaves over and over again.'

Grace jiggled the child up and down, watching in trepidation as Nan reached out with hands shaking convulsively. She prayed Nan wouldn't drop the teapot and break it. Under present circumstances, it might not be easy to replace. And although they got by — aided by the daily pint of milk Mrs Snell kindly gave them — there was never any money to spare.

It was as Grace really was beginning to wonder quite desperately what she should do with the caterwauling baby that she realized her mother had risen silently and unnoticed to her feet and had come up beside her.

'Let me have the poor little mite,' Temperance said with such calm serenity that Grace blinked at her in astonishment. It was the longest sentence her mother had spoken in months and her tone was so confident and normal that Grace couldn't believe her ears. She handed over the baby with a silent sigh of disbelief, and then turned her full attention to Nan.

'You mustn't give up hope just like that,' she attempted to soothe Nan's misery. 'You've only had the telegram, I take it? Well, someone'll write to you later with more details. No one can have reported seeing exactly what happened. It's absolute chaos out there, you know. Martin . . . told us so,' she explained, ignoring the stab of pain in her own heart. 'John could be wounded in a field station, got mixed up with another company, all sorts of reasons why he's not where he should be.'

'Does you . . . really think so?' Nan sniffed as her tears began to dry.

'Well, I know that you mustn't believe the worst. You've the tackers to think of. They'm too young to understand, so you must be strong for them.'

'But he don't even know about Jonty. It were awful, you knows, choosing a name without John being here. That's why I called him Jonty, after his daddy.'

Grace had to avert her eyes. Poor Nan. Grace hardly held John in high esteem, but she wouldn't wish him killed on the battlefield. And he was Nan's husband, whatever she thought of him.

Grace glanced across at her mother, suddenly aware that little Jonty had stopped crying. Temperance was rocking back and forth in her chair, crooning softly to the child as he sucked on the crooked little finger she had offered him. She lifted her head and Grace saw the radiant, golden smile that lit her face.

'There now. I think this little fellow deserves a proper feed now, doesn't you?'

She stood up and went across to Nan, waiting patiently while the young woman, feeling she couldn't disobey, unbuttoned her blouse. An instant later, Jonty was guzzling noisily at his mother's breast, Temperance gazing down at them in contented satisfaction. Grace observed her, a kernel of hope unfurling in her own heart.

* * *

'I'm so sorry I'm late, Martha. I were just finishing something off in the workshop. Oh.' Grace stopped short, glancing about the low-ceilinged room. 'Where's Mummy?'

'She'm gone home,' Martha answered enigmatically.

'Home? On her own?'

'Yes. She wanted to surprise you.'

'Well, she's certainly done that.' And as a gripping concern overtook Grace's thoughts, she asked anxiously, 'Is she all right?'

'I should say so, yes.'

Grace's forehead corrugated in bemusement. Certainly if Martha wasn't worried, then Grace was convinced. But Martha herself didn't appear her usual self.

'And is everything all right with *you*, Martha?'

The older woman sucked in her lips. 'Well . . . yes and no,' she faltered, sitting down at the table with a thump. 'Us had a letter from our daughter-in-law this morning. Our Stanley's been wounded. And he'll be invalided out of the army. You see, he's . . . lost an arm. His left one, so it might've been worse.'

Grace tried to stifle a sharp intake of breath. Stanley was the youngest of Martha and Barry's elder three boys and Grace had known him well. She had been about twelve when he had married and moved away to take up a job as farm labourer with a tied cottage. But it wasn't all that far and he visited on occasion with his young family, so it wasn't as if he was a vague figure from Grace's past. And anything that affected her dear friend affected her, too. 'Oh, Martha, that's awful!'

'*Is* it, though, cheel?' Martha's distraught gaze locked onto hers. 'At least he'm alive, and he'll be coming home. Though how he'm supposed to support a wife and three tackers with only one arm, I doesn't know.'

'Won't he get some sort of invalid pension from the government?' Grace put in optimistically.

'Aw, I doesn't know about that. Susan don't mention it in her letter. But it's not your problem.' Martha slapped her thighs as she stood up. 'Now you get on home and see what your mam's bin up to.'

'Yes, I will.' Grace planted a kiss on Martha's cheek. 'And let me know if there's ort I can do. Heaven knows you've done enough for us.'

'Bless you, cheel,' Martha smiled back, looking more like her old self.

Grace took the few steps to her parents' front door with a pensive frown. So, Martha almost welcomed the fact that one of her sons had lost an arm in the fighting. She looked upon it as his salvation. Dear Lord, the world had gone mad.

But Grace put the thought to the back of her mind as she opened the door to the tiny cottage. A delicious aroma wafted into her nostrils, mingled with the distinctive smell of ironing. She was astounded to see that her mother was half way through the pile of laundry she had expected to be tackling herself that afternoon, and a large pot of stew was simmering on the range.

Temperance looked up when she saw her and gave a proud smile. 'Thought I'd give you a surprise. Been sitting round on my laurels long enough. Relying on you to do

154

everything when you've enough on your plate. And I's certain they could do with you full time at the yard.'

Grace's jaw fell open in amazement. Since Nan's desperate visit a couple of weeks ago, Temperance had been far more communicative and had busied herself doing minor tasks about the cottage. But to see her suddenly taking on again the entire running of the home was quite a shock.

'B-but I were going to do that this afternoon,' Grace stammered.

'Well, I won't say no to some help. And later on, you can take over while I nip down to Nan's for a while. Poor girl could do with a hand, I'll be bound. Being left on her own with four chiller all under school age must be master hard on her. Put some extra carrots and onions in the stew I did to make it go further so I'll take some down to her, and all.'

Grace continued to stare at Temperance, her mouth dropping open even further. It was a miracle, and it had taken John's disappearance to inspire it. God certainly did move in mysterious ways sometimes!

* * *

'There's nothing stopping you now, Gracie,' Larry said sombrely.

Grace had been concentrating on chiselling a perfect dovetail joint. It didn't actually need to be perfect, but Geoffrey had said it would be good practice for her and George. They were having a competition to see who could produce the finest result in the shortest time, so Grace was more than a little irritated that Larry had come to disturb her, while George worked on with a conspiratorial grin as Larry winked at him.

'Stop me doing what?' she demanded crisply, pausing to blow away the minuscule wood shavings.

'Becoming a VAD. You said it's what you'd really like to do. Or are you exercising your woman's prerogative to change your mind?'

Grace's eyes flashed at him. 'No, I'm not,' she retorted. 'I'd still love to do it, only I can't afford it, as you know jolly well. So kindly stop mocking me and let me get on with this.'

Larry stood back with a short laugh, his hands in the air. 'As you wish. But I thought you might be interested in what I have to say.'

'What? You're determined to make me lose, aren't you?'

'No, but that's not important. Come outside for a minute, Grace,' Larry said persuasively, taking her gently by the elbow. 'That's really good, George, by the way. Better than Grace's.'

She opened her mouth in protest, but then noticed the teasing light in Larry's chestnut eyes. And perhaps he really did have something to discuss with her, so she allowed herself to be propelled outside. Larry walked her to the little bridge and perching on the low parapet, invited her to do the same.

'So, what's so urgent you have to ruin my chances of winning our little competition?' she wanted to know.

Larry paused infuriatingly as he wet his lips. 'Well, it really is about training as a VAD nurse,' he said at last. 'That's if you do still want to do it.'

Grace drew in a breath and released it in a steady stream. She recognized when Larry was being serious. 'Yes, I would. It's so awful what some of those men have been through, and I really think I could help.'

'So do I.'

'Do you? But how can I?' she sighed. 'I could barely afford the uniform, let alone be able to support myself.'

'No. But I could.'

There was a stunned silence during which Grace wondered if she wasn't dreaming, but then Larry went on, 'Look at it this way, Gracie. Your mother's found her feet again, even helping Nan so much, so you're free to do whatever you want. I know you give most of your wages to your family, but I could make that up as well. And before you ask, yes, I can afford it. The business will all be mine one day. But until it is, I get my share of the profits. Not a huge amount, it has to be said, but until I have a wife and family of my own, I've little to spend it on. And that's unlikely ever to happen. I mean, who'd ever have me with this wretched leg? So, if you think you could cope with all the dreadful things you're likely to see, I can't think of a more worthwhile thing to do with my money.'

Grace had been listening to him, a thread of intangible excitement tangling itself into a knot in her belly. Did she have inside her what was needed to help those poor souls? But as her mind drifted back over what she had seen, her heart strengthened with determination.

'But . . . don't you need me here? In the workshop?'

'Yes. But I'm sure we can get round it somehow. Gladys and Elsie are gems, and George is getting on so well. I know he's been with us less than a year, but he's a complete natural. And I think it would be good for Mother to do the paperwork. She used to, you know, back along.'

Grace met his level gaze, watching his eyes crease slightly at the corners. Larry, whom she would trust with her life. 'And you'd do all that for me?'

'Yes, I would.'

'But . . . why?'

'Because I can,' he answered, his voice deep and low. 'And because I believe *you* can. I've watched you with your mother and your own brothers and sisters. With Nan and her brood. Some people are meant to be carers, and you're one of them, Grace. And with Martin. You *understood*. And it's because of him, too. In his memory.'

Grace looked into his eyes, saw the moisture collecting against the lower lids. And felt her own eyes mist over.

'Then I shall write to Mrs Franfield,' she announced determinedly. Somewhere inside her, a little bird fluttered its wings.

CHAPTER SIXTEEN

'Well done, Nurse Dannings,' Sister Guscott beamed. 'Top marks in your exams once again.'

Grace felt her chest swell with pride. It was six weeks since Mrs Franfield had welcomed her to Mount Tavy Hospital, offering her a bed in the former servants' wing at the back of the house just along a passageway from the galleried landing and the stunning glass atriums in the roof. Six narrow beds had been placed in the room for the benefit of those who, like Grace, had nowhere else to live within a sensible distance. Grace was sharing with four other young women who had been volunteers for some while, and another who had arrived the day after Grace.

'You were due here yesterday,' Grace recalled Ling Franfield frowning at the girl as she waltzed into the grand hall. 'I hope this isn't going to be an example of your punctuality — or rather your lack of it. A hospital relies on strict time-keeping, you know.'

'Sorry, Matron. My maid hadn't finished packing my trunk.'

'Well, I'm certain you won't need the half of what's in it. Leave it there and I'll ask the porters to bring it up when they have a spare minute. Not that it's their job to run around after nurses. You'll be sharing with Nurse Dannings here — who arrived on time yesterday,' Ling said pointedly, turning to Grace who was tired from her first day but still effervescent with excitement. 'Just going for your break, Nurse Dannings?'

'Yes, Matron,' Grace answered, preening herself at being addressed as 'nurse' already. 'Sister said I should go now.'

'Well, would you mind taking Nurse Palmer here to the dormitory and showing her around, please? Obviously you can't change into your uniform until your trunk is unpacked, Nurse Palmer, so you'll have to come to tea in your civilian clothes.'

The girl's head retracted on her neck in offence at Ling's sharp tone, and Grace mouthed the words *Yes, Matron* at her. Fortunately she appeared to latch on, repeating them aloud. Ling dipped her head as if satisfied, and headed off in the direction of the office.

'Lordy-love, is she always as brusque as that?'

'Oh, no,' Grace replied, not quite sure how to take the newcomer. 'She'm wonderful, really. But she expects everyone to be as efficient as she is.'

'I'll have to watch out, then,' the girl winked, and held out her hand. 'Selina Palmer.'

'And I'm Grace. In private, anyway,' Grace grinned back, warming to her as she led the way up the grand staircase. 'There'll be six of us sharing up here.'

'Six? Well, I hope no one snores,' Selina declared, scanning the room when they reached it. 'And the bed's like a block of granite,' she pronounced, sitting down on the bare straw mattress.

'You have to make it in a special way,' Grace told her, nodding at the pile of bedding. 'Same way as you make the patients' beds. I'll show you later. But first of all, we have twenty minutes for tea, and then I think I'll be serving dinner to the men on my ward. And then after our own supper, it's study time.'

'No peace for the wicked, then?'

'No, none at all!' Grace laughed back.

And so the two of them had started training together on Sunshine Ward, the one which accepted amputees and assessed their mental ability to cope, and was where Martin had been a patient. Being one of only two wards for those who were recovering from physical wounds, cleanliness was essential. For Grace, washing walls and floors and disinfecting cabinets and bedsteads came as second nature, but for Selina, who had never so much as lifted a duster in her life, it was a completely new and not altogether welcome experience.

'Urgh, I think I'm going to be sick,' she declared a few days later, coming into the sluice room with a used bedpan, and indeed began to retch.

'Not great, is it?' Grace sympathized, taking from her the offending item which she emptied and put to soak in disinfectant. 'But just think how embarrassing it must be for the patient.'

'That's as maybe, but I don't think I'll ever get used to all the smells.'

'Lucky you'm not out in the trenches, then,' Grace observed grimly.

'You can say that again! But come on, let's get out of here.'

'Why don't you try to get hold of some peppermint oil and dab some on the inside of your collar? Then you can sniff at it when you'm dealing with bedpans.'

'Oh, you're a genius, Nurse Dannings! Hate these wretched starched collars, though, don't you? Chafe your neck something rotten.'

'Makes us keep our heads up and look dignified, Matron says, and she's right, I reckon.'

'Not so bad, is she, once you get to know her?'

'I think she's lovely. She were so good when my friend were a patient here. That's what made me want to be a VAD.'

'You're a dark horse!' Selina chuckled. 'A male friend, I take it?'

'Oh, nort like that. He were more like a brother. He weren't an amputee, mind. He *were* wounded, but he recovered from that. He were here because he had mild shell-shock, I suppose you'd call it. Only . . .' Grace paused as the flush of sorrow washed through her. 'He were sent back to the Front and were killed in action soon after.'

'Oh, my goodness, I'm so sorry. I shouldn't have pulled your leg—'

'You weren't to know.' Grace gave a wistful smile. 'He were on Sunshine Ward, same as us. I think Matron wanted me to face those memories from the beginning.'

'Talk of the devil,' Selina whispered under her breath as a familiar figure came towards them.

'Nurse Palmer, your cap still isn't folded correctly. Get Nurse Dannings to show you again tonight.'

'Yes, Matron. All very well for her to say so,' Selina grumbled once Ling Franfield was out of earshot. 'I bet she's not as exhausted as we are by the end of the day. It's all I can do to write up our notes for the day before I fall into that torture rack they call a bed.'

'Oh, I don't know. I reckon she gets just as tired. And did you know she and Dr Franfield have a son at the Front, and a daughter who's a nurse and has just gone out to France? That must be such a dreadful worry. And Sister were telling me they have a younger son, too, William, who wants to be a doctor like his father. He'm at school during the week, but comes here at the weekends.'

'Expect we'll meet him, then. But come on. We've got one of the nicest parts of the day to look forward to, serving dinner and helping those who can't manage on their own. I don't mind doing that, and talking to the men. And helping with the painting sessions, I like doing that.'

'It's the best part, isn't it, helping them relax and enjoy themselves?' Grace agreed as they entered Sunshine Ward again. And just for a second, she imagined she felt Martin's ghost tap her approvingly on the shoulder.

* * *

161

'Thank you very much, Sister,' Grace replied proudly. She had indeed worked hard for all the tests she had been set in those six weeks. Basic nursing skills and anatomy weren't strictly necessary for the volunteers on most of the other wards, but patients on Sunshine arrived with only partially healed wounds, and the VADs needed to have extra knowledge. But Grace relished in her studies and wanted to excel. It was like a fever with her, and she was astute enough to recognize why. Every bandage she applied perfectly, every question she answered correctly, paid homage to Martin and to Stephen. A tiny slither of grief removed from her heart. And she wanted to prove to dear Larry that his faith in her had been justified.

'I wish Nurse Palmer had your ability and dedication,' Sister Guscott sighed. 'I really think we should consider moving her to a different ward, or even asking her to leave altogether. I'm not at all sure she has what it takes. And we'll need everyone up to scratch. Heaven knows what injuries the poor lads will have who'll be coming through to us from this new offensive we're hearing about.'

'Near Ypres, a place called Passchendaele, you mean?'

'Something like that, yes. Read the papers a lot, don't you, Nurse?' Sister observed quite impressed.

'When I can find the time. I used to follow events with Larry. Martin's . . . Lieutenant Vencombe's brother.'

'Ah, yes. I was so very sorry to hear what happened to young Martin. None of us considered he should have been sent back to the Front. But sadly, that's war. And why I for one will be glad when it's over and I can go back to civilian nursing. But in the meantime, I'm mighty glad you were allocated to me. You might have been sent to Sister Hammett.'

Grace had to suppress a smile. She much preferred homely Sister Guscott, the nursing sister Dr Franfield had purloined from Tavistock Cottage Hospital to help set up this auxiliary military establishment. Sister Hammett was officially the Superintendant of the voluntary detachment, and from what Grace had seen of her, was much more fearsome.

162

'So you think we'll be full up again soon?' Grace asked, glancing at the three empty beds on the ward.

'Definitely. And we'll have to hurry these present patients on, too, I shouldn't wonder. Most of them have come to terms with their disability and I think can probably go home. And if last summer is anything to go by, we might have to squeeze in a few more beds besides.'

Grace nodded and closed her lips softly. The injuries, mainly amputations, of all the patients she had tended so far had been partially healed, but with the number of casualties soaring, it seemed obvious to her that they might well receive men whose wounds — to say nothing of their mental trauma — were far fresher. 'Well, when they come, let's hope there aren't too many as bad as the patients on Happiness Ward,' she sighed. 'I know it's amazing what Dr Franfield's doing, but it would be better if they weren't like that in the first place.'

'Amen to that. His work there interests you, doesn't it?'

'Very much so. When we came to visit Martin and we saw some of them, it was what struck me most and made me want to be a VAD.'

'Well, you certainly have a very sensible head on your shoulders for your age. I'll ask Dr Franfield if you can spend some time on Happiness Ward. It would have to be in your spare time, mind. I really couldn't spare you from your duties here.'

'Would you?' Grace replied with enthusiasm 'I would be grateful.'

'I don't see why not. I'll ask him next time I have a chance.'

'Oh, thank you, Sister!' And a little bud of excitement blossomed inside her.

* * *

'They'll be arriving any minute,' Elliott Franfield announced, his steady, green-blue eyes moving along the rows of faces so that each member of staff felt that he was addressing them personally. 'As you know, they will all be suffering either from shell-shock in one form or another, or will have some new disability thrust upon them which we have got to help them come to terms with as well as assist in their physical recovery. It isn't going to be easy, and many of you are inexperienced. But I expect every one of you to conduct yourself in a calm and professional manner. Reassure your patients and treat them with dignity. I've been informed there are some head injuries, and we all know that can lead to confusion, aggression and offensive language. But remember, these men have been through hell, and many of them won't have come from the privileged backgrounds that most of you have. So, good luck, and remember that I and the senior nursing staff are here to help you.'

Grace wet her lips, feeling the rush of apprehension coursing around her body. She was, of course, among the least experienced, and they wouldn't know exactly what they were dealing with until the casualties arrived. And now, through the open doors, she could hear the thrumming of an engine, and when it was turned off, the plod of horses' hoofs coming up the drive as the motley agglomeration of whatever transport could be rustled up arrived from the railway station.

Grace felt Selina squeeze her hand, and, as she glanced at her companion, she saw the girl was staring ahead, white as a sheet. Oh, Lord. Then Grace caught Sister Guscott's eye, and the older woman gave that beaming, apple-dumpling smile. Grace's gaze snapped back to Dr Franfield, tall, confident, his thinning hair fading to a silvery grey that spoke of maturity and experience. And Mrs Franfield, too, composed and calm. And Grace knew that she could trust either one of them as the couple led their staff outside to welcome the new arrivals.

The peaceful tranquillity of the old house was instantly shattered. For the next half hour, the chaos was tangible as weary soldiers, their faces either still etched with fear or sagging with relief, were assisted into the great hall. Some of them were carried in on stretchers and laid on the floor, and

Grace stood for several seconds, overwhelmed by the sheer numbers. There must be approaching forty of them altogether. There were two, she noticed, curled up in balls, their bodies convulsed in twisted tremors, one of them jabbering senselessly. Severe shell shock and destined for Happiness Ward, no doubt.

Grace and Selina worked together as they had been instructed, helping, with the other two VADs on Sunshine Ward, to settle in the patients who were allocated to them. They had squeezed in two extra beds, making ten, so however were they to cope? Three of the men had their heads bandaged, one of whom was only semi-conscious and was brought in by stretcher, while another had an empty sleeve as well. All the others, too, were amputees of one sort or another, so it was obvious Dr Franfield would regularly be present in the room. Grace gritted her teeth. Dear God, what had she let herself in for? What had *Larry* let her in for? But she had wanted desperately to be of use to these poor, broken victims, and must get on with it.

She and Selina approached their next patient, little more than a boy, with the sparse stubble of adolescence on his chin. He had been left sitting up on the bed, a weak smile scarcely moving his pale lips as the two young nurses came up to him. Already in hospital blues, he could do nothing to remove the shapeless jacket and red tie. Both his sleeves were empty.

Grace had to take a firm hold on her emotions. *Poor sod*, she could hear Larry's voice in her head. That was what he had said when she had told him of Martha's son Stanley who had lost an arm, and this young lad had lost both. At that moment, Grace didn't know whether to curse or bless Larry for enabling her to be there to help, since just now she would rather have been a million miles away. But she had two good arms and two good legs and must thank her lucky stars.

She began to unbutton the poor fellow's jacket with an encouraging smile. 'I'm Nurse Dannings,' she introduced herself, 'and this is Nurse Palmer. We'll help you into some pyjamas so you can get into bed and have a good rest.

You must be exhausted after such a long day. Now, Private Fletcher, isn't it? Are you in any pain?'

The boy nodded bravely. 'Bit,' he managed to mumble.

'I'll tell Sister and she'll give you something, but let's get you comfortable first. Let's take off this jacket. There. And now your shirt if you can just sit forward a little.'

She bobbed her head at Selina as together they slid the shirt from his shoulders — and had to clamp her jaw tightly. The stump of one arm ended below the elbow. It was the least healed she had witnessed, but there would be the chance of having a prosthetic limb of some sort in the future. But on the other side, oh, good God Almighty, there was nothing. Absolutely nothing. It was a shoulder amputation and it was horrendous. The boy had been lucky to have survived. Or perhaps he had been *unlucky*.

Grace instantly swallowed down her shock. She mustn't let her own anguish show. But as she glanced across at Selina, she saw that her colleague's face had turned grey, and the next instant the other girl had slumped over the pillows behind their patient.

'Can someone help, please?' Grace called, thankful that young Private Fletcher couldn't see what was going on behind his back. A second later, Grace was inundated with relief when one of the other VADs took Selina's place and Sister Guscott led Selina away, waving a tiny flask of sal volatile under her nose.

'Take her upstairs, would you, Nurse Dannings?' Sister instructed a few minutes later when the young soldier had been settled in bed and Selina was sitting in Sister's chair, her face still ashen. 'Treat her for mild shock, and come back as quickly as you possibly can. Goodness knows we could do without this.'

'Yes, Sister,' Grace answered, pulling Selina to her feet.

She half dragged her through the still crowded great hall and up the staircase to the dormitory. Selina moaned without actually saying anything intelligible as Grace deposited her on the bed, removing her starched collar and tightly tied apron, and then unfastening the front of her uniform.

'Thanks, Grace,' Selina mumbled. 'Oh, God, I feel sick.'

'Head between your knees, then. And, here, have a little water.'

She waited while her friend took the glass in a shaking hand and drank a few sips before handing it back. Grace could feel her fingers itching, cross at her own frustration. She should be back on the ward, and yet she didn't want to leave Selina. She filled with relief when at last Selina lifted her head and rolled herself onto the bed.

'I'll prop the bottom of the bed up,' Grace said, remembering what she had learnt and searching for something with which to do so. Ah, Selina's trunk was stored underneath. Well, at least it had been of some use in the end!

'Will you be all right now, do you think?'

'Yes, of course,' Selina croaked. 'Go on. They need you far more than I do.'

Their eyes met. They both knew that she was right, much as she would have preferred Grace to stay with her. Grace nodded, paused for a second to gird up her courage, and then hurried out of the room.

CHAPTER SEVENTEEN

Grace was surprised to discover the great hall to be empty of all the newcomers by the time she returned. The staff had certainly been busy allocating places to the new patients and so Grace went straight to Sunshine Ward. She glanced swiftly about the room. All the patients had been helped out of their uniforms and into bed and were now resting after the long hours of uncomfortable travelling. A large tea-urn had been rolled in on a trolley, the two other VADs handing out much needed cups of the hot brew, and Grace made to go and help them.

'Is Nurse Palmer all right now?' Sister Guscott asked in a low voice as Grace passed her desk. 'I'm not sure the poor girl is really up to it. The whole idea is to help these poor lads come to terms with their injuries, not to faint at the sight of them. Perhaps it would have been better if she'd gone on a VAD training course first, and she'd have realized she wasn't suitable before she started. Pity, though. She's such a nice girl. But it means we'll be extra busy. And for you, Nurse Dannings,' she winked, 'I have a particularly interesting case. Total identity loss.'

Grace tipped her head, intrigued, as she followed Sister Guscott down the ward. 'You mean the patient doesn't know who he is?'

'Exactly so,' she confirmed, stopping at the foot of a bed whose occupant was the semi-conscious man with his head heavily bandaged who Grace recognized from earlier. 'Must have been caught in the blast from an exploding shell. Had shrapnel wounds to his head and upper body. Unconscious for at least twenty-four hours as far as anyone can tell, and not completely lucid even now. And so far, he doesn't remember anything about himself at all.'

'No identity-tag?' Grace questioned.

'Red one's missing, so someone must have thought he was dead and removed it. So some poor soul somewhere is going to get a telegram.' Sister gave a compassionate sigh. 'And the green one was destroyed by one of the pieces of shrapnel that entered his chest. Can you believe that for bad luck? The only fragment that's left is almost illegible. All we have are the letters SMI. So he's very likely somebody Smith.'

'Good Lord. And presumably nobody's recognized him?'

Sister Guscott shook her head. 'No. But can you wonder at it? It must be chaos out there. Battalions and regiments all muddled up, men getting separated from their units. And when your head's swathed in bandages, well . . . Doesn't mean his memory won't come back in time, mind. And that's where conversation with an intelligent girl like you comes in. Not that he's up to much conversation yet, as you see.'

'Well, when he is, I'll do my best,' Grace promised. 'He's an officer, mind. A lieutenant. Look at the stripes on his uniform. Martin explained about those to me.'

'Good girl.' Sister Guscott gave an appraising smile. 'And I can trust you not to faint over the young laddie Nurse Palmer did, I hope?'

'Yes, Sister. Especially now I've seen his injuries once, I'll know what to expect.'

'Good. Fortunately I don't think the poor boy was aware of what happened. Now, Dr Franfield will be here soon on his initial rounds, and I want you to give him the first report on our mystery man here.'

Grace felt her heart bounce in her chest. 'M-me?' she stammered.

'I know it's not usual procedure, but you're showing exceptional talent, and I'll be there to make sure you don't miss anything. And Dr Franfield won't bite. He must be the loveliest doctor I've ever worked with, and I'm certain he'll agree you're one of the most promising VADs we've come across. When the war's over, you should consider training as a nurse proper. Need to be totally dedicated, mind. So, no young man in your life, a pretty girl like you?'

Grace was aware of a rash of heat flushing into her face, a mix of pride and excitement but also of uncertainty. The thought had never crossed her mind. She was there because there was a war on and her heart had gone out to the victims she had seen at the hospital — and because she was doing it for Stephen and for Martin. But the idea that she should become a professional nurse after the war had never come into it. But if that war had never started, she would still have been a housemaid at the Snells' farm.

A million thoughts were suddenly racing about in her head. Might it be possible for her to have a career of which she could be thoroughly proud? It was something she had never dreamt of. And it would all be because of dear Larry.

'No,' she answered with happy conviction, confidence blooming inside her. 'There's no one in my life like that.'

'Then you must think about it,' Sister smiled back.

* * *

'Excellent, Nurse Dannings.' Dr Franfield raised an impressed eyebrow. 'Now, what observations should we be making?'

'Pulse, heart-rate and respiration. General levels of consciousness, and most importantly, pupil reaction.' Grace bit her lip anxiously as she searched the good doctor's face.

'Anything else?'

'Oh, er, colour,' she mumbled, cross with herself for forgetting.

'Very good. Our patient should be out of the danger period now. This must have happened a good week ago, but he's still drifting in and out of consciousness, so best to keep up the observations. Personally, I wouldn't have moved him yet, but I imagine conditions are pretty desperate at the clearing hospitals for them to be shipping the wounded home so quickly. So, perhaps you'd like to remove the bandages from his head, then, Nurse?'

'I . . . need to wash my hands first,' Grace faltered awkwardly, for surely Dr Franfield knew that.

To her surprise, he gave a light chuckle. 'Passed my little test. You have her well trained, Sister. Well, go and wash your hands, and we'll see what's what.'

Grace did as she was instructed, her heart knocking against her ribs. The day had thrown so much at her that her hands shook slightly as she unwound the bandages, rolling them up as she went. Despite his head having been half covered, she had made a vague mental note that her patient was quite an attractive chap, a little older than Larry, she judged by the faint lines radiating from his eyes, so possibly about thirty years of age. It saddened her to see that a deep laceration from the side of his nose across his cheek, doubtless from another piece of shrapnel, marred his pleasing looks, but she was gratified that it had been neatly stitched to minimize scarring. So some caring medic somewhere had taken time over it, despite being under terrible pressure.

It took Grace utterly unawares when the eyelids suddenly sprang open and two incredibly deep blue eyes seemed to pierce into her own. The patient sat bolt upright and gripped her wrist so fiercely that she could have squealed from the pain of it. His movement was so swift that nobody had time to react and come to Grace's aid.

Instinct forced the sweetest smile to her face, though her heartbeat thundered in her breast.

'Good afternoon, Lieutenant,' she said steadily, even though she was mentally holding her breath. 'Now you mustn't worry. You're in hospital, safely back in England.'

The gentian blue eyes blinked at her, swivelled round the other faces at the bedside and then returned to Grace almost like a drowning man clutching onto a lifeline. Then his gaze dropped to his hand painfully grasping her wrist.

'Oh,' he mumbled. 'I'm so sorry. I thought you were a Jerry.'

'No, there's no Jerries here,' Grace answered gently as he released his hold. 'But Dr Franfield needs to examine your wounds.'

The patient gave a visible sigh and then allowed Grace to finish unwinding the bandages from his head. Engrossed in her work, Grace was unaware of the glance exchanged between Elliott Franfield and Sister Guscott. A natural, this one, it said appreciatively. And her soothing words as she unfastened the soldier's pyjamas so that his other wounds could be inspected were no less professional.

'About time those stitches came out,' Dr Franfield announced. 'The degree of healing proves you were wounded over a week ago,' he went on, addressing the patient. 'Your head must have taken quite a blow in one way or the other, what with the shrapnel lacerations and possibly the blast as well. But not to worry, old chap. I'm sure everything will right itself in time. Sister will take the stitches out for you later, and then you'll be more comfortable. Just make it every other one on that larger wound across the chest, though, Sister. The rest can come out in a couple more days.'

'Yes, Dr Franfield.'

'I'll see you again tomorrow,' the doctor told the anonymous man. 'You're in good hands. So, then, Nurse, what can you tell me about your next patient?'

'Before I forget, Doctor,' Sister Guscott put in. 'Nurse Dannings would like to observe some of your work on Happiness Ward. In her off-duty time, of course.'

'Would she, by Jove? Well I think that could be arranged. Not the hypnosis sessions, I'm afraid, but you'd be most welcome to visit the ward.' He gave such a broad smile that it made Grace's heart soar.

* * *

'Well done, Lieutenant,' Sister Guscott beamed as she dropped the last stitch into the kidney bowl. 'You were very brave. Nurse, will you finish tidying up here, and then our patient can have a well deserved rest?'

Grace watched the sister walk off down the ward. It was the first time she had been given the opportunity to see stitches being removed and had observed with avid interest. Sister Guscott had shown her how to curve the thread carefully as it was teased out so that it caused the least discomfort. Their patient had been understandably tense and the process took some time with so many stitches to be removed from his head and upper torso, but Grace had found it so natural to encourage him, enquiring when he felt he needed a rest. And in her turn, Sister Guscott was giving Grace nods of approval at the way she was talking to the patient.

Now Grace collected up all the instruments and used sterile swabs from where a few of the stitch holes had oozed a spot of blood, and put them all in the kidney bowl.

'You don't want to keep the stitches, do you?'

The man's taut face tightened further. 'Whatever for?'

'Apparently some patients like to keep them as souvenirs, although personally I don't see the attraction,' Grace answered gently. 'I can dispose of these, then? And Sister was right. You *were* very brave. It can't have been pleasant having so many taken out. But I imagine not as bad as having them put in.'

The soldier gave an ironic grunt. 'As I can't remember a damned thing about it, I couldn't say. But thank you for being so kind. Am I . . . right in thinking that you're in training?'

'Well, when the war's over, I'd like to train as a proper nurse. For now, I'm just a VAD. That's Voluntary Aid Detachment.'

'Yes.' The fellow's frown deepened. 'I remember that. I can remember lots of things. Why we went to war, all the different battles. I can remember being there, in the trenches. All the noise, being scared and yet not wanting to let it show, because we all felt the same. I was there back in the winter, I'm sure of it. We're in summer now, aren't we? I can remember the cold and the mud, even if it is all a blur. But I can't remember any facts. *Exactly* where I was. Who I was with, not even which regiment I'm part of, let alone my battalion or company. Everything about me is a complete blank, and it's absolutely horrendous not knowing who I am.'

His voice had risen on a crest of frustration, and Grace squeezed his arm. 'It's bound to come back in time. Dr Franfield thinks so. You already seem better than when you arrived here just a few hours ago. And in the meantime, we'll call you Lieutenant Smith.'

'Lieutenant? Why does everyone keep calling me that?'

'The stripes on your uniform. The rips and bloodstains correspond exactly with your injuries, so we know it's yours. And this is what's left of your identity-tag.' Grace reached to the narrow, army-issue cabinet at the side of the bed, and handed over what remained of the lozenge of green, fibrous material. 'You can just make out SMI and the first digit of your roll number.'

'Huh, not a lot of help, is it?'

'You never know. It might trigger something. But you need to rest. It's been a long day for you.'

He nodded, and as Grace turned from the bed, she noticed his eyes lower to the scrap of bloodstained material in his palm before his fingers closed tightly about it.

* * *

'Oh, Selina, I'm really sorry you're leaving. We could have been such good friends.'

'I sincerely hope we already have been!' Selina grinned. 'I wouldn't have got this far if it hadn't been for you. I only came because my father had been on at me to do something useful for the war. But you . . .' She broke off, taking Grace's hands in hers. 'You're a natural. I know you're thinking about training properly when this horrible war is over. But if that's what you want to do, and you can find a way to do it, then I really think you should.'

Grace arched a rueful eyebrow. 'As you say, if I can find a way. But I'll cross that bridge when I come to it. The war could go on for years yet.'

'Hopefully not. Not now the Americans have actually started fighting at last.'

'Well, let's hope it makes a difference and we can beat the Boche and then start getting back to normal. But . . . Oh, I'll miss you, Nurse Palmer.'

'And I'll miss you! And it's not *Nurse* any more, thank God. Oh, come here and give me a hug. And you will keep in touch, won't you?'

'Of course I will,' Grace promised as they laced their arms around each other. 'And good luck with whatever you end up doing!'

'Well, I must go.' Selina broke away. 'My trunk's already been taken to the station by the carrier, and I'd better not miss my train. Look after yourself!'

'I will. And you, too!'

Grace watched as the other girl opened one of the glass doors to the vestibule, turned to give one last wave, and disappeared out through the portico. Grace shook her head. Selina had been like a whirlwind, a breath of fresh air. But Grace had the feeling that, despite all her promises, she would never hear of her again.

* * *

'Good morning, Nurse Dannings,' the sister in the dark blue uniform greeted Grace as they met on the galleried landing. 'I was told you'd be coming. You'll find this ward very different from your own, so I do hope you won't be overwhelmed.

Our patients' nervous systems are in such a state that it manifests itself in physical ways. But I believe that is what interests you?'

Grace met the direct look in Sister Freeman's eyes and nodded. 'Yes, Sister,' she replied, although she had to admit to herself that she suddenly felt somewhat daunted. But she had asked to visit the ward and wasn't going to change her mind now. 'That's why I'm here in my off-duty time. I'd love to be able to help.'

'Well, you're very welcome. Just as on your own ward, understanding is the key. Sunshine Ward assesses how well a patient is coping mentally with a new disability, but here, few of our patients have physical wounds.' She paused, almost as if she were summing Grace up merely by looking shrewdly at her. 'You know how other patients here undo their trauma through peace and quiet and working in the gardens or doing carpentry, basket weaving or whatever. But on Happiness, our patients don't even have the physical ability to do that. Their limbs and their hands simply won't do what their brains tell them. Well.' Her fingers closed about the handle of the door to what Grace knew had originally been the opulent master bedroom of the house. 'I'll introduce you to Nurses Miles and Trembath who are on duty today. You're very young for this type of work, but I'm told you have a mature head on your shoulders.'

Sister Freeman then gave a warm smile as if her introductory lecture was over, and led Grace through into the ward. It was a beautiful, spacious room with three large windows set in a semi-circular bay that echoed the shape of the great hall below. There was a spectacular view down over the sloping grounds and across the valley, and the room was flooded with sunlight, so Grace could appreciate at once why it had been chosen to soothe the souls of these most wounded of men. She noted that none of the eight patients was in bed. Some were seated in chairs attempting exercises, while others were struggling manfully to move about on twisted limbs that refused to behave normally. Two were on the floor in the wide bay that had obviously been cleared for them, their bodies writhing like slithering snakes.

'I have some paperwork to do,' Sister Freeman said, 'but Nurses Miles and Trembath will show you the ropes.'

'Of course, Sister. I'm Nurse Miles. Vera.' The taller of the two middle-aged VAD nurses introduced herself, her face creased in welcome. 'I see your attention's been drawn by our two prostrate patients. If you watch, you'll see they're actually playing tag. A game gives them some focus, you see. When they arrived here only three days ago, neither of them could move a muscle. At least, not in the way they want to. All they've had so far is one hypnotherapy session with Dr Franfield, so you can see the improvement already. One of them couldn't speak at all, but now he can make himself understood, at least.'

'That's amazing,' Grace replied, certainly impressed since she had indeed noticed the men when they had arrived. 'So, what can I do to help?'

'You could help me with Private Wicks,' the other nurse smiled. 'That would be a good place to start. Both his arms are contracted up, and we're giving him massage to try to relax the muscles. Come and I'll show you. Tresca Trembath, by the way. Right, here we are, Private. We have a helper on the ward today.'

Grace nodded a greeting to the young man who was curled up in an easy-chair in a defensive ball, arms crossed tensely across his chest and his hands like stiff sticks. His eyes, though, seemed to light up like stars when he spied the pretty young nurse and he presented her with a lopsided smile. For a few seconds, Grace felt a little uneasy, but as she joined Nurse Trembath in rolling up the fellow's pyjama sleeves, her nervousness fled and her heart filled with sympathy as she took in the poor man's condition.

'We rub on a little oil to make it more comfortable, don't we, Private Wicks?' Tresca Trembath explained to Grace, giving an encouraging smile to the patient. 'Then we gently but firmly stroke down the arms like so. The idea is to stretch out the muscles but without hurting the patient. Doesn't hurt the way we do it, does it, Private?'

'Specially not when I's got someone like this here maid to do it,' the young fellow slurred.

Grace tried not to blush as she concentrated on copying the older nurse's example. Her fingers tingled at the unfamiliar sensation of doing little more than caressing the stranger's limbs. She had learnt to dress partially healed wounds and amputation stumps, and had helped men in and out of bed, and to wash and shave. But the majority of the patients at Mount Tavy Hospital were over the worst of their injuries and no longer required frontline nursing. It really was their minds that were being given the chance to heal. And so for Grace it was the first time she had experienced such close intimacy with any of the soldiers, her touch directly on a man's skin in an almost sensual way, and it set her heart pounding as she worked on the tensed limb. Miraculously, however, she could feel the muscle begin to relax beneath her hands, and the satisfaction made *her* feel more at ease as well.

'Why don't you close your eyes and imagine you're somewhere you love?' she heard herself say as if her tongue had suddenly found a life of its own. 'In the countryside, perhaps? It's a lovely sunny day, so quiet and still all you can hear is the humming of a bee. It's so peaceful that you can feel something good blossoming inside you.'

Her voice had taken on a gentle, sing-song lilt, and she could feel her own mind drifting away. She was standing on the top of Peek Hill, her favourite spot on the moor, and there were Stephen and Martin and Larry . . .

'I doesn't need to imagine that.' The young soldier's chuckle made her jump sky high. 'I reckons I's already dead and gone to heaven with an angel like you tending to my needs.'

Grace felt the colour spreading into her cheeks and was supremely grateful when Tresca Trembath came to her rescue.

'Cheeky so-and-so,' the older woman chided mildly. 'But I can see we'll need to have Nurse Dannings here more often. I can feel you're more relaxed today, Private. At this rate, we'll have you back on your feet in no time.'

'Not too quickly, I hopes,' Private Wicks answered, winking surreptitiously at Grace.

'Now do be quiet and concentrate on relaxing, you naughty boy.'

'Spoil sport!' the fellow retorted with a mock grimace. But he held his tongue as they continued with the massage, working down his arms to his stiff hands. As Grace gently kneaded his fingers, she began to feel she was enjoying herself, so engrossed in her achievement that she found herself humming quietly. No one told her to stop, and she actually felt disappointed when Nurse Trembath declared the session to be over.

'Corporal Jenkins's turn now,' she announced.

'Lucky devil,' Private Wicks grumbled. 'But if you hums a bit louder like, I can still hear you.'

Grace couldn't stop the corners of her mouth curving upwards. 'Perhaps we can all join in a song?' she suggested. 'They have the piano downstairs, after all. Just because you can't get down there when it's being played doesn't mean to say you shouldn't enjoy some singing, does it? In fact,' she went on, excitement burgeoning inside her, 'maybe we could put on a concert? Get all the men and staff involved who want to be. And not just music. Poetry readings, comic sketches. What do you think, Nurse Trembath?'

'Well, there's been talk of it before. But no one's actually come forward to organize it. It's not up to me, of course, but I reckon Dr Franfield and Matron would agree if you think you could take it on.'

'Tell you what, mind,' Private Wicks put in, his frail, slurred voice becoming stronger each time he spoke. 'I feels better already. Concert sounds a grand idea to me. Clever cheel, you. Be a lucky bugger what catches you as his wife, I can tell you!'

'Language, Private Wicks!' Nurse Trembath chastised him with a grin.

CHAPTER EIGHTEEN

Grace lifted her head from the papers she had been poring over on Sister Guscott's desk. It was the third consecutive night she had been left in entire charge of the ward, but with strict instructions to wake Sister in her room if she considered it necessary. Grace was becoming accustomed to the strange atmosphere during the hours of darkness. The old house never slept in complete silence. Floorboards creaked as the night-duty staff in other wards moved about to check on patients, and there were periods of heavy snoring or mutterings, groans as men turned over in their sleep.

Grace did a round every hour and then logged her observations in the book by the light from the dim electric bulb in the desk lamp. It was one of many wonders at Mount Tavy, brightening the darkness at the flick of a switch. There was hot and cold running water, a sewerage system and even one of those telephone contraptions so that Dr Franfield could be summoned instantly from his home or the civilian cottage hospital. And the house was apparently heated by a system of hot water pipes which would soon be put into use now autumn was approaching. For Grace, it was a fascinating experience just living there, let alone all she had been seeing and learning on the wards.

Now, though, the sound that rumbled through the shadows was more than the usual mumblings of the sleeping men. Someone was having a nightmare. The unravelling of a tortured mind, Dr Franfield had explained. It was a healing process, and unless the patient was particularly distressed or appeared in physical discomfort, he was probably best left undisturbed. But every case should be investigated, so Grace got to her feet.

It was probably poor young Private Fletcher. He was devastated by his injuries, even more so now that his pain-killing drugs had been withdrawn and his awareness had returned to normal. He had dictated a letter to Grace for his parents who lived at the opposite side of the county. They had replied in a short, not too literate note that they could not afford the fare to visit him. Ling Franfield had at once sent them a postal order, and they were expected any day. But in the meantime, their son was suffering such violent nightmares that he had been prescribed a sleeping draught that night. Even so, he wasn't enjoying a peaceful slumber, poor boy.

When Grace reached his bed, however, she found that the medicine had indeed worked. It was Lieutenant Smith who was moaning in his sleep, the incomprehensible sounds growing in intensity as he thrashed from side to side until he cried out in anguish. Grace bit her lower lip. Was he reaching the stage when she should wake him? Beads of sweat stood out on his forehead, his face twitching restlessly. And then his eyes jerked open and he sat bolt upright.

'It's all right,' Grace soothed. 'You were just dreaming.'

She heard him draw a rasping breath and hold it for several seconds before releasing it in a strangling sigh. He blinked his frightened eyes wide open and then, focusing on Grace's face, fell back heavily onto the pillow.

'Nurse Dannings,' he whispered into the gloom.

'Yes. You're safe, remember. Now try to go back to sleep.'

She smiled down at him and saw him nod as he turned onto his side. Satisfied, Grace returned to the desk, noted his nightmare and went back to the concert schedule she had been contemplating. It was surprising the ideas the men were coming up with, whether or not they possessed any talent to perform. That was beside the point. The thing was that so many of them had found their spirits lifted. Arts and crafts were provided in the conservatory, basket-weaving and woodwork went on in the rooms in the coach-house, there were cards and other board-games provided in the great hall as well as an occasional sing-song, and a library of books in the study. But now groups of patients were taking themselves off to various locations to rehearse in private, and those who weren't involved were looking forward immensely to the performance.

'I've seen such an improvement in so many of the men as a result of this forthcoming event,' Dr Franfield had observed. 'And all down to you, Nurse Dannings. Thank you so much for taking on the organization of it.'

Grace had gloried in his praise, even though, together with her work, her studies and the time she spent on Happiness Ward, it meant she had no time for herself. She hadn't written to Larry for ages and felt guilty since his letters arrived regularly, but surely helping these damaged soldiers was more important.

Goodness, time for her next round already. She crept from bed to bed, pleased that each man was now sleeping soundly. Apart from Lieutenant Smith who was lying on his back, hands clasped behind his head as his alert eyes stared at the ceiling.

'Can't sleep?' she whispered.

He breathed in deeply through his nostrils. 'It was all so vivid, my dream. I was there again, in the trenches. We'd gone over the top. Noise, explosions all around. Shouting, smoke. The confusion. I even saw a shell land in front of me. I don't know if it was *the one*, or whether I was just imagining it.'

'Hush, now. It's all over.'

'No, it isn't. For me, maybe. Or maybe not. I could be sent back. But it's not over for all the poor devils who are still out there. And never for the ones who won't come back, or poor sods like Harry here. Private Fletcher.'

Grace nodded gravely. 'I know. Poor chap's taken it really hard.'

'Well, you would, wouldn't you?' Lieutenant Smith's tone was sharp. 'And he's so young. Makes my problem seem trivial.'

'Would you like a cup of tea?' Grace asked, wanting to divert the grim conversation.

'That would be kindness itself, Nurse Dannings. But I need the lavatory first. And don't offer me a bottle or a trip in a wheelchair. I want to walk there on my own two feet.'

'I'll have to check your notes to see if you're allowed. They'd have my guts for garters if you're not. You can feel proper groggy when you've been in bed for so long. *And* with a head injury.'

'Oh, come on, it must be well over three weeks by now—'

'But it were *serious*! You had severe concussion, you know, and a very deep head wound. No. I must check your notes first,' Grace told him firmly, and went off to do just that. She hadn't made one mistake since she had come to Mount Tavy, and she had no intention of doing so now.

'Well,' she conceded on her return. 'I see you've walked there twice this afternoon, but you have to be accompanied.'

'Fair enough. Mind you,' he said darkly as he swung his legs over the side of the bed, 'how a slip of a thing like you could catch me if I decided to faint, I have no idea.'

'I'm stronger than you might think. I used to work at a wheelwrights' afore I came here.'

'Wheelwrights'? Good Lord. Well, come on, then. And I promise I won't pass out on you,' he said with what passed for a smile.

Nevertheless, he leant on her quite heavily as they progressed down the ward, out into the great hall and along to the facilities. Grace found herself tucking her shoulder under his armpit, arm around his back and grasping his slender waist so that if he did keel over, she could take his weight safely.

The queerness of the situation struck her as they shambled along together. Here she was, in the middle of the night, her flank pressed tightly against that of a virtual stranger. And, although not alone since the house was full of patients and nursing staff, it certainly felt at that moment as if she was!

Lieutenant Smith, however, appeared unaware of her misgivings as she left him alone in the cubicle. She waited outside, her emotions on edge and swathed in confusion. She had to admit that his physical closeness had actually been quite thrilling. He was an attractive man despite the scar across his cheek, and he was well-spoken and always polite even if a little laconic at times. And she was a young woman, twenty years old and never been kissed, her senses smouldering and ready to burst into flame. If it hadn't been for the war, she might have been married by now, although to whom, she couldn't imagine. But the presence of this stranger, together with the close contact she had experienced with the few patients on Happiness Ward, had ignited something new and passionate inside her; a sense of yearning and wonderment, and the need to be fulfilled.

She had to concentrate hard on their way back to the ward. She really must not let these ridiculous feelings show!

'I'll get you that cup of tea now,' she said, grateful to get her patient back in bed.

'Thank you. And can you give me something for my head? It's absolutely splitting again.' And by the way his eyes were screwed against even the dim light, Grace could well believe it.

'I can only give you aspirin, I'm afraid. Unless I wake Sister Guscott.'

'No, don't do that. I wouldn't want to disturb her. Aspirin will do.'

Grace retraced her steps across the hall, but over to the kitchens this time. She turned on the gas, another miracle she still hadn't got used to. Perhaps the lieutenant would like a biscuit. Grace pulled herself up short as she realized she was making an extra effort to please him. Nevertheless, she placed a biscuit on the saucer before going back to the ward.

'There,' she said amiably. 'And here's some water to take the aspirin with. Is there anything else I can get you?'

'No, thank you. That's all very kind. Unless . . . If you have time, could we talk for a few minutes? I know it sounds silly when there are so many people all around. And I know you're all doing your best to make us feel at home. But . . . I feel lonely. I've lost so much time since we all arrived here. I'm sure I'm over that now, but . . . There's so much of me missing. Up here, in my head. I know it's nothing to what some of the other poor devils have got to learn to live with, and that makes me feel ashamed. But, not knowing who I am—'

'I don't think you realize how seriously you were hurt. And besides, it's what it means to you personally that counts. You can't compare it to other people's problems. We will find out who you are in time, even if your memory takes longer to come back. You know Matron's sent off one of the buttons from your uniform to identify your regiment, and they'll take it from there. It's a bit of a jigsaw, and with all the chaos, lists of the missing and so forth. But we will get an answer in the end.'

Grace met his gaze, noticing once again the intense sapphire of his eyes, and she saw his lips curl into a wry smile.

'Thank you. I hope you're right. It's just so unnerving not having a name.'

'We can give you one if you like. We'll stick to Lieutenant Smith until we know better, but we can make up a Christian name for you. Is there anything you've always wished you were called?'

'I wouldn't know, would I?' He raised a sceptical eyebrow. 'But I suppose under the circumstances, Oliver might be appropriate.'

'Oliver? You mean, after Oliver Twist? Because they didn't know who he were, either? Larry, a friend of mine, he got me reading some of Charles Dickens and I loved that one.'

'Yes. But why can I remember Dickens and Shakespeare and some of the Romantic poets when I can't remember my own name?'

'It's bound to come back eventually. In the meantime, I think Oliver will suit you quite nicely.'

'Suit me?'

'Well, yes. Somehow.' Grace tipped her head to one side to contemplate him. 'So we know you must be quite educated. And you're not from round here. At least, you don't have a Devonshire accent and we know you weren't in the Devonshire Regiment. I imagine you were sent here because of Dr Franfield's reputation with neurosis patients, and in all the chaos . . . But try not to think about it now. Drink your tea afore it gets cold.'

'Thank you for making it for me. And for staying to talk.'

'All part of the service. I'll be back on days on Friday and we can talk again then.'

'I'll look forward to it. And,' he faltered, his brow dipping into a frown, 'I'm not sure if it's allowed, but may I ask your given name? If I'm to be Oliver . . .'

'You're right. It's against the rules. Officially. But I'm Grace,' she said without hesitation. 'Only don't let anyone hear you call me that.'

'I promise, Nurse Dannings,' he answered. And for the first time since his arrival, she saw his serious face break into a grin.

* * *

'Nurse Dannings,' Ling Franfield addressed Grace a few days later. 'Nurse Palmer's replacement has arrived. She's up in the dorm changing into her uniform, but she'll need to be shown how to fold the headdress. If you wouldn't mind?'

'Of course not, Matron. I'm just going on my break so I'll go straight up.'

'Thank you. And I think you'll be pleased.' Matron gave a kind, almost mischievous smile. 'She comes from your neck of the woods. You're probably already friends.'

Grace gave a perplexed frown as she hurried up the grand staircase. Who on earth could the new VAD be? Did Matron mean Walkhampton when she referred to her *neck of the woods*? Grace couldn't think of anyone from the village who could possibly be in a position to join the detachment. Matron must have been mistaken or muddled the name of the village. Unless . . . it couldn't possibly be kind Mrs Snell, could it? Grace somehow couldn't imagine her volunteering as a nurse, although the prospect filled her with joyous expectation.

When she reached the top of the staircase, she almost ran along the narrow passageway to the dormitory even though running was strictly forbidden, and flung open the door. But the figure in the pale blue uniform with its back to Grace wasn't short and stout, but tall and slim and altogether far younger. She must have heard Grace enter the room and instantly turned around.

Grace stopped dead in her tracks. Unwelcome surprise scorched through her, followed at once by a swirl of bitter disappointment. It couldn't possibly be — but it was.

'Aggie!' The disgruntled cry of disbelief was out of her mouth before she pushed the door shut behind her. 'What the devil are *you* doing here?'

'Same as you, I imagine.' Aggie gave a casual shrug of her shoulders. 'I came because I wanted to help.'

'Help? Huh!' Grace retorted, astounded by her own bluntness. 'You've never wanted to help anyone in your life. Except yourself!'

Aggie, in her habitual infuriating way, was not to be perturbed. 'Well, maybe this time, it's different. Besides, I'm sick of sitting around at home doing nothing, like my mother does.'

'Ah, I thought there must be a selfish motive in it some-where! Well, you won't know what's hit you here, I can tell you. Never stick it, you won't.'

'Maybe that's where you're wrong.' Aggie's eyes flashed challengingly. But then her shoulders sagged in a dejected sigh. 'I'm determined to prove to my father that I'm not the useless imbecile he says I am. But he won't normally allow me to do anything to show what I'm capable of. At least this was *something* he approved of, and it got me away from him.'

'There we are, then!' Grace hissed acidly. 'You only came here because—'

'No, that's not true,' Aggie insisted, her brow wrinkled in earnest. 'I really do want to do something to help our soldiers. Because of . . .' She hesitated, lowering her eyes, and Grace noticed a catch in her voice when she continued, 'Because of Martin. You don't have a monopoly on grief, you know. And whatever you think of me, I *loved* him.'

Her eyes swam with moisture and Grace stared at her, chewing on her lip. Aggie could be play-acting. Heaven knew she was accomplished enough at that! Or it was possible that she was telling the truth. But whichever it was, Grace imagined that it must have taken considerable courage for Aggie to have sought her father's approval to leave home. Everyone in Walkhampton knew that despite being a preacher, he was a strange and dour individual who strode through the village peering down his nose at anyone who dared to speak to him. At the thought of him, a drop of sympathy escaped into Grace's blood. And if Aggie had genuinely loved Martin . . .

'Matron asked me to show you how to fold your headgear,' she said grudgingly. 'It takes a bit of practice to get it right. Look, like this.'

Grace smoothed out the starched white material on Aggie's bed, made some folds, explaining how it would then be secured at the back of the head, and then opened it out again. To her surprise, Aggie made such a passable effort when she tried herself that Grace felt able to transfer it to the girl's head and fasten it for her. What surprised Grace even more, though, was that Aggie had cut her hair into the short bob that was becoming fashionable.

'Had your hair cropped, I see,' she couldn't stop herself from commenting.

'I thought it'd be easier to manage if I'm going to be so busy,' Aggie answered coolly.

Well, well. Even Grace hadn't done that. And of course, Larry had forbidden her. Not that his opinion would have stopped her if she had really wanted to. But perhaps Aggie was actually as genuine as she was making out.

'Come on. I'll show you where the kitchens are,' Grace surprised herself by saying in a more friendly tone. 'There's just enough time to swallow a cup of tea, and then you can help me wash Private Fletcher. I must warn you, though, he has what we call a shoulder amputation on one side, and his other arm ends below the elbow.'

Aggie's face dropped into an expression of horror. 'You mean . . . both?'

'Yes. Poor devil can't do ort for himself. It's the worst thing I've seen. But . . . this is reality, Aggie. Do you think you can cope with it? Selina, the volunteer you're replacing, she fainted when she saw him.'

She watched as Aggie swallowed hard and then straightened her back.

'Thank you for the warning. But I won't faint. And I'm going to surprise you, Grace Dannings.'

'I hope you do,' Grace answered.

CHAPTER NINETEEN

'That's really good, Oliver!'

Grace had come into the conservatory where all the arts and craft material was kept to see if any of her charges occupying themselves there needed any assistance. It was astonishing what emerged from the conservatory. In many ways, Grace thought creative activities must provide an even greater release than any of the outdoor pursuits available. And those weren't an option anyway for most of the amputees. Like Harry Fletcher, for instance. When the tenderness eventually eased, his stump would be fitted with some sort of prosthetic which would give the poor fellow a shred of independence again. But in the meantime, Grace had suggested he tried painting using his feet.

'Don't be so daft,' he had complained wretchedly, looking as if he might dissolve in angry tears.

'What a splendid idea!' Oliver declared. 'Slippers off, everyone. Even you, Mark. No excuse only having one foot. Come on, chaps.'

It had lapsed into one of the most hilarious afternoons anyone could remember. Oliver had everyone squelching about in trays of paint with their bare feet and then making patterns on paper spread on the floor. Friendly rivalry bantered about the conservatory as men tried to outdo each other, and Harry Fletcher had laughed for the first time since the exploding shell had blown off both his arms. The clear-up operation, however, had taken so long that it had been decided not to indulge in that particular activity again. But everyone had relished in the jolly memories for days, and Harry had been lifted out of his world of misery.

'Why don't you try holding a paintbrush in your mouth?' Grace had suggested a few days later when Harry was enviously eyeing his partners in crime in the conservatory.

'I'll take some brushes over to the lads in the woodwork shop,' Oliver offered. 'Get them to cut the handles shorter to make it easier for you.'

Harry had opened his mouth in doleful protest, but Oliver was already out of the door, Grace smiling gratefully at his tall, strong back. Kind was Oliver, with a wicked sense of humour when his frequent, crippling headaches and his own problems allowed him. And Grace . . . No. She mustn't think like that. It was strictly forbidden between any member of staff and a patient. But she could feel a warm sensation curling up inside her whenever he was near.

Harry's first mouth painting was a furious dash of angry black streaks across the paper, but as the days passed, he gained more control, added colour, and shapes resembling flowers began to emerge. Harry seemed altogether brighter. Another patient excelled at cartoons lampooning the Germans and the Turks, while another, who was often found cowering under his bed, worked out his trauma in charcoal sketches of the trenches under attack, hardly works of art, but he threw all his fear and hatred onto the paper and out of himself.

Now Grace was contemplating the painting of a little boy on Oliver's easel. She could see something of Oliver in the child's face, and it brought an unfathomable uneasiness to her heart.

'Do you know who it is?' she asked hesitantly, not wanting to destroy any flicker of enlightenment it might be causing in his fragile mind.

'No,' he answered flatly, and Grace saw a shuttered look veil his expression. 'I've been seeing the face in my dreams and I wanted to capture it before it goes away again.'

'But you don't think it means anything?'

'No.'

It was almost as if he *wanted* it to be meaningless. Afraid that it might be a clue. So Grace persisted very carefully. 'But it might mean something in time. It looks like you. Perhaps it's you when you were little.'

Oliver's eyebrows arched in frustration. 'I really don't know. Perhaps if I stare at it for long enough, it might spark some memory . . . Your friend's settled in well, hasn't she?' he continued, deliberately changing the subject, it seemed. 'She tells me you're from the same village.'

'Yes. But I wouldn't exactly describe us as friends.'

'Ah-ha! Do I detect a little tension there?' Oliver gave a teasing wink. 'Bit of rivalry?'

'Rivalry? Hardly! Aggie's, well, she were always out to cause trouble. But I have to admit she seems different here.'

'Maybe she's found her feet? This war is changing so many things. I don't suppose life will ever be the same for so many of us. I doubt *my* life ever will. If I ever discover what it used to be.'

Grace contemplated him for a moment or two. His mood could swing so suddenly between jocularity and despondency. Dr Franfield had explained that the blow to his head from the piece of shrapnel that had embedded itself in his skull was directly to blame. But the ensuing memory loss and the anxiety it was causing Oliver was in itself making matters worse. A vicious circle so to speak.

'They'll work it out eventually,' Grace assured him. 'I reckon it's just not a priority, and there'll be thousands of names to go through.'

'Yes, but . . . When they do, what if it still doesn't mean anything to me? Or I don't like who I really am?'

His eyes met hers, deep and intense with pain. And Grace felt her heart fragment.

* * *

'Congratulations on the concert!' Sister Freeman greeted Grace as she entered Happiness Ward. 'I understand you're already working on another one for Christmas?'

'I am, yes. I'd like to talk to some of the men here about it, if I may.'

'Be my guest. Just watch Private Wicks, mind. Getting a little too familiar, he is.'

'Don't worry, Sister,' Grace chuckled. 'I think I can keep him at arm's length.'

'I'm glad to hear it. Could you possibly help Nurse Trembath with Captain Evershed while you're here? Nurse Miles is off with a heavy cold.'

'Poor soul. I hope she gets better soon. But of course I'll help with the captain. Really beginning to make progress at last, isn't he?'

Grace stepped straight across to the bay where Tresca Trembath was helping Captain Evershed to lurch from one window to the next, staggering on his crooked limbs and attempting desperately to keep his balance. But when Grace considered that on his arrival barely three months previously, he could do little more that wriggle on the floor and his speech was practically non-existent, it was a miracle. Each hypnosis session he underwent with Dr Franfield resulted in a marked improvement, and even though his words were slightly slurred, he could now hold a normal conversation.

Grace felt proud that she had played some small part in his progress. She loved her work helping the amputees come to terms with their disabilities — at least most of them did with care and understanding — and seeing them go home to their loved ones to await their prosthetics with a positive attitude. But the achievements on Happiness Ward were no less satisfying — and it was one time when she could escape Aggie's presence, although during their off-duty time, Aggie invariably disappeared into the town.

'Are you all right this morning?' Grace plucked up the courage to ask a little later as she and Tresca Trembath took their morning break. 'You seem a bit preoccupied.'

'I am,' the older woman admitted quietly. 'Had a letter from Callum, our eldest. He's been wounded. Took a sniper bullet in his arm. He'll mend, but I can't help worrying.'

'Of course you can't. And the other two?'

'All right as far as we know. But every day, I expect to get a telegram. This dreadful fighting that's still going on at *Wipers* as they jokingly call it. Though I can't see anything funny in it myself.'

'Me neither. I think it's just a way of keeping their spirits up. Let's just pray it all comes to an end soon. And in the meantime, if you visit Vera, tell her I hope she gets better soon. Been friends a long time, haven't you?' Grace asked, trying to cheer Tresca up by changing the subject.

'Yes, ever since I came to Tavistock with my father back along when they were building the second railway through the town.' She paused, and her eyes took on a far-away look so that when she spoke again, it took Grace by surprise. 'But my Morgan and I have been so happy together all these long years. I'm so thankful for that. I just wish we could have the boys safely back home.'

Grace nodded her head. She had heard of more than one instance where all the male members of one family had been wiped out. In the Parish of Walkhampton, there was a case where two brothers had lost their lives, and who knew if the third would survive the carnage? To lose one family member was unbearable, but to lose all the young men didn't bear thinking about. For Tresca and her husband it must be unimaginable to have all three sons in the thick of the fighting — including Liam whom Grace now knew had been the young lad manning the gate on her and Larry's first visit to Martin.

Grace found herself staring into her teacup. She had lost three brothers in her life, and her heart still ached whenever she thought about it. No wonder her poor mother had lost her mind for so long. But surely the war must end before George was old enough to be conscripted, especially now the Americans were involved? But it had already been raging for well over three years when back in the summer of 1914, everyone was convinced it would be over by Christmas.

Well, not quite everybody. Sadly people like Larry had been proved right. And Grace thanked God that he was one person in her life who would always be there.

* * *

'You have a visitor, Nurse Dannings,' Ling Franfield told Grace who was making the beds on Sunshine Ward with Aggie's help.

'A visitor? But I'm on duty and I'm not expecting anyone.' And then panic gripped her in a fist of iron. 'Oh, my God, it's not bad news?'

'Not at all. Forgive me, my dear, I should have said. And don't worry about being on duty. Heaven knows, no one has put in as much extra time here as you have. Off you go. He's waiting in the vestibule. Take as much time as you like.'

He? Whoever could it be? Her father perhaps, Grace wondered as she made her way towards the door. But why would he come now when he should be at work on the Snells' farm? Despite Matron's assurances, Grace prayed it was nothing to do with her mother. As she crossed the great hall, she was oblivious to the group of soldiers in hospital blues playing cards. But then she recognized a familiar figure through the ornate glass doors to the vestibule.

'Larry!' she cried as she went through. But her eyes immediately snapped in irritation. 'What are you doing here?'

'If Mohammed won't come to the mountain,' he answered darkly, catching her fierce gaze.

'What do you mean?'

'Is that the best welcome you can muster when I've come all this way?' he retorted. 'I thought you'd be pleased to see me.'

'Of course I am. But I'm on duty. You should have written and we could have arranged a time when I'm free.'

'And would you have read any letter?' Larry's voice was a blend of suppressed anger and hurt. 'I write to you almost every week, but you haven't replied in ages. You only came home to visit your parents a couple of times shortly after you came here, and your notes to them are so brief. I was worried about you, but I see there was no need.'

His eyes locked with hers, but the underlying distress in them filled Grace with remorse.

'Oh, I'm sorry, Larry. It's just that I've been so busy. It becomes a way of life here. Wait and I'll get my coat. I know it's drizzling but we can still walk around the grounds.'

'That would be nice,' Larry replied stiffly, but then Grace saw the taut lines about his mouth slacken. 'And I must say you look very fetching in your uniform.' His eyes had softened and Grace felt the tension between them easing.

'It isn't supposed to be fetching,' she chided. 'So it's probably as well that I'll have my coat on over the top. Matron said she doesn't mind me taking a while, and it's because of you that I'm here, after all. But I still shouldn't be too long.'

'Neither should I. We're still pretty busy at the yard.'

'I'll be half a minute. The dorm's just upstairs.'

She slipped quickly through the doors and up the staircase, her heart feeling lighter. It was so good to see Larry again and she was cross with herself for her ungracious greeting. But Larry wasn't one to bear a grudge and he threw her a tentative smile as she returned to the vestibule, shrugging into her coat.

'Come on,' she invited him, threading her arm through his elbow. 'Pity the weather's so miserable. You can't see the view properly.'

'It wasn't the view I came to see,' Larry said drily as they stepped outside. 'Besides, I've seen it before. When we came to visit Martin.'

196

'Yes, of course.' Grace momentarily lowered her eyes. 'It's a pity anyway. I'm sure the view and the beautiful house help to lift our patients' spirits. I'm so lucky to work here.'

'You really enjoy it, then?'

'Oh, Larry, I really do!' Grace enthused as they meandered across the steep lawn that was peppered with fallen autumn leaves. 'Of course it's so awful that these poor souls need to come here in the first place. But it's so satisfying when you see them improving. We send men home to a reasonable future when they arrived here as quivering wrecks.'

'Pity the hospital wasn't able to do something for Martin, then,' Larry muttered under his breath, and Grace felt his listing gait come to a halt. When she glanced up, he was staring into the mist, his face set.

'Yes,' she agreed solemnly. 'But treatment methods were in their infancy then, and Martin *wanted* to return to the Front. It made it a difficult case.'

'I know. But I'm glad you're finding your work fulfilling anyway.'

'I can't tell you how much! The neurosis side is so fascinating, but I love the nursing side and studying the human body and everything so much as well. So much so that I've decided that I want to train as a proper nurse when the war's over.'

She looked at Larry, her face aglow with enthusiasm, but her heart sank when Larry's expression hardened.

'And how do you propose to do that?' he demanded. 'I can see it'd be a real outlet for your intelligence. You're even talking differently, working with all these educated people. But have you thought what it would mean? With the war on, they'll accept any volunteers who come forward, married or not. But under normal circumstances, don't they expect total dedication? It's like being a nun. You have to be married to your vocation. You'd be denying yourself a normal life. A husband and children.'

'Trust you, Larry,' Grace pouted. 'But who would I marry, anyway?'

She didn't see that little twitch at the corner of his mouth. 'Well, think very carefully, Gracie.'

'Oh, I will.' And as the image of Oliver's face slipped into her head, she felt a seed of doubt in her mind. 'Anyway,' she went on with deliberate brightness, 'how's life back in Walkhampton?'

Larry shrugged. 'Much the same. Your mother's being a tower of strength to Nan. Amazing when you consider how she was herself not so long ago. And George is doing famously. He's shot up since you saw him last. Oh, I understand dearest Aggie has come here as a VAD, too. See much of her, do you?'

'*Too* much!' Grace complained, rolling her eyes. 'Matron thinks we must be friends and puts us together all the time. We even sleep in the same room. The only time we're not together is when we're off duty and she always goes into the town. But I have to say, she's turned out to be a brilliant nurse. She works hard, nothing's too much trouble. She gets on really well with the patients — without flirting even! And she's very quick to learn. I'd never have believed it of her.'

'Maybe it was just what she needed. Just like your mother needed poor Nan's situation to get her back on her feet. I have to say I've always felt sorry for Aggie, having no friends—'

'That were her own fault.'

'Maybe. Or maybe not. Having such a tyrant for a father can't be easy for anyone. Her odd ways could be the result of being browbeaten all the time.'

'You could be right. She's certainly surprised me. But we were making the beds together before you came, so I'd better get back.'

'Yes, of course. But, Grace, about the other business. Remember what I said. You've a lot of love in your heart to give. And I'm not sure giving a lifetime of it to strangers on a hospital ward would be enough for you.'

'Well, I won't be making any decisions until the war's over, whenever that might be. We've finally won at

Passchendaele, but who knows what difference that'll make? It's taken months and months, and with hundreds of thousands of casualties . . .'

'Let's hope with the Americans with us now, next year will see an end to it all.'

'My God, I hope so,' Grace agreed as they turned back towards the house. But at the thought that she would be spending the rest of the day in the same room as Oliver Smith, Grace put all thoughts of the war aside, and her heart gave a little flutter of pleasure.

CHAPTER TWENTY

'Off you go, Grace,' Aggie insisted. 'I can manage here.'

'Are you sure you don't mind? I mean, there are a few finishing touches—'

'Go on, shoo! I can give Harry here his dinner and take over your other duties. Don't mind, do you, Harry?'

'Course not. Just can't wait for this here concert.' Private Fletcher actually grinned. And he rather liked Nurse Nonnacott who couldn't give a damn about the rule of not using first names on the ward. Who the bloody hell cared when you had to face the rest of your life with no arms?

'Oh, bless you, Aggie dear!'

Grace shot out of the door and into the great hall where the Christmas concert was to take place in less than two hours. For a split second, she found herself dumbstruck. She would never have imagined using such a term of endearment towards Aggie! But then she spied Oliver fixing the final piece of scenery at the back of the stage which had been built in sections in the woodwork room. Grace had found a task for virtually everyone in the hospital, and all hearts were poised in eager anticipation of the evening ahead.

Grace's gaze moved over the makeshift theatre. Chairs had been brought in from wherever they could be found with space left for those who would be in wheelchairs. There wouldn't be room for everyone, so those who were physically capable would line the upper gallery and look down on the proceedings instead. The study had been turned into a dressing-room, but other performers who didn't need costumes would be coming onto the stage from their seats in the audience.

It was as perfect as it possibly could be, and as Grace's eyes settled on the scenery, she felt that delicious sensation sizzle in her breast again. Oliver had turned out to be a gifted artist, something that perplexed him deeply, but it had meant that Grace had spent considerable time working with him. With every minute they shared each other's company, an enchanted thread of understanding seemed to be weaving itself about them. Now, as Oliver saw her, his face lit up in a smile that overwhelmed her in happiness.

But there was no time for that now. Grace had to check the props list, make sure her schedule had not gone missing, start getting men into their costumes. Her stomach churned with nervousness since really the whole affair was her responsibility. The only thing she hadn't been able to control was the lighting system that one of the men had managed to rig up.

The excited tension was palpable as men arrived in the study, wriggling into costumes, laughing as they slapped on outrageous make-up. Outside, they could hear the noisy buzz as the audience took their seats. Grace felt her heart thumping as the opening moment drew close. And then, beside her, Oliver squeezed her shoulder, and she relaxed as she stood by the study door. The lights went down, the audience fell silent, and Grace ushered on the first act.

A line of men with bare, hairy legs and dressed in scarlet skirts, cavorting about the stage to the booming rhythm of the Can-Can being thumped out on the piano, was met with tumultuous applause, wolf whistles and raucous guffaws. A comic sketch set in the trenches followed, then two serious acts with a soldier reciting a couple of poems he had penned himself, and the pianist proving that he was in fact an accomplished musician, capable of interpreting beautifully some Strauss waltzes and Tchaikovsky's rousing Piano Concerto Number One. A barbershop quartet sang in dulcet harmony, the Can-Can dancers followed up with a hilarious interpretation of Swan Lake, and a hopeless ventriloquist using another patient as a dummy was almost booed off the stage amidst delirious laughter. A magician who could make none of his tricks work was followed by a slapstick act and two stand-up comedians, and all was interspersed with singers both amusing and serious and finished with a jolly sing-song.

'You're a triumph, Grace!' Oliver winked at her during the interval as he went to dress in his costume for the pantomime which had been written by the men themselves and was based on nursery rhymes. Oliver was the back half of the cow that jumped over the moon. As he changed, Grace glimpsed yet again his strong, muscular torso. Sadly marked by several battle scars, his bare chest nevertheless did something to Grace's pulse that she delighted in, and she had to force her mind back to the task in hand.

All went without a hitch, the audience almost falling off their chairs in howling laughter. At the end, while the cast took their bows to an explosion of clapping and shouting, Grace slipped up the back stairs to join Matron and all the nursing staff waiting at the top of the grand staircase. As the lights were dimmed, Grace led the procession slowly downwards as they sang carols in unaccompanied, angelic voices. The whole effect was stunning, transcendent. As the heavenly choir gathered on the stage to invite the audience to join in *Oh, Come all ye Faithful*, Grace's brain was whirling with joyous pride and relief that it had all gone so well.

She noticed, though, that one of the vestibule doors had opened and a telegram boy slid inside. He spoke briefly to the soldier in the first seat, who pointed along the back row to where Dr Elliott Franfield was singing along with everyone else, his sixteen-year-old son, William, by his side. Grace saw him take the telegram, read it and then slide it into his pocket. Grace's heart dropped like a stone, and the gladness drained away. Elliott Franfield didn't sing another note.

'Well done, Nurse Dannings!'

'Hasn't laughed so much in my life, I hasn't!'

'Marvel you are, cheel!'

Grace accepted with a modest smile the praise heaped upon her. Even Oliver giving her a brief hug left her soul cold. Something had happened, and an overpowering sorrow swept through her.

It wasn't until later that she discovered what it was. The men were all abed, quiet ripples of excitement still rumbling through the old house. Grace and Aggie finally left the ward together, crossing the hall from which the chairs had been cleared, leaving the empty stage to be dismantled the following morning.

'You were wonderful, Grace,' Aggie whispered. 'I reckon you deserve a cuppa before we go to bed.'

'Yes, I think I need one,' Grace agreed, and so they made for the kitchens.

As they passed Matron's office, the door was slightly ajar and they both caught the distressing sound of a woman's sobbing. Grace's stomach tensed. It was that telegram, wasn't it? Natural compassion drew her to peer through the gap. Ling Franfield was weeping in her husband's arms, and Elliott was attempting to comfort her while talking with William.

'But Artie will be all right?' Grace heard the young lad say in a shaky voice. 'Plenty of people survive being blown up, don't they?'

'Yes,' Dr Franfield answered gravely. 'Thank God it was a grenade and not a shell. But Artie . . . he has serious wounds to his lower body. And, well, put it this way. He'll never father any children.'

It didn't take much imagination to realize what the good doctor meant, and Grace's blood ran cold. She drew back, exchanging glances with Aggie. The two girls tiptoed away, the ebullient atmosphere from the concert utterly ruined.

'Poor souls,' Grace breathed. 'They do so much for others, and to have that happen seems so unfair. But I bet they'll be working tomorrow as if nothing has happened.'

'Do you think we should make them a cup of tea?' Aggie suggested, her face taut with compassion.

'Nice idea, but better to leave them alone, I reckon,' Grace answered, and as she lit the gas under the kettle, she wondered quite how it was that she and Aggie were becoming friends. But it had taken the deaths of millions of men and the maiming of so many more for it to happen.

* * *

'Oliver, is anything the matter?'

It was a bitingly cold, crisp February morning, but inside the great hall, the atmosphere was warm and comforting. The sunlight that shimmered on the blanket of hoar-frost outside streamed in through the large window, casting patterns on the polished floorboards. Grace had noticed that Oliver was lounging in one of the armchairs, staring sightlessly out over the wintry grounds, his expression frozen and lost in thought.

He glanced up at Grace's question, his eyes veiled in confusion. 'I'm not sure.' He held out his closed fist and slowly uncurled his fingers. In his palm sat a round, silver badge. *For King and Empire* — *Services Rendered*.

'Your Silver War Badge,' Grace stated steadily. 'You've been officially invalided out.'

'Yes. Remember the army quack came a few weeks ago to assess a group of us? He agreed with Dr Franfield that the awful headaches I still get and the fact that my memory still hasn't come back could make me unreliable on the battlefield. The certificate caused a bit of a problem, hence the delay in it coming through. At least it should make them get a move on trying to discover my real name. But for now, they've put me down as Oliver Smith, identity to be confirmed. I'm under oath, mind, to inform them if I remember who I am before they manage to work it out.'

His words ended in bitter irony, and Grace sank onto her haunches before him. 'Aren't you pleased, though, that you won't be going back to the Front?' she questioned him, since she herself was overflowing with relief that this man who had lit something inside her was to be saved from the continuing carnage.

His eyes when they met hers were dark and troubled. 'I don't know. No man in his right mind would want to go back, and of course I don't. But I feel such a fraud. Most of the time, I'd make a perfectly good soldier.'

'And so would many of our shell-shock patients,' Grace argued passionately. 'But suddenly something could trigger it all again. Even the smallest sound on the ward if someone drops something can have them diving for cover or turning back to senseless wrecks just like that.' She paused just long enough to click her fingers. 'It could be something similar with you. You've got to accept that there's still something very wrong inside your head, Oliver, and you could be a liability on the battlefield. I know you try to hide it, but I've seen you almost staggering with pain when one of those headaches comes on. And they still make you sick sometimes.'

Grace stopped, burning with exasperation. Oliver had sucked in his cheeks, but now one side of his mouth curved in a wry smile. 'Not much escapes you, does it?'

She felt the heat prickle beneath her starched collar. 'And I had to report it each time, too, I'm afraid. So I'm partly to blame for your honourable discharge.'

She watched, relieved as his smile broadened. But then a sudden, tearing sigh escaped his lungs and he sprang to his feet.

'I need some air,' he declared from between clenched teeth. 'I'm going to take a walk around the grounds. Unless . . . unless you'd like to join me?'

A sudden joy bubbled up inside her. She had accompanied Oliver on strolls on numerous occasions just as she had with other soldiers hundreds of times. Sometimes she had taken them down to the town. It was part of the rehabilitation process to see how they reacted to the hundreds of soldiers garrisoned there, or the noise of the motorized vehicles and the two train lines that ran through Tavistock. But somehow the issuing of Oliver's Silver War Badge had made the close relationship Grace had shared with him over the past months blossom into intimacy.

'I'll just check Sister doesn't need me for anything,' she replied, fighting to keep her emotions in check. 'And then I'll fetch my coat.'

'I'll wait for you on the bench under the portico.'

Within a few minutes, Grace stepped out into the frosty morning, the glacial air making her face tingle after the warmth inside the great house. But deep inside her, something was glowing. Oliver stood up when he saw her, and her heart turned over. He looked so tall and handsome in his greatcoat unlike the shapeless hospital blues he wore beneath. He was bare-headed, and his hair, which had been left to grow back longer than the normal army cut in order to hide the deep scars from his wounds, had a lustrous sheen to it. Grace hardly saw the ugly slash across his cheek she was so used to it. Besides, she had seen inside him as a man, and that was what counted.

They walked slowly, absorbing the pleasant tranquillity of the morning. They weren't the only ones to be enjoying the stillness, but the grounds extended to over forty acres and soon they were well away from the house and virtually alone. Grace waited for Oliver to speak first, sensing he needed time to untwist the tangled thread of his emotions. It wasn't until they came into a copse hidden down by the river that ran through the estate that Grace became aware of him beginning to relax.

'You're right, of course,' he said at last, although there was still a hint of irony in his voice. 'But then you usually are. I should be relieved and utterly grateful to be honourably discharged. I just don't like the feeling that I've let somebody down somewhere.'

'But you haven't. You've fought for king and country and been seriously wounded in the process. You've done your bit, and you need to accept it. So . . . ?'

She peered up at him cajolingly, her head tipped to one side. He met her gaze and his face slowly spread into a smile.

'Yes, Nurse. I must look forward. To the future. Which will be easier when they tell me who I am. But in the meantime, I promise to be more positive. You know I'm to be discharged soon?'

'No?' A black shiver darkened Grace's present pleasure, but she knew she mustn't allow it to show.

'Matron told me this morning. There's nothing more they can do for me, and some other poor sod could do with my place here, I'm sure.'

'But . . . where will you go?' Grace faltered, feeling as if she's been run over by a steamroller.

'Not far, if I can help it. I've no home to go to, after all. At least, not as far as I know. And I need to be near, anyway. If news comes through about my identity, it'll come to the hospital first. But . . .' He put a hand on her arm, halting her and turning her towards him. As he fixed his gaze on hers, his eyes were deep pools of emotion. Grace gulped, and her stomach filled with butterflies as she stared intently into his tense face.

'There is another reason why I don't want to go far,' he croaked, wetting his lips. 'There is someone . . . It was all such a blur when I first came here. But every time I came to my senses, there was someone there. Smiling at me. Encouraging me. And it came to be that this angel was in my mind even when I was unconscious, so that often I wasn't sure if she was real or not. But as I got better, I knew that she *was* real. And she was just as beautiful and sweet and caring as she was in my dreams. I came to look for her the minute I woke up each morning. And over the weeks and months that she's been caring for me, she became my reason for living.' He paused, the breath trembling in and out of his lungs. 'Tell me I'm a poor deluded fool, but, Grace Dannings, I love you. And I pray that when this ridiculous business is over, we can be together for the rest of our lives.'

Every nerve, every muscle in Grace's body was totally stilled. Her mind emptied of all thought, and that tiny light that had been flickering inside her for so long burst into flame. She watched, head tilted upward, as Oliver's eyes searched her face. She waited, the breath quivering at the back of her throat, longing. And when, in the quiet depths of the copse, his mouth barely touched her, enraptured joy rushed through her veins.

Oliver drew back, a frown wavering on his brow. 'Did you . . . ? Could you . . . ?' he choked.

The words Grace yearned to say lodged in her throat. And so she raised herself on tiptoe instead, pulling him towards her, arms around his neck. Her lips found his again, sending shockwaves down to her belly and tingling out to her fingertips.

They drew apart, and Grace's hand went over her mouth as she gazed back at him.

'I've just broken one of the sacred rules,' she gasped. 'I'm not supposed to fall in love with any of my patients.'

Oliver threw up his head with a roar of laughter. 'I take it that means you have, then?' he crowed. 'I was so frightened you wouldn't feel the same. And it's all right because I won't be your patient for much longer and you won't be breaking any rules. Oh, my darling girl!' His arms came about her, crushing her to his chest. 'You've made me so happy, I can't tell you! I'll find somewhere to live in Tavistock. Get a job, hopefully.'

'And I can tell you where! Tresca Trembath — she's one of the volunteer nurses on Happiness — her husband owns a hardware shop. His assistant's just got his call-up papers, poor fellow, so he needs a replacement. Perhaps he'll take you on. He's starting to expand into this new electricity business. And there's a flat over the shop that goes with it. They live in Bannawell Street themselves.'

'Sounds perfect, if they'll have me!' Oliver's eyes shone like stars as he smiled down at her.

'I'll go and ask her as soon as we get back. That'll be two good pieces of news they've had today. All three of their sons are in the Ninth Devons. By some miracle, they all survived Ypres with only minor injuries—'

'God, that *is* a miracle!'

'And now the Eighth and Ninth are being sent to Italy where they should be relatively safe.'

'Poor devils, they deserve it. I do remember being out there somewhere, you know. It was hell on earth. The noise of the big guns, shells exploding and machine-gun fire. The stench of the mud. There must have been hundreds of bodies decomposing in the slime that filled the craters. You had to try not to slide off the duckboards because if you did, you were likely to drown before you could be pulled out. And that was without the bloody fighting.'

His face had taken on that terrible, distraught look again. It was no wonder his damaged brain had decided to blank out vast tracts of his memory, except that it had chosen the wrong ones. But Grace didn't want their moment of elation to fade.

'Let's not think about that now,' she urged. 'Let's just think about ourselves and our future. And,' she said, smiling coquettishly, 'I rather liked that kiss, so please may I have another one?'

So Oliver happily obliged.

CHAPTER TWENTY-ONE

The shop doorbell clanged as they stepped out into the April sunshine in buoyant mood, Grace's fingers laced about Oliver's crooked elbow. A grey, niggling fear still rumbled deep in her soul, but she stubbornly refused to let it mar her happiness on her afternoon off. She had waited for Oliver as usual at the bottom of the stairs in the back room of the shop, leaving the door slightly ajar for propriety's sake so that Morgan Trembath could glimpse them through the gap — if he wanted to! But for a few moments, they had drawn back into the stairwell and enjoyed a long, passionate kiss that had sent an electric charge sparking down Grace's spine.

Once or twice during the two months Oliver had been living and working at Trembath's hardware store, while Morgan had been busy with a customer, Oliver had pushed the door to and they had taken advantage of those brief minutes to snatch a quick cuddle. Oliver had slipped a hand beneath Grace's cardigan, cupping her breast through her blouse and underwear. At first she had gasped with shock, but Oliver had never attempted to go any further. And the rapturous enchantment that plunged down to her loins once she had become used to his gentle touch almost made Grace wish that he would!

Now they sauntered down the steep hill of West Street, passing a long queue outside a grocer's shop. What with food shortages, the recently introduced rationing of certain items, and the hundreds of soldiers garrisoned in the town, it was impossible to forget that the country was still at war. There were also those who, like Oliver, bore the Silver War Badge on their civilian lapels but whose injuries were more obvious than his. However, when passers-by saw the gash gouged out across his otherwise handsome face, their expressions displayed just as much sympathy.

'Oh, good, I've found you.' Ling Franfield's voice startled them from the blissful reverie they had both fallen into. Straight away, Grace's attention was drawn to Matron's face, but she couldn't fathom the expression she found there. A knot of apprehension tightened in her stomach, for why had Matron apparently sought them out on purpose?

She had her answer almost at once.

'It's up to you what you do when you're off duty, of course,' Ling went on. 'I can't say I altogether approve, for your own sakes' as much as anything. And I have some news,' she announced, using her eyebrows to indicate the brown envelope in her hand. 'Perhaps we should go somewhere quiet? There's a bench in the churchyard.'

'Yes, of course.'

Oliver's voice was grave, and when Grace looked up at him, the colour had drained from his cheeks. Her own heart had begun to hammer painfully so that she could feel the tremor of each beat. Oh, God. That envelope, she knew, contained the key to their future. Oliver yearned desperately to discover his identity, and yet what if it were something neither of them wished to hear? As he took her elbow and steered her towards the churchyard in Matron's wake, not a word was spoken. Oliver sat down between them on the bench, and Grace was glad to be seated since her flying pulse-rate was making her feel faint.

Matron opened the envelope and removed what was evidently an official letter. 'It's from *The Queen's Own Royal*

West Kent Regiment,' she began with quiet efficiency. 'That was what your tunic buttons told them.'

She paused, waiting for Oliver's reaction. 'Kent,' he said pensively. 'Yes. Do you know, I think I have a picture in my head of Tunbridge Wells? And everyone says from the way I speak that I could be from the Home Counties.'

Beside him, Grace dared not look into his face. An apple had stuck in her throat so that she could not speak, so she nodded instead. Kent. Yes. It made sense.

'They can't be absolutely sure,' Ling continued, eyeing them both shrewdly, 'but by a process of deduction, they believe you might possibly be one Lieutenant Clarence Smith-Haddon.'

'*Clarence*!' Oliver's cry of horror was instantaneous. 'Oh, dear heavens, *Clarence*?'

The hint of an amused smile played about Ling's mouth. 'I'm afraid so. You were listed as killed in action last summer at Ypres, but no body was ever recovered. But sadly that's common enough, of course. If they're right, you drew some sketches for the *Wipers Times*. That would fit in with your artistic talents, of course. If it is you, you're thirty-three years old, and in peacetime, you were a solicitor, as you mentioned just now, in Tunbridge Wells.'

Grace heard Oliver draw in an enormous breath. She herself was scarcely breathing at all, feeling the blood coursing round her body. Her muscles were locked in paralysis, dreading what was to come next and yet still hoping beyond hope . . .

Ling Franfield rose to her feet and turned to face them both, her gaze steady and level. 'We'll know for certain tomorrow. As we speak, the lady believed to be your wife is travelling here by train. Poor soul, if it's all wrong, well, you can imagine what she's going through. But if you *are* Clarence Smith-Haddon, you have two lovely little boys aged six and three. Now then, I'm afraid I must leave you to ponder the news together. My own son, Artie, is being brought home from the specialist hospital later this afternoon, and Elliott and I wish to be with him, of course. But I shall expect you in my office at ten o'clock tomorrow morning, Lieutenant. In the meantime, I think you two will have a lot to discuss.'

She replaced the letter in the envelope and held it out to Oliver who took it in trembling fingers. He sat forward, resting his elbows on his spread knees and turning the envelope over and over in his hands. Grace watched him, her heart deadened. Waiting for the crippling pain to subside. She was like a fledgling, ready to leave the nest and soar into the sky, to experience the world and the magical joy of love — only to discover that she was really a bird without wings. Her soul, everything that made her who she was, had crashed to the ground, shattering into a million pieces like broken glass.

'They could be wrong,' she heard Oliver croak at last. 'This woman might not be my wife.'

Grace stared ahead, seeing nothing. Feeling the fight pulse out of her. 'If it's not her,' she barely ground the words from her throat, 'it'll be someone else. You're a lovely man, Oliver. And attractive. You're bound to be married. Deep down, I've thought it all along, but just refused to let myself believe it.'

'Perhaps any wife I might have will be put off by this,' he said wryly, fingering the disfiguring scar on his cheek.

'No. Not if she really loves you. Like . . . like . . .'

'Like you do,' Oliver finished for her.

'Yes. And if you *do* have children, they'll need you.'

They looked at each other, eyes clinging, crazed. Defeated. And knew that the truth was there only to crucify them.

* * *

Grace walked, unsteadily, across the great hall. She had seen Oliver arrive, hovering as if he hoped to have a brief word with her, but Matron had appeared and astutely whisked him into her office before he had the chance. Perhaps it was for the best. To say another goodbye as they had the previous afternoon, knowing it might well be the last moment they ever truly shared, would simply destroy her.

She saw Mrs Smith-Haddon arrive a few minutes later, looking lost, worried, charged beyond hope. Her expression said it all. But if she *was* Oliver's wife, Grace wanted to hate her. She went over to ask if she could help, seething, craving to find something she could despise about her. But the pretty young woman appeared distraught, her hands fluttering nervously.

'I've come to see if the man you've been calling Lieutenant Smith is my husband,' she said shakily. 'I can't believe it. All this time I thought he was dead. I just hope to God . . . I couldn't bear it if it isn't him. It would be . . . like losing him all over again.'

Tears clung to her lashes, and Grace's heart melted. How could she have been so selfish? But she *loved* Oliver, and this was all . . . so cruel.

'Have they warned you that he has a nasty scar across his cheek?' she asked gently, since it could be a shock to the woman if she didn't know. But if she wasn't Oliver's wife, it wouldn't matter. Oh, please, *please* God . . .

'Yes, but I don't care. If he's alive, that's all that matters.'

So Grace pointed out Matron's office. But she simply couldn't bring herself to show Mrs Smith-Haddon inside. She went back to her work, although her mind was a million miles away, crushed and yet clinging to some reckless hope. It seemed an eternity but was in fact no more than twenty minutes before the door to Matron's office opened again, and Grace's heart crashed against her ribs. She hardly dared look. But she must, though the very core of her screamed out in protest.

She knew instantly. Mrs Smith-Haddon was grasping Oliver's arm as if she would never let it go, and her face gleamed as if lit by a torch of joy. Grace met Oliver's bewildered gaze across the hall, and her soul splintered. Time fragmented and became meaningless — life a fathomless void.

214

'Nurse Dannings!' Oliver's voice, strange and cracked, called across to her. And somehow her legs carried her to him. 'This is apparently my wife, Nicola.' And then looking down on Mrs Smith-Haddon with a blend of despair and compassion since this poor woman had suffered as much as any of them, he said, 'Nicola, this is the nurse who cared for me so well while I've been here.'

'Yes, we met earlier.' Nicola Smith-Haddon beamed with sublime elation. 'I can't thank you enough!'

She shook Grace's hand in a gesture that spoke of the deepest sincerity. Behind her, Grace read the tearing anguish on Oliver's — Clarence's — face. Was there any hope for them? But she knew, didn't she? Oliver would do what was right and proper. And he would be less of a man in her eyes if he didn't.

'Just doing my job,' someone answered. Was it her? But there was something she had to know. 'But . . . do you recognize your wife?' she asked falteringly.

Oliver screwed up his lips. 'No.' Grace saw Nicola's jaw tremble at his reply. But then he continued, 'Show Nurse Dannings the photos, would you?'

'Of course.' The smile, more tentative this time, returned to Nicola's face as she rummaged in her handbag. Grace knew her own hand was shaking as she took the photographs. What if Nicola saw? But just now she was past caring. Her eyes fell on a wedding portrait — of Oliver and Nicola smiling jubilantly into the camera. And then two little boys, like peas in a pod except for being a few years apart in age.

Grace gasped. 'Your painting,' she breathed.

'Yes.' Oliver gulped. 'So there is a memory there somewhere.'

A torrent of emotions welled up in Grace's breast. 'Good. I'm so pleased.' She somehow nailed a smile on her face. 'And I truly hope that your memory comes back properly and that you find happiness again.' Despite her efforts, a rogue tear escaped her eye and she dabbed it away. 'Forgive me, but this is a wonderful moment,' she lied. And scraping herself together, she asked, 'What are you going to do now?'

'We're going *home* tomorrow,' Oliver answered pointedly. 'To build a new life somehow. Or to find our old one again. So . . . this is goodbye. And thank you once again for everything.'

Their eyes met in one final, desperate glance, and then Oliver held open the vestibule door for his wife. Grace watched them, her heart bleeding. But she couldn't let Oliver go. Just one moment more. Please. She sprang forward, out of control.

'Lieutenant!'

'Yes?' He turned back, his eyes glistening. 'And it's *Mister* now, thank God.'

'Of course. I were just going to say, if you wouldn't mind, do let me know how you progress. Yours has been such an interesting case.'

'Yes, I will.'

'Take care of yourself, then. And good luck to you both.'

Oliver nodded, Nicola's beaming smile widened again, and Grace saw them outside. She waited, grief swallowing her into a great black hole, while they walked away down the long driveway, crossed the bridge, and disappeared out of her life for ever.

* * *

Curiously enough, it was in Aggie's arms that she wept that evening. The other girl patted her shoulder, smoothed her hair. And as the broken sorrow gradually washed out of her, Aggie held her tightly.

'I know just how you feel,' Aggie crooned softly. 'I've . . . I've been seeing someone all these months. In my off-duty time. I met him in the town. He was home recovering from trench-foot. Not bad enough to need any amputation, but you know it can take ages to clear up. But . . . it's better now, and he's just been sent back to his battalion. The

Second Devons. And with all this fierce fighting started up again . . .'

Her words filtered slowly into Grace's brain, and she pulled away, sniffing back her tears. 'I wondered why you kept going into town. But . . . you never said.'

'No. Well, I knew what you'd think. Aggie Nonnacott, the flirt. The slut. First Martin, and now Keith. I never thought I'd ever love anyone ever again after Martin was killed. But it is possible to fall in love again. And I *truly* love Keith, and I hope to God—'

'Yes, of course.' Grace took her hands. 'At least I know Oliver's alive. And God willing, he'll find happiness again. And, though it breaks my heart that it can't be with me, I must learn to be grateful for that. Oh, Aggie, this war is so awful. Not just all those soldiers dying or being maimed, but what it's done to *everyone*. But at least it's made us friends, hasn't it?'

Aggie's distressed face moved into a wry smile. 'I never thought I'd hear you say that, Grace Dannings. Never in a million years. But I'm so pleased you have.'

'And do you know, so am I?' Grace replied.

CHAPTER TWENTY-TWO

'That's tremendous, Captain! Well done!'

Captain Evershed's face radiated with triumph as he reached the bottom of the grand staircase. His left leg still had a slight tremor, but it was nothing that anyone would notice unless they knew of his medical history.

'When I think that when I came here last summer,' he answered proudly, 'I just lay on the floor, writhing out of control and unable to speak, it's an absolute miracle. What everyone's done for me here is beyond words. Soon I'll be going home to my family as a proper man again, and you, Nurse Dannings, were part of it.'

'Oh, I only came for a couple of sessions a week,' Grace protested, flushing with embarrassment.

'I know. But we all missed you when you didn't come for that couple of months. Private Wicks especially,' the captain ended with a knowing wink.

But even mention of the cheeky young private couldn't stop the knife from twisting in Grace's side. 'I . . . had other things on my mind for a while,' she murmured. But she had succeeded in thrusting her misery aside and was determined not to let it raise its ugly head again. 'So, let's see you go back up again.'

She followed the captain back up the staircase, biting her lip as the tearing memories flooded back. She had buried them deeply by hurling herself back into her work. She was planning another concert, and every other moment of her off-duty she spent helping on Happiness Ward. It was so satisfying to see men being discharged to civilian life, and watching the progress of the new patients who took their places. It had all helped to cement Grace's aspirations for the future. Her relationship with Oliver had made her doubt whether she wanted to sacrifice a normal life for the sake of becoming a properly trained nurse. And, of course, Larry had pointed that out to her as well. But now that sacrifice would be her salvation. If she couldn't devote herself to Oliver, she would devote herself to a career helping others.

She had told Larry all about Oliver. How could she not when he was her dearest, lifelong friend? She couldn't bear to have any secrets from him and, of course, they shared that one, appalling secret about Martin. Nobody else in the world knew the entire truth apart from Reg. But having received an honourable discharge following his wounds at Passchendaele, he been sworn to secrecy and they knew they could rely on him.

Once Oliver had been discharged so that their feelings for each other no longer broke the rules of Grace's employment, Grace had revealed all to Larry. He had written back, wishing them well and hoping everything would work out for them. Later, when Oliver's identity had been established, Grace had written to Larry of her broken heart. She had said, quite truthfully, that she couldn't be jealous of Nicola Smith-Haddon. If Grace had been in her shoes, she could imagine how the poor woman felt. It didn't make her own pain any easier. Larry had written by return in the sensible, comforting way she knew he would, not gushing over with meaningless platitudes, but simply stating that war made a mess of people's lives in so many ways, and that he would always be there for her.

Now, as she followed Captain Evershed's slow progress up the stairs, Grace's mind drifted back to when, towards the end of May, she had managed to get a full day off-duty, making it worth her while to go home. She got off the train at Horrabridge, walking the couple of miles across Knowle Down to reach Walkhampton, her heart eased to be out in the countryside again with views up to the rugged moorland that was in her blood.

As she neared the village, Grace kept her eyes open — unsuccessfully — for her father or Farmer Snell. Never mind. Her father always came home for lunch and if Grace had time, she would call into the Snells on her way back.

She opened the door to the little cottage, expecting to be greeted by the usual chaos. To her surprise, it was unusually tidy and although Temperance wasn't there, a tasty-smelling stew was simmering on the range. Grace guessed her mother might be at Nan's helping with the four young children, so she set off on the short distance down the hill.

'Larry!' she cried excitedly at the familiar figure coming towards her.

'Morning, Grace. What are you doing here? Come to see your parents at last?' he said with a hint of bitterness.

Grace felt somewhat miffed. 'Yes. I managed to get a whole day off — *at last*,' she answered with a flash of her eyes. 'I'll call in to see you later. Is Mummy at Nan's, do you know?'

'I think so. But I won't have time to chat. We're really busy. I'm just getting something from the timber yard. Have a good day.'

He limped past her towards the yard, leaving Grace staring, slack-jawed, at his back. Her forehead compressed into deep folds. It wasn't like Larry to be so short. Grace shrugged, and continued on her way. Perhaps she had mistaken his attitude, and she had enough to deal with in her struggle to heal the hurt over Oliver.

It wasn't easy with so much to remind her of him all around her every day. Captain Evershed's innocent comment just now jolted her thoughts back to the present and she swallowed down her agony. And then, just as they reached the top step, Aggie brushed past them in a blind, headlong rush towards the dormitory. She was off-duty, too, and Grace knew she had gone into town to seek news of her young man from his parents. By her behaviour, Grace was convinced something was wrong.

'Will you excuse me, Captain?' she asked politely, and then dashed after Aggie.

The other girl was lying face down on her bed, banging her fists on the pillow, her body racked with violent sobs. Oh, no. A solid knot tightened inside Grace as she put a tentative hand on Aggie's shoulder.

'Aggie?' she whispered.

Aggie at once turned and flung herself into Grace's arms. 'Oh, Gracie, he's dead!' she squealed. 'There's been this awful battle going on the last ten days. Biggest German bombardment ever, they say. And . . . they used masses of gas and . . . Oh, Grace, he died later from the gas. It . . . would've been horrific. He'd have suffered so dreadfully . . .'

Dear God. Grace's blood froze. But she must find the strength to comfort and soothe poor Aggie, even though she knew her words would be futile. 'Oh, Aggie, try not to think about it. There's nort to be done, and it's all over now.'

'No, it's not,' Aggie wheezed. 'I'm pregnant and his parents don't want to know.'

Grace's jaw fell open and she had to suppress a gasp of shock. Oh, Jesus. 'Are . . . you sure?' she dared to ask.

'Oh, yes. We only did it once, after he got his recall papers. It was a sort of leaving present. I never thought . . .' Aggie seemed less hysterical now and sat back, though she wrung her hands in her lap. 'I won't even get a war widow's pension, and his parents threw me out saying he'd never have done it and that I'm a liar and a slut.' She sniffed, lifting her head proudly. 'And I expect you think so, too.'

'Aggie, no, I—'

'Remember when you found Martin and me down by the brook? The look on your face—'

'That were a long time ago,' Grace insisted, but Aggie cut her short again.

221

'I was always so jealous of you, having Larry and Martin and Stephen. Always together, having fun, when I had nobody. I remember when you followed them jumping off Huckworthy Bridge into the river and Larry had to save you. I was so jealous, I wished you'd drowned. I was hiding nearby, watching you, as I often did. My father would've killed me if I'd got my clothes wet or dirty as you did all the time. The slightest smear of mud on my boots and he'd beat me.'

'*Beat* you?'

'Oh, yes,' Aggie spat viciously. 'I'd have done *anything* to get away from him. That's why I always wanted to seduce Martin. Don't misunderstand me. I loved Martin with all my heart, but I wanted to get pregnant so that he'd marry me and take me away from my father. He'd have agreed to *that*,' she snorted. 'The Vencombes were some of the few people in the village he approved of. But for me, it had to be Martin. I know he never loved me, but I loved *him*. And I couldn't seduce Larry. He was always too upright. Besides, he was always yours.'

'*Mine?*' Grace was incredulous, her head whirling with Aggie's confession.

'Of course.' It was Aggie's turn to be astonished. 'All those nasty things I did, it was a way of hitting back because I was so envious of you all. And now I've got my comeuppance. I'll have to tell my father, though he'll likely murder me.'

'Not if I come with you.' The words were out of Grace's mouth before she could stop them, but a bitter argument with someone was just what her pent-up emotions needed just now. 'Come on. It's Saturday afternoon. Your father'll be at home. And we're off-duty for the rest of the day.'

'Oh.' Aggie's face had turned to paper. 'Do you . . . ?'

'Strike while the iron's hot,' Grace answered grimly.

It wasn't until they were on the train that reality rushed at her and her stomach sickened. What in God's name had she let herself in for? But she couldn't let Aggie down now, could she?

* * *

'Oh, Gracie, I be that pleased to see you!' Nan Sampson, four small children around her skirt, shrieked as they came into Walkhampton. 'I's just had a letter. From John! He's been alive all this time! He were dreadful wounded and took prisoner. But now he's better, and he'll be kept in the camp till the war's over. So he *will* be coming home one day! And he says to tell you he's been thinking about you. And he's going to be a much better husband when he comes home.'

Grace blinked at Nan's jubilant face. Under other circumstances, she would have been delighted for her. And who knew, John might come home a more considerate husband? If so, the upset of all the arguments Grace had had with him would have been worthwhile.

'That's wonderful news, Nan. But I can't stop now. We're going to see Mr Nonnacott.'

'Nasty Nonnacott?' Nan frowned, and looked Aggie distastefully up and down. 'What does you want with *him*, Gracie?'

'It'll be all over the village soon, so you might as well know now,' Aggie sighed. 'I'm having a baby and the father's been killed and we're on our way to tell my father.'

Nan's eyes stretched like saucers in her round face. 'Rather you than me!'

Grace pulled a wry grimace. 'I'm not exactly looking forward to it. But don't worry about us. You go and celebrate.'

'I will. But you be careful,' Nan frowned, watching them move on.

'You don't have to do this,' Aggie croaked a few moments later as they turned into her parents' front garden.

'Well, we've come this far,' Grace answered, steeling her courage.

Five minutes later, she wasn't at all sure it had been the right decision. She had felt convinced that confronting Mr Nonnacott in the presence of another person would have lessened his reaction. How wrong she had been. His face worked like some hideous gargoyle as he absorbed the news, turning a vivid puce and his eyes bulging as if he would burst open with rage. Grace, her own skin slicked in nervous sweat, watched his wife cowering in the corner, while Aggie, despite her earlier bravado, simply withered on the spot.

'You little whore!' her father exploded, the veins on his neck standing out like ropes. 'Bringing sin and ignominy upon our heads!' He towered over Aggie until their noses touched and she shrank onto her knees. Grace watched in appalled fascination, disbelieving, as he slipped off his belt in one practised movement and slammed it down on Aggie's back.

Grace couldn't believe her eyes. She could understand why poor Aggie used to be the unpleasant character she once was if her entire life had been dominated by such a monster. And as for his poor wife, no wonder she had turned into a recluse! It was as the belt found its target for a second time that Grace broke free from her shock and catapulted forward, hurling the volcano of pain and anguish of all she had seen and suffered over those past four years onto Mr Nonnacott's arm. She clung to him in a frenzy of anger, but though she was tall, her willowy frame was no match for the burly man. The next instant, she was thrust back against the wall, winded and slithering to the floor.

'It's your fault, isn't it?' the demented voice bellowed over her. 'You led her on, you trollop, the way you've always cavorted around with the Vencombe boys!'

A furious eruption of red-hot indignation lifted Grace's head, her mouth open and ready to protest. She hardly saw the belt whipping through the air before a searing pain slashed across her neck and chin. The force of it sent her sprawling, and before she could pick herself up, agony sliced across her shoulders again and again, battering her into the carpet.

Somewhere through a black shroud she heard the door slam open and a roar of outrage echoed in her ears. Crashes and thumps banged about the room until all suddenly went quiet apart from the rapid, heavy breathing of someone quite close. Grace dared to peer out. Larry had pinned Mr Nonnacott to the floor and was sitting astride him, fist raised lest the devil tried to struggle free.

'You bastard!' he barked, swiftly drawing the back of his hand across the red stream that dripped from his torn lip. 'Thank God Nan told me what had happened and I followed them up here. Now you, Mr Nonnacott, are going to make out a cheque for fifty pounds' compensation to Miss Dannings—'

'Fifty pounds!'

'An amount I'm sure you can afford and precious little for what you've just done to her. And on Monday you're going to set up a monthly allowance for your daughter. Then I'm going to report all this to Constable Rodgers with instructions that if I ever hear you've harmed a hair on either of the girls' heads, or your wife's for that matter, or you stop Aggie's allowance, he's to arrest you for assaulting Miss Dannings.'

'You wouldn't dare,' Mr Nonnacott sneered, although Grace nonetheless detected defeat in his voice.

'Wouldn't I? And I'm sure Miss Dannings here would be perfectly willing to press charges, wouldn't you, Grace?' And before Grace could do more than nod in the affirmative, Larry added for good measure, 'And I promise you I'd also reveal to the world what a cruel, vicious piece of work you really are, and that wouldn't do your precious reputation among the Methodists much good, would it? So.' He scrambled to his feet, jerking Mr Nonnacott upwards by the collar. 'Get up, you blackguard, before I horsewhip you.'

The next few minutes passed in a grey fog. Grace peeled herself from the floor, her shoulders and neck on fire with pain. Aggie was clinging onto her, and then Larry, who had taken the other man to write out the cheque, was back in the room, stony-faced as he glared at a scowling Mr Nonnacott.

Then he grasped the two girls each by an arm and dragged them outside.

'What the *hell* possessed you?' he demanded as they staggered down the road.

Grace turned her head, forcing aside the scorching pain that seemed to pierce every inch of her body. Her eyes narrowed, ready to do battle. But this was Larry, and her coiled fury was suddenly washed away by a riptide of unstoppable tears. She collapsed against him, feeling his strength and his goodness enter her heart like a soothing balm.

'You're a bloody idiot, Grace Dannings,' she heard him sigh in tempered exasperation. 'But that fifty pounds can go towards your nurse's training when the war's over. Good job I opened that bank account to pay in your allowance. I suggest you pay in that cheque first thing on Monday morning before he changes his mind. I'm certain he wouldn't want me to tell his fellows in the Methodists what he's really like, but I have no idea if the legal threats I made would hold water.'

Grace glanced up at him through a blur of tears. 'Don't you?' she croaked.

'No, I don't.'

And that old, familiar smile slid onto his face, making him wince from his torn lip and flooding Grace's heart with a river of emotion.

CHAPTER TWENTY-THREE

Dear Nurse Dannings

I hope this finds you well and happy.

I apologize for not writing before, but the months since leaving Tavistock have flown. It is an unimaginable experience piecing together a stranger's life, knowing that it is in fact your own. My sons are adorable. I vowed for their sakes that I would behave towards them like their proper loving father, and they are such a delight that I really do feel as if that is what I am. Of course there was that small memory at the back of my mind, and I am gradually having more and more flashbacks.

Grace paused, resting the letter in her lap. When Matron had handed her the envelope, her pulse had begun rattling erratically when she saw the Kent postmark. By her mid-morning break, however, when she could sit outside alone in the late September sunshine, she found herself oddly calm and driven to read on by curiosity rather than any other emotion.

We live in a pleasant house on the outskirts of town. Little things are familiar as if I'd seen them in a dream. Going into the office where my senior partners treat me like a long-lost son, and studying old case notes, has triggered my knowledge of the law. I'll need to brush up on it, but on the whole it has come flooding back, and it has brought other more personal memories with it.

As for Nicola, she is such a beautiful, kind and warm person that I can understand why I married her. There is definitely something deep-down inside me, bursting to be reawakened, but even without that, I have found myself falling in love with her all over again. I really do feel that, as time passes and in familiar surroundings among people who know and love me, my memory will return in large part if not entirely, so that I can look forward to a happy and fulfilling future.

It would seem that this horrific war will soon be over. We've been driving the Germans back for weeks and from what I have read in the newspapers, we'll break through the Hindenburg Line any day and Germany will be forced to capitulate. Pray God it happens soon and the world can return to some semblance of normality. I recall you planned to train as a civilian nurse afterwards, and I wish you every success. I will never forget your kindness towards me and the other men at Mount Tavy.

Take care of yourself, and good luck
Your grateful patient
Clarence Smith-Haddon

Grace released her breath in a deep sigh. She had expected to feel tears pricking in her eyes, but instead she was lulled in warm, if wistful, contentment. Oliver had found happiness, and Grace was delighted for him. The grief had lessened as the weeks passed. She had come to accept that there could never be a future for their whirlwind romance, and from the tone of Oliver's letter, so had he. His memory would always linger in her heart, but it was time to close the door on it — and open another.

Nursing. She would stay at Mount Tavy as long as she was needed, and then find out where she stood financially. She had that fifty pounds that Larry had extracted from Aggie's father, but how far would that go? Ah, Larry. He had set up that allowance to fund her as a VAD nurse, but she couldn't expect him to help her further. She wouldn't let him. Dear, kind, thoughtful Larry, who was as much a part of her as she was herself.

That awful day when she had gone with Aggie to confront Mr Nonnacott kept haunting her. It came into her head now, obliterating the view over the hospital grounds. Her shoulders and neck had stung agonizingly, but the pain had eased in the safety and protection of Larry's arms of steel. The feel of his broad, strong chest as she leant against him had comforted her aching spirit like a healing salve, and she had wanted to stay locked in his embrace forever. It was hardly the first time he had rocked her in his arms, and always she had dragged herself away with reluctance.

Larry had always been in her life as a dear brother she had trusted and loved. What was it Aggie had said? That Larry was always hers? What had she meant? Had Aggie, of all people, seen beyond what Grace had been able to herself?

Grace's mind had been turning cartwheels ever since. Oliver had awakened something inside her, a woman's passion, but had it been simmering there for years, all her life perhaps? And had she been too close to recognize it for herself? All she knew was that it was Larry and not Oliver who was constantly in her thoughts.

She wrote to Larry every week now, exchanging news and commenting on the Allies' massive and continuingly successful offensive. And yet there was something else in the letters Larry wrote by return, something gentle and affectionate, all friction gone. When Grace thought back, had Larry been hiding a deep hurt? Could it be that he had feelings for her? She kept remembering that on the couple of occasions she had gone back to Walkhampton since, she had greeted him with a tight, lingering hug, and had read some deep sensitivity in his eyes.

Grace rose to her feet, shaking her head in confusion, grateful that she must go back inside since duty called.

* * *

It was the second Monday in November, a grey, dank, miserable morning. On Sunshine Ward, life was going on as normal. Grace was teaching a newcomer who had lost his left foot how to use his crutches and had just taken him through to the great hall where there was more room to practise. Hot drinks and biscuits were being served from the tea-trolley to the other patients who were relaxing in the peaceful surroundings of the beautiful room.

A sudden booming explosion, followed by several more, shattered the tranquil atmosphere. Chaos broke out in seconds. A couple of shell-shock patients dived for cover, others cried out and almost went into convulsions. Terrified looks were exchanged. Several mugs were dropped and smashed on the floor.

'God, we'm being invaded!'

Grace glanced swiftly around the room. The distant crashes had stopped, and she frowned in bemusement. 'No, it's all right!' she called out reassuringly. 'We can't be! Listen, it's stopped. And . . .' She met several pairs of frightened eyes, but her own ears were straining. 'Can anyone else hear church bells? What are they doing ringing at this hour? Unless . . .'

It was a moment everyone would remember for the rest of their lives. Murmurs ricocheted within the hall walls, the air all at once palpable with unleashed expectation. Could it possibly be . . . ? A soldier in hospital blues standing by the window pushed the lower section upwards as far as the sash-cord allowed. The peal of church bells blared into the room, interrupted almost at once by the sirens from the laundry and the town's factory. There must have been a train at one of the stations as the distinctive whistle of a railway engine joined in the cacophony, and a dart of confused hope pierced Grace's breast.

She picked up the hem of her uniform and ran outside. The noise was even louder, resonating across the valley. And then, pedalling like fury up the drive, was the newspaper boy, and Grace flew down to meet him.

'War's over, Nurse!' he shouted between breathless gasps. 'Us heard about five minutes ago, just in time! Boche signed at five o'clock this morning, and it all stopped at eleven. The marines let off some detonations bang on the dot. Will you tell everyone? Got other places to tell, I has.'

'Yes! Yes, of course!'

Grace spun on her heel, racing back up the slope, no thought in her head. Just an eruption of pure joy bursting out of her heart. 'It's over!' she screamed at the men who had spilled outside. Then she pushed past astonished, jubilant faces, shouting out the news to everyone still inside, scurrying from ward to ward, leaving a trail of exultation in her wake.

The rest of the morning passed in a blissful haze. The clamour of voices raised in rejoicing resounded through the old house, patients and nursing staff hugging each other with tears of celebration running down their cheeks. Dr Franfield ordered the opening of some crates of beer he had recently secreted in the storeroom in anticipation of the event. And rousing choruses of *It's a long way to Tipperary*, *Keep the Home Fires Burning* and other such songs broke out periodically. A further visit from the newspaper boy revealed that there was to be a procession through the town that evening led by the Salvation Army Band and followed by a thanksgiving service in the ancient Parish Church. Afterwards, the Royal Marine Light Infantry stationed in the town were to give a free public entertainment in the town hall.

'Nurse Dannings, you couldn't drum up an impromptu concert for tonight, could you?' Matron asked, face aglow.

'Oh, yes, why not?' Grace grinned back.

She dashed about the rooms, seeking out the men she knew would be willing to perform at such short notice. Who cared if it wasn't rehearsed and polished? It would simply be an expression of relief, the overwhelming elation that filled every breast.

It wasn't until after she had helped serve what turned into a riotous lunch that Grace was able to take her own break. But she was too overflowing with emotion to eat. A corkscrew had clamped down inside her stomach, and she felt suffocated, gasping for air, and despite the wretched weather, she escaped outside.

A few patients were wandering about the grounds, but she stood outside the front entrance alone, staring out through the vapour that enshrouded the valley and the town hidden in its depths. It was over. Indescribable release welled up inside her, and yet with it came a magnitude of sorrow, of jumbled bewilderment. Yes, it was over. But the world had gone mad, deranged, and could never be the same again. *Her* world would never be the same. Not without Stephen and Martin. All the men enjoying the raucous celebrations inside, in all the towns and villages all over the country, in France and everywhere else, none of their lives would ever return to normal. And, as she stood there among all the revelling abandonment, Grace wanted to weep until her heart was washed clean of its misery.

She sniffed hard. Blinked back the moisture that misted her eyes. She mustn't cry. Not among all this happiness. She bit her lip, staring sightlessly down the steep sweep of the drive. Materializing from the drizzling mist was the figure of a tall man in an overcoat limping over the stone bridge. A patient gone for a walk to clear his head. He didn't use a stick. In fact, there was an air of purpose in his step as if he were unaware of his disability. The gait was unusual and yet oddly familiar, and Grace found herself walking towards him. As they drew nearer, she could see that the coat was unbuttoned, yet there was no flash of hospital blues beneath. A civilian, then. But . . . who . . . ?

Grace's heartbeat quickened in her breast, and her legs began to walk faster. A quiet, calm and steady euphoria seeped through her sadness, scattering her grief to the four winds, and that tiny flame that had flickered inside her all her life suddenly flared out in a dazzling blaze of glory.

Larry.

She broke into a run. Her heart took wing, spiralling heavenwards. Her senses dropped away, her entire being wreathed in the enthralled rapture of seeing his beloved face. Not the fountain of enchantment of some passion that had suddenly bewitched her, but a strong, unbreakable thread that had always been there, but too close, too familiar for her to recognize. She had been blind, but now the truth came, joyously, to claim her.

He was the one person in the entire world that she yearned for, needed, just then. And he had known.

He was hobbling towards her in what passed as a run. But then, as she came within a dozen feet, they both instinctively came to a halt, their eyes holding each other's gaze, nerves stretched, drenched in unspoken love and devotion. Grace saw his face, tight and intense.

'You came,' she said.

'Yes,' he answered hoarsely. 'Stephen.'

'And Martin.'

'And everyone else.'

His eyebrows swooped, his eyes troubled pools. Grace stepped into his arms, and he held her, close and unmoving, his love emptying into her until she lifted her head, offering her lips to his. He answered at once, his mouth brushing hers, soft as summer rain, and her lips parted to receive that joyous wonder she had hungered after, she knew now, all her life.

'I've waited for this for so long,' he murmured against her.

She pulled back. 'For me to grow up,' she stated. And they both understood.

'I thought I'd lost you.'

'Thank God you didn't.' She stared up at him, head spinning as intoxication streamed through her. Watching his face twitch with anguish.

'Finish your work here,' he grated thickly. 'However long it takes. And then come home, Grace, where you belong. Come home and marry me. And help me make wheels till I'm an old, old man. That's if you can put up with a grumpy old peg-leg.'

'Oh, Larry,' she whispered, breathless. 'Yes.' And for good measure, she pulled his head down towards her, and kissed him again, long and deep, feeling her body crushed against his and wanting to melt into him forever.

She vaulted away, dancing, uncontained, grasping his hand and pulling him up the slope towards the great house. 'Come inside and join in the celebrations!' she crowed. 'I can introduce you as my fiancé!'

Larry's face stilled. Clouded. 'Are you . . . really sure, Grace?'

She threaded her arm through his, smiled up at him impishly. 'Absolutely!' she cried back.

And as they walked, slowly now, up the driveway, linked in love and bottomless understanding, she knew that she had never been so sure of anything in her entire life.

THE END

ACKNOWLEDGEMENTS

My most sincere gratitude will always go to the late Dr Marshall Barr, international authority on medical history, who contributed so much to the medical information in so many of my novels. He taught me so much, and I will never forget his clarity, his patience and his generosity.

Huge thanks go also to my wonderful agent without whom my career would not have flourished as it has.

I must also thank the following for their contribution to this particular novel: Peter Shapcott for sharing his knowledge of Walkhampton Mill's history and its machinery; historical wheelwright, Greg Rowland, for teaching me about the construction of both agricultural and military wheels; Mary Lillicrap, born and bred in Walkhampton, for sharing her lifelong memories of the village; the staff of Mount House School, formerly the First World War Mount Tavy Hospital; Tavistock historian Gerry Woodcock; last but not least, Dartmoor Guide and historian Paul Rendell for his continued support.

AUTHOR'S NOTE

A century after the Great War, Walkhampton remains a quiet, tranquil village but one which retains a strong community spirit. You are welcome to visit, to stand on the bridge and see the launder that once fed the waterwheel, identify the buildings in my story and visit the inn — which I describe as it was at the period and not as it is now. I would ask you, though, to respect the privacy of the village's residents, and note in particular that the workshop is now a private dwelling. Although the waterwheel is still there, it stands on private land and cannot be visited.

It is commonly believed that guncarriage wheels were made at the mill during the Great War, but I could not find any records of this. Greg Rowland suggested that, with its strong reputation, it is quite possible that Walkhampton's wheelwrights were on occasion sub-contracted to do so, that is the line I have taken in the book. What is now Mount House School on the edge of Tavistock, however, was most definitely Mount Tavy Hospital which specialized in shellshock and was renowned for its concerts.

ALSO BY TANIA CROSSE

THE AMBULANCE GIRL
THE WHEELWRIGHT GIRL

Don't miss the latest Tania Crosse release,
join our mailing list:

www.joffebooks.com

FREE KINDLE BOOKS